DEATH IN THE DEVIL'S ACRE

Murder was hardly rare in the slums of London in 1887, but the discovery in the infamous Devil's Acre, on a bitter January night, was enough to stun even the most hardened residents of that quarter...
Why should a respectable doctor have been stabbed to death and brutally mutilated in a London slum? Inspector Pitt of Bow Street is mystified as he stands watching the police surgeon carrying out his examination in the cold morning light. There are few clues to help Pitt in his hunt for the killer, but with his wife Charlotte he embarks on a race to unravel a mystery which will leave no one—not the lowest brand of ruffian nor the noblest aristocrat—totally unscathed.

DEATH IN THE DEVIL'S ACRE

DEATH IN THE DEVIL'S ACRE

by
Anne Perry

Magna Large Print Books
Long Preston, North Yorkshire,
England.

British Library Cataloguing in Publication Data.

Perry, Anne
  Death in the devil's acre.

A catalogue record for this book is
available from the British Library

ISBN 0-7505-0466-8

First published in Great Britain by Souvenir Press Ltd.,
1991

Copyright © 1985 by Anne Perry

Published in Large Print 1993 by arrangement with Souvenir
Press Ltd.

Printed and bound in Great Britain by
T.J. Press (Padstow) Ltd., Cornwall, PL28 8RW.

CHAPTER 1

P.C Withers sneezed as the icy January wind howled up the alley off the Thames. It was still three hours before dawn, and the gas lamps of the main streets barely lit this dismal passage on the very edge of the Devil's Acre, swarming with filth in the shadow of Westminster itself.

He sneezed again. The smell of the slaughterhouse fifty yards away was thick in his throat, along with the stench of the drains, old refuse, and the grime of years past.

Now that was funny—the yard gate was open! Shouldn't be rightly—not at this time of the morning. Not important, probably; some apprentice boy forgot to do his job—careless, some lads were. But what meat there was would likely be safe in cold rooms. Still, it was something to do in the long boredom of walking the pavements.

He crossed the alley to the cold rooms. Better just look inside, see everything was in order.

He poked his head around. It was silent—just one old drunk dossed down right in the middle. Better move him on, for his own sake, before the slaughtermen arrived and kicked him out. Apt to make a bit of sport of the old boys, some of them were.

' 'Ere, dad,' he said loudly as he bent down and shook the man's ample shoulder. 'Best be gone. You've no business in 'ere. Although as why anyone'd want to choose a place like this to kip, I dunno.'

The man did not move.

'Come on, dad!' He shook him harder and lifted his lantern for a better look. Surely the poor old fellow was not frozen to death? Not that he would have been the first P.C Withers had seen, by any means—and not all of them old either. Plenty of kids not more than a few years froze to death in a hard winter.

The light shone on the man's face. Yes, poor old basket, he was dead; the eyes were open and glazed.

'Funny,' he said aloud. 'Them as freezes to death usually goes in their sleep.' This face had a startled look, as though his death had taken him by surprise. He moved the lantern farther down.

'Oh, God Almighty!' The crotch and thighs of the body were drenched in blood; the brown woollen trousers had been slit open with a knife and the genital organs completely removed. They were lying useless between the knees—bloody, unrecognizable flesh, a mass of scarlet pulp.

The sweat broke out on P.C Withers' face and froze instantly. He felt sick, and his legs shook uncontrollably. Great God in heaven—what sort of a creature would do that to a man? He staggered backward and leaned against the wall, lowering his head a little to overcome the nausea that engulfed him.

It was several moments before his head cleared enough so he could think what he must do. Call help, that was certain. And get away from here, and from that abomination lying on the ground.

He straightened up, made for the gate, and closed it hard behind him, glad for the slicing wind from the east, even though it carried the raw iciness of the sea with it. Murder was hardly rare in the teeming slums of London in this year of Our Lord, 1887. But this was an act of bestiality unlike anything he had seen before.

9

He must find another man to stand guard; then he could report in and get his superiors to take charge. Thank heaven he was not senior enough to have to sort out this one!

Two hours later, Inspector Thomas Pitt, holding a lamp, closed the slaughterhouse gate and stood in the yard. He stared down at the corpse, still lying exactly as the constable had found it. In the grey morning light it looked grotesque.

Pitt bent down and lifted the shoulder of the corpse to see if there was anything under it—a weapon perhaps, or further injury. This dismemberment by itself would not account for his death. And surely a man so appallingly violated would have made some attempt to protect himself—to staunch the fountain of blood? The thought was sickening, and he forced it out of his mind. He ignored the cold sweat running on his skin, soaking his shirt.

He looked down the body. There was no blood on the dead man's hands, none at all. Even the nails were clean, which was extraordinary for anyone who frequented an area like this, let alone slept in a slaughterhouse yard!

Searching further, he found a wide, dark stain under the man, matting the cloth of his jacket. It was near the spine, straight through the ribs to the heart. He held the lamp higher for a closer look, but there was no blood anywhere else on the stones. He let out his breath and stood up, unconsciously wiping his hands on the legs of his trousers. Now he could only look at the face.

It was a heavy-jowled, broad-nosed face; the skin was faintly plum-coloured, the mouth marked with lines of humour. The eyes small and round—the face of a man who enjoyed good living. The body was portly and of barely average height, the hands were strong, plump, and immaculately clean; the hair was grey-brown.

The clothes were made of thick brown wool, baggy in places from wear, and wrinkled over the stomach. There were a few crumbs caught in the folds of the waistcoat. Pitt picked one up, crushed it experimentally in his fingers, and sniffed it. Cheese: Stilton, if he was not mistaken, or something like it. Inhabitants of the Devil's Acre did not dine on Stilton!

There was a noise behind him, a scuffle

of feet. He turned to see who it was, glad of company.

'Morning, Pitt. What've you got this time?' It was Meddows, the police surgeon, a man capable of insufferable good cheer at the most inopportune times. But instead of seeming offensive, his voice this time was like a sweet breath of sanity in a terrible nightmare.

'Oh, my good God!' He stood beside Pitt and stared down. 'Poor fellow.'

'He was stabbed in the back,' Pitt said quickly.

'Indeed?' Meddows cocked an eyebrow and looked at Pitt sidewise. 'Well, I suppose that's something.' He squatted down, balanced his bull's-eye lamp at precisely the right angle, and began to examine the body with care. 'Don't need to watch,' he remarked without turning his head. 'I'll tell you if there's anything interesting. For a start, this mutilation is a pretty rough job—just took a sharp knife and sliced! And there you are!'

'No skill?' Pitt asked quietly as he stared over Meddows' head at the dawn's light reflected in the slaughterhouse windows.

'None at all, just—' Meddows sighed. 'Just the most god-awful hate.'

'Insane?'

Meddows pulled a face. 'Who knows? Catch him and then I'll tell you—maybe. Anyway, who is this poor devil. Do you know yet?'

Pitt had not even thought of searching the body. It was the first thing he should have done. Without answering he bent down and began going through the man's pockets.

He found everything he would have expected, except money—and perhaps he had not really expected that. There was a gold watch, very scratched but still working, and a key ring with four keys on it. One of the keys appeared to be a safe key, two were door keys, and one was for a cupboard or drawer, judging by its size—just what any middle-aged, moderately prosperous man might have. There were two handkerchiefs, both grubby but of good Egyptian cotton with finely rolled hems. There were three receipted bills, two for quite ordinary household expenses, the third for a dozen bottles of a highly expensive burgundy—apparently a man of self-indulgence, at least as far as the table was concerned.

But what mattered was that his name

13

and address were on the bills: Dr Hubert Pinchin, 23 Lambert Gardens—a long way from the Devil's Acre, in social standing and every other aspect of the quality of life, if not so very far as the London sparrow flies. What was Dr Pinchin doing here in this slaughterhouse yard, appallingly murdered and maimed?

'Well?' Meddows asked.

Pitt repeated the name and address.

Meddows' face creased into comic surprise. 'How very unlikely,' he observed. 'By the way, he was probably unconscious and damn near dead by the time they did this to him.' He gestured toward the lower part of the body. 'If that's any comfort. I suppose you know about the other one?'

'Other one? What are you talking about? Other what?'

Meddows' face tightened. 'Other corpse, man. The other one we found castrated like this. Don't say you didn't know about it?'

Pitt was stunned. How could he have failed to hear of such a monstrosity?

'Some gambler or pimp,' Meddows went on. 'Other side of the Acre—not your station. But, as I said, he was emasculated, too, poor sod, though not as badly as this

14

one. It looks as if we've got some kind of maniac loose. Managed to keep the papers from making too much of the first one. Victim was the sort of man that's always getting knifed—they do in an occupation of that kind.' He stood up slowly, his knees cracking. 'But this one's different. He'd seen better times, perhaps, but he still ate well. And I'd say at a guess that his shabbiness might be more of an eccentricity than a lack of means. His suit is pretty worn, but his linen is new—and reasonably clean, not had it on more than a day, by the look of it.'

Pitt thought of the Stilton cheese, and the immaculate fingernails. 'Yes,' he said flatly. He knew Meddows was staring at him, waiting. 'All right. I suppose if you've finished here we'd better have him taken away. Do a proper autopsy, and tell me anything else—if there is anything.'

'Naturally.'

Now came the worst part; once again, Pitt mentally debated whether he could delegate the task of informing the family— the widow, if there was one. And, as always, he could not escape the conviction that he must do it himself. If he did not, he would feel he had betrayed both the junior he sent and the bereaved he might have comforted.

He gave all the necessary orders to the men waiting outside. The body must be removed, the yard sealed off and searched for anything at all that might render a clue as to who had done this thing. A search must be initiated for vagrants who had been in the area, for lodgers who might have been returning home, for idle prostitutes, for someone who might have seen something.

Meanwhile he would go to 23 Lambert Gardens, and inform the household—at this hour probably just sitting down to breakfast—that their master had been murdered.

Pitt was met at the door by an extremely competent butler. 'Good morning, sir,' the man said politely. Pitt was a stranger to him, and it was too early for a social call.

'Good morning,' Pitt answered quietly. 'I am from the police. Is this the residence of Dr Hubert Pinchin?'

'Yes, sir, but I am afraid Dr Pinchin is not at home at the moment. I can recommend another doctor to you if your need is urgent.'

'I don't require a doctor. I'm sorry, I have bad news for you. Dr Pinchin is dead.'

'Oh dear.' The butler's face tightened but his composure remained perfect. He moved back a step, allowing Pitt to enter. 'You had better come in, sir. Would you be good enough to tell me what happened? It might be easier if I were to break the news to Mrs Pinchin. I am sure you would be most tactful, but...' He delicately left the obvious in the air.

'Yes,' Pitt said with a relief that struck a spark of guilt in him. 'Yes, of course.'

'How did it happen, sir?'

'He was attacked, stabbed in the back. I think he probably knew very little pain. I'm sorry.'

The butler stared at him in a moment of immobility; then he swallowed. 'Murdered?'

'Yes. I'm sorry,' Pitt repeated. 'Is there someone who can identify the body—perhaps someone other than Mrs Pinchin? It will be distressing.' Should he mention the mutilation now?

The butler had regained his self-possession; he was in command of himself and of the household. 'Yes, sir. I will inform Mrs Pinchin of Dr Pinchin's death. She has an excellent maid who will care for her. There is another doctor in the neighbourhood who will attend her. The footman, Peters, has been with us for twelve years. He will go and identify the body.' He hesitated. 'I suppose there is no doubt? Dr Pinchin was a little less than my height, sir, very well built, clean-shaven, and of a rich complexion...' He let the vague hope hang in the air. But it was pointless.

'Yes,' Pitt answered. 'Did Dr Pinchin have a suit of rough brown tweed. I should judge of some years' wear?'

'Yes, sir. That is what he was wearing when he left home yesterday.'

'Then I am afraid there can be little doubt. But perhaps your footman should make sure before you say anything to Mrs Pinchin.'

'Yes, sir, naturally.'

Pitt gave him the address of the mortuary, and then advised him of the nature of the other wounds, and that the newspapers would inevitably make much of it. It would be a kindness to keep the reporters out of the house for as long as possible, until some other event superseded the murder in the public eye.

Pitt left without meeting the widow at

all. She had not risen from her bed, and only in his imagination did he see her shock, followed by disbelief, slow acceptance, and finally the beginning of overwhelming pain.

He must, of course, go to see the officer dealing with the other murder that appeared to be so similar. The two crimes may or may not be connected, but to ignore the possibility would be absurd. Perhaps he would even find himself relieved of the case. He would not mind in the least; he felt no sense of proprietorship, as he had in some cases. Whoever had committed this crime had entered a realm far outside the ordinary world of offence and punishment.

As he trod on against the squally wind fluttering rubbish off the pavements, he reflected that he would not mind in the least if they took this one away from him. He crossed the road just before a hansom cab clopped past. A boy who was sweeping a clear path from the horse droppings stopped and rested on his broom. His small hands were chapped red, and his fingers jutted out of the ends of his gloves. A brougham swished by and splattered them both with a mixture of mud and manure.

The boy grinned to see Pitt's irritation. 'Oughter've walked on me parf, mister,' he said cheerfully. 'Then yer'd not get yerself mucked.'

Pitt handed him a farthing and agreed with him wryly.

At the police station he was greeted with an unexpected warmth. 'Inspector Pitt? Yes, sir. I suppose as you've come about our murder, sir—it being the same as your one this morning, like?'

Pitt was taken aback. How did this young constable know about Hubert Pinchin? His face must have reflected his thoughts, as it often did, because the constable answered the question before Pitt asked it.

'It's in the afternoon extras, sir. Screaming about it, they are. Downright 'orrible. Course I know they write up things something chronic, adding bits to shock people into 'ysterics. But all the same—!'

'I doubt they added anything to this one,' Pitt replied dryly. He unwound his muffler and took off his hat. His coat flapped loose, one side longer than the other; he must have done it up on the wrong buttons again. 'May I speak to whoever is in charge of your murder, if he's in?'

'Yes, sir, that'll be Inspector Parkins. I reckon as 'e'll be real glad to see you.'

Pitt doubted it, but he followed the constable willingly enough into a warm, dark office that smelled of old paper and wax polish. It was larger than his own, and there was a photograph of a woman and four children on the desk. Parkins was a dark, dapper man; he sat dismally looking at a sheaf of papers in his hand. The constable introduced Pitt with a flourish.

Parkins' face lost its lugubrious expression immediately. 'Come in,' he said heartily. 'Come in—sit down. Here, move those files—make yourself comfortable, man. Yes, disgusting affair. You want to know all about it? Found him in the gutter! Dead as mutton. Quite cold—of course no wonder, weather we've been having! Filthy! And it'll get worse. He'd been stabbed in the back, poor devil—long, sharp blade, probably kitchen knife, or something like it.' He paused for breath and pulled a face, running his hands through his sparse hair. 'Man was a procurer—corpse found by a local prostitute. At any other time, I would have said that was not inappropriate.

21

I suppose you'll want to take the case now, since it's almost certainly connected with yours.' He made it a statement.

Pitt was startled. 'No!' he said involuntarily. 'I thought you—'

'Not at all.' Parkins waved his arms as if declining some favour. 'Not at all. Senior officer, much more experience than I have. Admired you for the way you handled that Bluegate Fields business.' He saw Pitt's surprised expression. 'Oh, we get to hear the odd thing, you know. Friends, a word here, word there.' He held up a finger and waved it in some vague gesture of understanding.

Pitt was surprised and flattered. He was vulnerable enough to like having his courage admired—it was a singularly warming feeling. And he had been afraid during the Bluegate Fields investigation; he had risked more than he could afford to lose.

'Our fellow was only a pimp,' Parkins went on. 'Better off without him—not that it'll make any difference, of course. Soon as he's gone, someone else'll step into his place—probably have already. Like taking a bucket of water out of the river. Tide comes and goes just the same—can't see where it's been. No, not at all! Your fellow was a doctor? Decent chap. You better have all the papers we've got—autopsy report, and so on. And I suppose you'll want to see the body.'

'You still have it?' Pitt asked.

'Oh, yes—only a week ago, you know. Weather like this, cold enough to keep bodies for ages. Yes, you'd better see it. Never know, might be able to tell if it's the same maniac.'

Pitt followed him silently to the mortuary. Parkins opened the door and had a quiet word with the attendant, then conducted Pitt inside. The room was chilly and dry, with a faint musty smell, like old medicine.

Parkins went to one of the white, sheet-covered tables and pulled the cloth off entirely, showing not only the face but the whole naked body. It was a curiously indecent gesture, even toward the dead. Pitt's instinct was to seize the sheet and cover the lower part again, but he knew it was ridiculous. After all, that was what he had come to see.

But the wound was not identical. This was a messy and extremely inexpert castration. The glands had been removed

23

and the organ all but severed.

'All right.' Pitt swallowed, his throat rough.

Parkins replaced the sheet and looked at Pitt, his mouth twisted with wry, sad humour. 'Nasty, isn't it?' he said quietly. 'Makes you feel sick. Don't suppose you know him, by any chance? Not likely, but you can never tell.' He turned the sheet back at the top.

Pitt had not even looked at the face. Now he did so, and instantly felt a prickling sense of shock. He had seen those dark, surly features before, the heavy eyelids and curling, sensuous mouth. At least he was almost sure he had.

'Who is he?' he asked.

'Max. Used two or three different surnames: Bracknall, Rawlins, Dunmow. Kept more than one establishment. Very enterprising fellow. Why? Do you know him?'

'I think so,' Pitt replied slowly. 'At least he looks like someone I dealt with a few years ago—murders in Callander Square.'

'Callander Square?' Parkins was surprised. 'Hardly the area for a creature of this sort. Are you sure?'

'No, I'm not sure. He was a footman.

His name was Max Burton then—if it is the same man.'

Parkins' voice lifted with curiosity. 'Can't you find out? It could be important.' Then his tone fell again and he smiled bleakly at himself. 'Although I hardly suppose so. He's changed his style of living more than somewhat since then!'

'I expect I can,' Pitt said thoughtfully. 'Shouldn't be too hard. Oh, where was the wound that caused his death?'

'Here,' Parkins replied, as if he too had momentarily forgotten it. 'Stab in the back, about so.' He indicated on Pitt's body a place close to the spine, an inch or two to the left. It was lower than the wound in Pinchin's back, but only by a fraction, and on the same side. But then Max had been taller than Pinchin.

'What kind of weapon? How long? How broad?'

'About eight inches long, and an inch and a half broad at the hilt. Could have been a kitchen knife. Everybody has one, ordinary enough. Sorry.' Parkins raised one eyebrow, understanding perfectly. 'Same as yours, is it?'

Pitt disliked the reference to Pinchin as 'his' but he knew what Parkins meant.

'Yes,' he conceded. 'Almost exactly.' He was compelled to add, 'Only, in today's case, the man's entire genital organs were slashed away, and placed between his knees.'

Parkins' face tightened. 'Catch him,' he said quietly. 'Catch this bastard, Mr Pitt.'

Pitt had not been back to Callander Square since the murders three years ago. He wondered if the Balantynes still lived there. He stood in the bitter afternoon under the bare trees; the bark was wet with rain gathering on the wind. It would be dark early. He was only twenty feet away from the place where the bodies had been found that had first brought him here to question the residents of these elegant Georgian houses, with their tall windows, and immaculate façades. These were people with footmen to answer doors, parlourmaids to receive, and butlers to keep their pantries, guard their cellar keys, and rule with rods of iron their own domains behind the green baize doors.

He pulled his collar up higher, set his hat a trifle rakishly on his head, and plunged his hands into his pockets, which already bulged with odd bits of string, coins, a knife, three keys, two handkerchiefs, a piece of sealing wax, and innumerable scraps of paper. He refused to go to the tradesmen's entrance, as he knew would be expected of him, but instead presented himself at the front door, like any other caller.

The footman received him coldly. 'Good afternoon...sir.' The hesitation was slight, but sufficient to imply that the title was a courtesy, and in his opinion one not warranted.

'Good afternoon,' Pitt replied with complete composure. 'My name is Thomas Pitt. I would like to see General Balantyne on a matter of business that is most urgent. Otherwise I would not have called without first making sure it was convenient.'

The footman's face twitched, but he had been forestalled in the argument he had prepared.

'General Balantyne does not receive callers merely because they happen by, Mr Pitt,' he said, even more coldly. He looked Pitt up and down with an expert eye. Obviously, dressed like that, he was not a person of quality, in spite of his speech. Such clothes were surely the product of no tailor, and as for a valet—any valet worthy of his calling would cut his own throat rather than let his master appear in public in such total disarray. That waistcoat should not have been matched with that shirt, the jacket was a disaster, and the cravat had been tied by a blind man with two left hands.

'I am sorry,' he repeated, now quite sure of his ground. 'General Balantyne does not receive callers without appointment—unless, of course, they are already of his social acquaintance. Perhaps if you were to write to him? Or get someone else to do it for you?'

The suggestion that he was illiterate was the final straw.

'I am acquainted with General Balantyne,' Pitt snapped. 'And it is police business. If you prefer to discuss it on the doorstep, I shall oblige you. But I imagine the general would rather have it pursued inside! Considerably more discreet—don't you think?'

The footman was startled, and he allowed it to show. To have police at the house—and at the front of it—was appalling. Damn the man's impertinence! He composed his face, but was annoyed that Pitt was taller than he by some inches, so even with the advantage of the step he could not adequately look down on him.

'If you have some problem of theft or the like,' he replied, 'you had better go round to the tradesmen's entrance. No doubt the butler will see you—if it is really necessary.'

'It is not a matter of theft,' Pitt said icily. 'It is a matter of murder, and it is General Balantyne I require to speak to, not the butler. I cannot imagine he will be best pleased if you oblige me to come back with a warrant!'

The footman knew when he was beaten. He retreated. 'If you will come this way.' He refused to add the 'sir.' 'Perhaps if you wait in the morning room, the general will see you when he is able.' He walked smartly across the hall and opened the door of a large room whose grate held the embers of a fire that took the chill from the air but was not hot enough to thaw Pitt's hands or warm his body through his clothes.

The footman looked at the ashes and smirked with satisfaction. He turned and went out, closing the polished wooden door with a click. He had not offered to take Pitt's hat and coat. Five minutes later, he was back, his face pinched with anger. He took Pitt's outer clothes and ordered him to follow the parlourmaid to the library.

In that room a fire was blazing, reflecting bright scarlet in the leather bindings of books and glinting off the polished trophies on the far wall. The general stood behind a great desk littered with inkstands, pens, paperweights, open books, and a miniature field cannon in brass—a perfect replica of a Crimean gun. He had not changed outwardly since Pitt saw him last: the same broad, stiff shoulders, the proud face, the light brown hair perhaps greying a little, although Pitt was not sure. It was a face dominated by strength of bone, and the colouring was incidental.

'Well, Mr Pitt?' he said formally. He was a man who did not know how to be casual. All his life had been spent in observing rules, even in the face of terror or extremity of pain. As a boy soldier, he had stood appalled on the ridge above Balaclava and seen the charge of the Light Brigade. The carnage of the Crimea was indelible in his memory. He knew the men of the 'thin red line' who had held against all the might hurled at them by the Russian Army, men who had kept their ground in face of the impossible. Hundreds had fallen, but not a man had broken ranks.

'My footman says you wish to speak to me about a murder? Is that correct?'

Pitt found himself standing a little straighter—not quite to attention, but definitely with his feet together and his head up. 'Yes, sir. A week ago there was an extremely unpleasant murder in an area known as the Devil's Acre, hard by Westminster.'

'I know where it is.' The general frowned. 'But surely that was this morning?'

'I'm afraid there was a second one this morning. The first did not make much of a mark in the newspapers. However, I was called in for this one today, and when I heard of the earlier one, naturally I went to see the body.'

'Naturally,' the general's frown deepened. 'What is it you wish of me?'

Now that it came to the point, Pitt felt rather embarrassed at having to ask this man to come and look at the corpse of a dead procurer of whores. What did it matter if it was or was not the man who had been his footman at the time of the Callander Square murders? It could make no real difference now.

He cleared his throat; there was no avoiding it. 'I think the man may be someone you knew.'

The general's eyebrows rose in amazement. 'Someone I knew?'

'Yes, sir, I think so.' Pitt explained as briefly as he could the circumstances of Pinchin's death, and what Inspector Parkins had shown him at the mortuary.

'Very well,' the general said reluctantly, and reached for the bell cord to summon the carriage.

The door opened and, instead of the footman, one of the most striking women Pitt could recall ever having set eyes on came in: Lady Augusta Balantyne. Her face was as fine as bone china, but without any of porcelain's fragility. Her clothes were magnificent, in the subdued taste of those who have always had money and therefore never felt the compulsion to display it garishly. She stared at Pitt with distaste; her very posture appeared to demand an explanation, not only for his presence in her house but for his very existence.

Pitt refused to be intimidated. 'Good afternoon, Lady Augusta,' he said with a slight bow. 'I hope I find you well?'

'I am always well, thank you, Mr—' She could not have forgotten their past meetings; the subject was too bizarre, too painful. 'Mr Pitt.' She arched her eyebrows very slightly, and her eyes were glacial beneath them. 'To what unfortunate occurrence do we owe your visit this time?'

'A matter of identification, ma'am,' he answered smoothly. He felt the general relax, even though he could barely see him at the edge of his vision. 'A man General Balantyne may be able to name for us, and if so, that might assist us greatly.'

'Good gracious—can the man not name himself?'

'People do not always tell the truth, ma'am,' he said dryly.

She coloured at her own clumsiness for not having seen the obvious.

'And in this case I understand he is dead anyway,' the general added tartly. 'It is nothing for you to concern yourself with, my dear. It is my duty to be of assistance, if I can. I dare say I shall not be long.'

'Have you forgotten we are dining with Sir Harry and Lady Lisburne tonight?'

She ignored Pitt as if he had been one of the servants. 'I do not intend to arrive late. I will not be thought ill-mannered, whatever you may imagine your duty to be.'

'The man is in a mortuary not half an hour away.' The general's face flickered with irritation. He disliked dinner parties, and, with Harry Lisburne as host, this one was likely to be more tedious than ever. 'I have only to look at him and say whether I know him or not. I shall be back before dark.'

She blew down her nose with a little sigh, and went out without looking at Pitt again. General Balantyne walked into the hall, collected his coat from the waiting butler, and accompanied Pitt out into the rain just as the coachman drove around from the mews and stopped at the curbside for them.

They rode in silence. Pitt did not want to prejudice the identification by discussing the case beforehand, and he felt no compulsion to make small talk of other things.

The carriage stopped a short distance from the mortuary, and Pitt and the general alighted and walked up the path, still silent. Inside, the duty attendant appeared startled to see a gentleman of Balantyne's obvious quality, but he recognized Pitt, and conducted them to the body without hesitation.

'There you are, sir.' He whipped back the sheet with the air of a conjurer producing a rabbit.

Like Pitt before him, the general's eyes went straight to the mutilation, not even glancing at the face. He took a deep breath and let it out. He had seen death before, a great deal of death, almost all of it by the violence of war or the ravages of disease. What made this uniquely appalling to him was that it had happened deliberately, here at home in the streets of London. The inexpert dismemberment was not the accident of random cannonfire, but looked to be the result of a passionate and individual hatred for one man in particular.

What man? The general looked up at the face. Pitt, watching him carefully, saw the start of recognition.

'General?' He lifted his voice only a little.

Balantyne looked up slowly. Pitt could not read the emotions in his eyes. Balantyne was an exceedingly private man, unused to the comforts of fellow sympathy. Pitt could never really understand him; their backgrounds were worlds apart. Balantyne was the last of generations of soldiers who had served monarch and country with unquestioning sacrifice in every foreign war since the days of Agincourt, whereas Pitt was the son of a country gamekeeper convicted unjustly of some petty offence. Pitt had grown up on the estate of his master and been educated to his excellent, almost beautiful diction, to provide companionship to the son of the house and to encourage the boy in his studies. Pitt's hunger had been a challenge, and not infrequently a reproach to spur the boy out of indolence.

Yet he liked Balantyne, even admired him. He was a man who lived as strictly by the code he believed in as had any ancient knight or monk.

'Do you know him?' he prompted, although the question was now no more than academic; the answer was in the general's face.

'Of course,' Balantyne replied quietly. 'It is Max Burton, who used to be my footman.'

CHAPTER 2

Gracie came rushing into the parlour with the early editions of the afternoon newspapers. Her face was suffused with colour, her eyes as round as gooseberries. 'Oh, ma'am! There's been an 'orrible murder—most terrible in London's 'istory o'crime, it says 'ere. Doin's as'd make a strong man go white to 'is knees!'

'Indeed?' Charlotte did not stop her sewing. Newspapers always dealt in hyperbole—who stops in a January street to buy a paper that tells of the ordinary?

Gracie was horrified of her indifference. 'No, ma'am—I really means it! It was dreadful! 'E was all 'acked to pieces, in a place as wot a lady wouldn't even know of! Leastways not as she'd put words to and still call 'erself a lady. The papers is right, ma'am. There's a terrible maniac loose in the Devil's Acre—and maybe them preachers is right and the Last Days is come, and it's Satan 'isself!' Gracie's face went pale as the apparition formed in her mind.

37

'Nonsense!' Charlotte said sharply. She could see that if she was not careful she would have a case of hysterics on her hands. 'Here, give me the papers, and go and get on with the vegetables or we shall have no dinner. If the master comes home out of this weather and there is nothing hot for him, he will be most displeased.'

It was an idle threat. Gracie held Pitt in immense respect; he was the master, after all. And beyond that he was a policeman and therefore represented the Law. And then there were the fascinating and dangerous things he must know! Shocking things! Worse than in the papers! But she was not in the least afraid of him. He was not the sort of person to put a servant out on the street for one neglected meal, and she knew it.

'It's 'orrible, ma'am,' she repeated, wagging her head to prove she had been right from the beginning. 'Do you want as I should use that cabbage tonight, or the turnips?'

'Both,' Charlotte replied absently, already absorbed in the newspapers herself.

Gracie accepted the dismissal and went back to the kitchen, turning the morning's events over in her mind. It was a source of great satisfaction to her that she worked for a lady—a real lady—not one of your jumped-up social climbers as fancied theirselves better than they was, but one as was born into the Quality, and grew up in a house with real servants, a Staff, a butler as had a pantry of his own, and a separate cook and kitchenmaids and parlourmaids and upstairs maids and the like—and footmen! None of Gracie's sisters or friends had a mistress like that! Gracie enjoyed considerable distinction because of it, and was able to tell other girls what was what and how things should be done proper.

Of course Charlotte had come down in the world a bit since then: a policeman was not a gentleman—everyone knew that. But still there were times when it was very exciting! The tales she could tell—if she chose! But of course such things were far better hinted at than recounted in detail. She had her loyalties.

And, to tell the truth, she did not entirely approve of the way her mistress sometimes got herself involved in police goings-on. More than once she had actually had some face-to-face contact with people as had done murders. Looking for people like that, even if they turned out to be from the Quality, was no thing for a lady to do.

Gracie shook her head and tipped the turnips out into the sink and began to wash and peel them. Unless she was very mistaken in her judgment, her mistress was shaping up nicely to start meddling into something again. She had that restless look about her, fiddling with things and putting them down half done, writing letters to her sister Emily as was now Viscountess Ashworth. Married above herself, that one. Not that she wasn't very nice, the few times that Gracie had seen her. More often Charlotte went to visit her at her grand house in Paragon Walk. And who could blame her for that?

Gracie drifted into a pleasant dream of what a Viscountess's house might be like. No doubt she would have beautiful footmen, all tall and handsome, and wearing livery, too! A man did look good in livery, no matter what anyone said!

In the evening when Pitt came home, Charlotte was waiting for him. She had read the newspapers thoroughly because the appalling corpse had been discovered in Pitt's area; she knew it was quite likely that the call he had received before dawn that morning had to do with the murder.

Of course the case was not one in which she would be able to give any help, unfortunately. She was ready for the challenge, even the danger of another investigation, but the man had been found in a location she knew nothing whatsoever about, except by repute. And Lambert Gardens, where apparently he had lived, was not part of her family's social circle, so she could offer no assistance there either.

Still, perhaps if he was prepared to discuss it with her, she could at least use her wits. She had not been unskilled at divining motives in the past, and the nature of human beings had much in common whatever the circumstances.

She hurried to meet her husband as soon as she heard the front door close, even before Gracie could get there. She took his coat, hung it up to dry, and then turned immediately to kiss him. His face felt cold. She knew he must be tired; it was over twelve hours since he had left, without breakfast. Her senses told her to restrain her curiosity at least until he had finished supper. She led the way into the parlour and talked about nothing of consequence while Pitt thawed out in front of the fire until Gracie served the meal.

By nine o'clock she considered that tact had been paid more than its due. 'The constable who came for you this morning,' she began. 'Was that because of the corpse in the Devil's Acre?'

A trace of bleak humour flickered across his face. When Charlotte tried being subtle with him, he usually saw through it, so she had abandoned the effort. Anyhow, she had not had time to prepare and approach the whole subject in a more devious fashion.

'Yes,' he said guardedly. 'But Lambert Gardens, which is where he lived, is not your family's social circle. There is nothing you can do to help.'

She was not tactically inept. 'No, of course not,' she said. 'But it is impossible not to be interested. The newspapers are full of it this evening.'

He pulled a face.

She changed her line of attack. 'Do be careful, Thomas. It sounds as if there is some dreadful madman loose. I mean, it isn't a sane sort of crime, is it? What do you suppose a man like Dr Pinchin was doing in the Devil's Acre anyway? Did he have a practice there? The newspapers said he was a very respectable man.' She was not entirely convinced; she had known plenty of 'respectable' people herself. All the adjective really meant was that they were either clever enough or fortunate enough to have maintained an excellent façade. Behind it there might be anything at all.

Pitt smiled, his eyes uncomfortably clear. 'Thank you, my dear, but you have no need to be anxious for me. I don't expect to prowl the Acre alone. I shall be in no danger from madmen.'

She debated whether to be hurt and pretend he had misunderstood her, but decided rapidly that it would not work. 'Of course not,' she said. 'Perhaps I was being silly. I dare say Dr Pinchin was not nearly as respectable as the newspapers suggested. After all, they would have to be very careful of what they said, and the poor man is only just dead.' She looked up, wide-eyed and totally candid. 'Did he have a family?'

'Charlotte!'

'Yes, Thomas?'

He let out his breath in a sigh. 'This is not a case you can involve yourself in. Dr

Pinchin was not the only victim—he was the second that we know of, and whatever is going on, it has its cause in the Devil's Acre. The other body was found there, too. It is not a domestic crime, Charlotte. It does not involve the sort of motives you are good at.'

She ignored the compliment. 'Another one? I didn't know that! The newspapers didn't say anything. Are you keeping it secret? Who was it?'

There was a momentary flash of irritation in his face. Charlotte was not sure whether it was directed at her or at circumstances.

Pitt waited several seconds before he answered, and when he did there was resignation in his voice. 'Actually, it was someone you have already met.'

Shock tingled through her, not unmixed with a sense of excitement that she was ashamed of the instant after she felt it.

'I've met?' she repeated incredulously.

'Do you remember General Balantyne—in Callander Square?'

The excitement turned to horror so intense it almost made her sick. The room swam and she thought she was going to faint. To imagine the general, with his

44

fierce, inarticulate pride, his loneliness, his veneration of duty—how could he have descended to the Devil's Acre to die not in service or battle but exposed in such a horrible manner.

'Charlotte!'

Surely there must be some way it could be kept quiet? It was the last way on earth such a man deserved to die!

'Charlotte!' Pitt's voice cut through her thoughts.

She looked up.

'It wasn't Balantyne!' he said sharply. 'It was his old footman, Max—do you remember Max?'

Of course! How could she have been so ridiculous? She took a deep gulp of air. 'Max—yes, of course I remember Max. Perfectly odious. He always gave me the feeling that when he looked at me he could see through my clothes.'

Pitt's face dropped in alarm, then changed to a wide-eyed amusement. 'How graphic! I had no idea you were so perceptive.'

She felt herself colouring. She had not meant to let him know she understood that look so well, especially in the eyes of a footman. She ought not have!

'Well...' She attempted an explanation, and gave it up.

He waited, but Charlotte refused to dig herself in any more deeply. 'What was Max doing in the Devil's Acre?' she asked. 'I didn't think people in that sort of area had footmen.'

'They don't. He was keeping a brothel—in fact, more than one.'

She maintained her composure. Over the years Charlotte had had cause, one way or another, to learn quite a lot about poverty and the prostitution of both adults and children.

'Oh.' She remembered Max's dark face, with its hooded eyelids and heavy, sensuous mouth. He had always given her an acute consciousness of physical power, of an appetite that was his servant as well as his master. 'I should imagine he would do that sort of thing rather well.'

Pitt looked at her with surprise.

'I mean—' she started, then changed her mind. Why should she explain? She may not know as much as he did, but she was not a total innocent! 'In that case, he must have had rather a lot of enemies,' she continued reasonably. 'If he had several establishments, then he was doing very well—and I imagine in that sort of trade people are not very scrupulous about how they dispose of competition.'

'Not very,' he agreed with an expression that showed such a mixture of feelings she found it quite unreadable.

'Perhaps Dr Pinchin kept a brothel as well,' she suggested. 'Sometimes very respectable people own property in places like that, you know?'

'Yes, I do know,' he said dryly.

She caught his glance. 'Of course you know. I'm sorry.'

'There's nothing you can do in this case, Charlotte. It isn't your world.'

'No, of course not,' she said obediently. At this point it would not be to her advantage to pursue the matter because she could think of no argument to put forward. 'I don't really know anything about the Devil's Acre.'

Nevertheless, the following morning as soon as Pitt was out of the house, Charlotte began making arrangements to be absent for most of the day. Gracie, who far preferred to look after children than blacken the stove, polish the passage floor, or scrub the doorstep, greeted Charlotte's instructions with enthusiasm—and a tacit promise of silence. She knew a conspiracy when she met it, even if she did not entirely approve. A lady's curiosity ought to be restricted to other people's romances, who was wearing what, and how much it cost—and even then she should always keep her dignity. If a gentleman was murdered, that was one thing—but not a doctor who practiced in the Devil's Acre and was obviously no better than he should be! Gracie had heard about places like that—and people!

Charlotte had said she was going to see her sister Emily, but Gracie had her own ideas of what that was for! She knew perfectly well that Lady Ashworth was not above a good deal of meddling in shocking affairs herself.

'Yes, ma'am.' She bobbed a neat curtsy. 'I 'ope as you'll 'ave a nice day, ma'am. An' come 'ome safe.'

'Of course I'll come home safely!' Charlotte switched her skirt past a chair and accepted her coat from Gracie's outstretched hands. 'I'm only going to Paragon Walk.'

'Yes, ma'am, I'm sure.'

Charlotte gave her a sidewise look, but

apparently considered she had already said enough about discretion. Anything more might only make Gracie's suspicions worse.

'What shall I say to the master, ma'am?' Gracie asked.

'Nothing. I shall be home long before then. In fact, if Lady Ashworth has an engagement, I may even be home by luncheon.' And with that she swept out the door, down the front step, and went briskly toward the corner where the public omnibus stopped.

Paragon Walk was classically elegant in the winter sun. Charlotte walked smartly along the footpath and up the smooth carriageway to Emily's front door. The footman opened it before she had reached up for the bellpull. Naturally, in a well-ordered house the pantry would look out onto the drive and guests would be anticipated.

'Good morning, Mrs Pitt,' he said courteously.

'Good morning, Albert,' she replied with satisfaction, accepting his tacit invitation and stepping inside. It was a very comfortable feeling to be recognized so easily. It gave her the temporary illusion of belonging to this world again.

49

'Lady Ashworth is writing letters,' he said almost conversationally as he walked ahead of her across the large hall. On its walls were the Ashworth family portraits stretching back to the days of ruffled collars and Elizabethan pantaloons, with gorgeous slashes of colour. 'But I am sure she will be pleased to see you.'

Charlotte, knowing how Emily disliked letter-writing was also sure. And she would be even more pleased when she heard Charlotte's extraordinary piece of news.

The footman opened the morning-room door. 'Mrs Pitt, m'lady,' he said.

Emily stood up, pushing her pen and papers away before Charlotte was even through the door. She was not quite as tall as Charlotte, and had fairer hair that turned to curls with a softness Charlotte had envied all her life. She came forward and hugged Charlotte impulsively, her face alight with pleasure.

'How delightful of you to come! I'm bored to pieces with letters. They are all to George's cousins, and I can't bear any of them. Really, you know, the young girls out this Season seem to be even sillier than last year. And heaven knows they were light-witted enough! I refuse to think

50

what next year will be like! How are you?' She stood back and surveyed Charlotte critically. 'You look far too healthy to be in the least fashionable. You should appear delicate, like a lily, not some great bursting rose! That is the thing these days. And don't you know that it is vulgar to look so excited? Whatever has happened? If you don't tell me, I shall—' A suitable chastisement eluded her; she went over to the comfortable chair in front of the fire and curled up in it.

Charlotte joined her on the sofa opposite, feeling warm, comfortable, and smug. 'Do you remember the murders in Callander Square?' she began.

Emily sat up a little straighter, her eyes bright. 'Don't be idiotic! Whoever forgets a murder? Why? Has there been another?'

'Do you remember that dreadful footman, Max?'

'Vaguely. Why? Charlotte, for goodness' sake stop being so obscure! What on earth are you talking about?'

'Did you read of the murder of Dr Hubert Pinchin in the newspapers yesterday, or this morning?'

'No, of course not.' Emily was on the edge of her seat now, her back ramrod stiff. 'You know George doesn't give me anything but the society pages. Who is Hubert Pinchin, and what has it to do with that unpleasant footman? Really, you can be extremely irritating!'

Charlotte settled more deeply into the cushions and recounted everything she knew.

Emily clenched her hands, crushing the shell-pink silk of her dress. 'Oh dear—how very disgusting! But I never liked that man,' she added frankly. 'He left the Balantynes, didn't he—before the end of that affair, anyway?'

'Yes. It seems he became very successful as a procurer of women.'

Emily winced. 'Then perhaps it was rather suitable that he was found in a gutter. And by a prostitute. Do you suppose God has a sense of humour? Or would that be blasphemous?'

'He created man,' Charlotte answered. 'He must at the very least have a pronounced sense of the absurd. The newspapers say that Dr Pinchin was perfectly respectable.'

'Then what was he doing in the Devil's Acre? Did he take charity cases or something of the sort?'

'I don't know. I expect Thomas will find out.'

'Well, any man of quality who wanted to pick up a loose woman for the evening would go to a music hall, or the Haymarket. He wouldn't go to some dangerous slum like the Devil's Acre.'

Charlotte felt a little crushed. The mystery was fast dissolving in front of her. 'Perhaps the women in the Haymarket were too expensive. If Max kept a brothel, there must be customers in the Devil's Acre! If Dr Pinchin was one of them—'

'Why kill him?' Emily interrupted with an irritating display of reason. 'Nobody but an idiot kills his own customers.'

'Maybe his wife did.'

Emily raised her eyebrows. 'In the Devil's Acre?'

'Not personally, stupid! She may have hired someone. You would have to hate a person very much and in a particular sort of way to do that to him.'

Emily's face lost its spark of amusement. 'Of course you would. But, my dear, all sorts of men use loose women from time to time, and as long as they do it discreetly, a wife with any sense at all does not inquire into it. If a man does not offer explanations of where he has been, for the sake of one's own happiness it is wiser not to press for them.'

Charlotte could think of no reply that was not either painful or naïve. People must deal with their own truths as they were able.

Emily's mind was on a different train. 'Fancy that dreadful footman turning up again. He always made me uncomfortable. I wonder who provided the money for him to set up a brothel? I mean who owned the property and paid for an establishment? Perhaps it was Dr Pinchin.'

But a far uglier thought forced itself into Charlotte's mind, linked with memories of the Balantyne house, murder and fear in the past, and Max's sudden, silent departure.

'Yes,' she agreed abruptly. 'Yes, that may very well be so. I dare say Thomas will discover that.'

Emily gave her a narrow look, a flicker of suspicion, but she did not pursue it. 'Will you stay for luncheon?'

As Charlotte was preparing for her visit with Emily, Pitt alighted from his cab and walked up to the front door of number

23 Lambert Gardens. It was a high house with a handsome frontage, though today, of course, the curtains were drawn and there was black crêpe on the windows and a wreath on the door. The whole effect was one of a curious blindness.

There was no point in putting it off; he lifted his hand and knocked on the door. It was several minutes before an unhappy-looking footman opened it. Death in the house made him awkward; he had no idea how much grief he was expected to show, especially in these grotesque circumstances. Maybe he ought to pretend to ignore it. After all, what could he possibly say? The kitchenmaid had already given notice, and he was considering doing the same.

He did not recognize Pitt. 'Mrs Pinchin is not receiving callers,' he said hastily. 'But if you care to leave your card, I am sure she will accept your condolences.'

'I am Thomas Pitt, from the police,' Pitt explained. 'I do convey my sympathy to Mrs Pinchin, of course, but I am afraid it is necessary that I also speak with her.'

The footman was painfully undecided about which of his duties was paramount: on the one hand, preserving the sanctity of mourning from such a crass invasion by a person of this sort, or, on the other hand, his undoubted allegiance to the majesty of the Law.

'Perhaps if you call the butler?' Pitt suggested tactfully. 'And permit me not to wait upon the step while you do so. We do not wish to attract the attention and the gossip of the neighbours' maids and bootboys.'

The footman's face was almost comical with relief. It was the perfect solution. Gossip would be inevitable, but he had no intention of being blamed for adding to it.

'Oh—yes, sir—yes—I'll do that. If you come this way, sir.' He led Pitt across the hall, which was filled with a faint odour as if none of the doors had been opened for days. The mirrors were black-draped like the windows. There was an arrangement of lilies in a pedestal vase; they looked artificial, though they were in fact real, and undoubtedly extremely expensive at this time of year.

The footman left Pitt in a room with a black-leaded grate and no fire. It was dark behind the drawn blinds, and it seemed as if the whole household were determined that even if the corpse of the master could not lie in his own home, they would order their domestic arrangements to imitate the chill of the grave.

It was only a few moments before Mr Mullen, the butler, arrived, his thinning, sandy hair brushed neatly back and his face determined. 'I am sorry, Mr Pitt.' He shook his head. 'I'm afraid it will be another half hour before Mrs Pinchin is able to receive you. Perhaps you would like a dish of tea while you wait? It is a very inclement day.'

Pitt felt warmer already. He had respect for this man; he knew his job and seemed to perform it with more than ordinary skill.

'I would indeed, Mr Mullen, thank you. And if your duties permit, perhaps a little of your time?'

'Certainly, sir.' Mullen pulled the bell rope and, when the footman answered, requested that a pot of tea be brought, with two cups. He would not have presumed to take refreshment with a gentleman caller, and a tradesman would have been sent through the green baize door to the kitchen. But he considered Pitt to be roughly his social equal, which Pitt realized was something of a compliment.

A butler was in many senses the real master of a household, and might rule a staff of a dozen or more lesser servants. He might also have greater intelligence than the owner, and certainly inspire more awe from his fellows.

'Have you been with Dr Pinchin long, Mr Mullen?' Pit began conversationally.

'Eleven years, Mr Pitt,' Mullen replied. 'Before that I was with Lord and Lady Fullerton, in Tavistock Square.'

Pitt was curious about why he had left an apparently superior employment, but was unsure how to ask him without giving offence. Such a question, as well as being against his regard for the man, would be professionally foolish at this point.

Mullen supplied the answer of his own accord. Perhaps he wished to clear himself from suspicion of incompetence. 'They took the habit of going to Devon every winter.' A shadow of distaste crossed his face. 'I did not care for the travel, and I have no wish to remain idle in an empty town house with a caretaking staff for several months of each year.'

'Indeed,' Pitt agreed with some sympathy. An estate in the home counties would be an entirely different thing, with hunt balls, shooting parties, and guests for Christmas, no doubt. But a retreat to the silence of Devon would be a form of exile. 'And I should imagine Dr Pinchin was not an uninteresting employer?' he said, trying to probe a little deeper.

Mullen smiled politely. He was far too honourable to repeat the vast and intimate knowledge he had acquired of the Pinchin household. Butlers who betrayed that trust were, in his opinion, contemptible and a disgrace to their entire profession.

He misunderstood deliberately, and both of them knew it. 'Yes, sir, although not a great deal of his practice was conducted from this house. He has offices in Highgate. But we have had some distinguished gentlemen here to dine, from time to time.'

'Oh?'

Mullen repeated the names of several surgeons and physicians of eminence. Pitt made a mental note of their names, to call upon later for whatever they might add to his picture of Hubert Pinchin, although he knew from past experience that all professionals seem to defend their colleagues, even to the point of ridiculousness. However, there was always the hope of stumbling upon some personal or professional jealousy that might loosen a tongue.

He learned from Mullen a little more about Pinchin's habits, particularly that he quite frequently returned home very late in the evening. It was not unknown that he should be out all night. No explanation was offered other than the discreet supposition that illness does not confine itself to convenient hours.

A few moments later, the lady's maid knocked on the door. Her mistress was ready to speak to Mr Pitt, if he would care to come to the breakfast room.

Valeria Pinchin was a woman of Wagnerian stature, broad-bosomed, blue-eyed, with a sweep of fading hair above her wide forehead. She was dressed in unrelieved black, as became a new widow in the deepest mourning, not only for the untimely death of her husband but the appalling notoriety of its nature. Her face was pale, and set in grim and defensive determination. She looked at Pitt warily.

'Good morning, ma'am,' he began with suitable reverence for the occasion and some genuine pity. 'May I offer my sympathy in your bereavement?'

'Thank you,' she replied, with a very slight sniff and a lift of her powerful chin. 'You may sit down, Mr—er, Pitt.'

He took the chair opposite her across the table. She sipped at tea without offering him any. After all, he was an extremely distasteful necessity, part of the trappings of the sordid disaster that had overtaken her—like the ratcatcher, or the drainman. There was no need to treat him as a social equal.

'I'm sorry, ma'am,' he began again, 'but I am obliged to ask you a number of questions.'

'I can be of no help to you whatsoever.' She stared at him, bridling at even the suggestion. 'You cannot imagine I know anything of such an unspeakable—' She stopped, unable to find a word extreme enough.

'Of course not.' She was not a woman Pitt found it easy to like. He had to force to his mind some of the other shocked people he had spoken with, their various ways of protecting their wounds.

Mrs Pinchin was slightly mollified, but still her eyes glittered at him and her black-beaded bosom rose and fell with indignation.

'You can help me learn a great deal more about your husband,' he said, trying again. 'And therefore whoever might have believed him an enemy.' He wanted to be as courteous as possible, but ultimately the facts must be pursued to their logical end. Hubert Pinchin had been murdered. Someone had believed he had reason; a simple robber does not emasculate his victims.

She started to say something, then changed her mind and took another sip of tea.

Pitt waited.

'My husband was...' She was obviously finding it difficult to express her thoughts without betraying a part of her life that was far too private—and too painful—to be acknowledged, let alone paraded before this—policeman! 'He was an eccentric man, Mr Pitt,' she said. 'He chose to practice medicine among some very peculiar people. I hesitate to say "unworthy." ' She sniffed. 'I do not wish to be hard upon the unfortunate, but he could have had an outstanding career, you know. My father'—her chin jutted forward—'Dr Albert Walker-Smith. No doubt you have heard of him?'

Pitt had not, but he lied. 'A very famous man, ma'am,' he agreed.

Her face softened a little and Pitt feared for a moment that he would be called on to make some relevant comment. He had not the faintest idea who Albert Walker-Smith had been, except that obviously he was the man Mrs Pinchin wished her husband could have lived up to.

'You said Dr Pinchin was eccentric, ma'am,' Pitt said. 'Was that true in any way other than not pursuing his career to its best advantage?'

She crumpled a napkin in her large hands. 'I am not sure what you mean, Mr Pitt. He had no unfortunate habits—if that is what you imply!' All the half guessed-at aberrations of masculinity, practices her woman's ignorance conjured from the darkness of imagination, hovered behind her words.

Pitt looked at her hopelessly. She was so armoured in dignity and so conscious of the formalities of grief that he knew he would accomplish nothing with these predictable questions. Her mind was running in channels as entrenched as those of an old river falling to a long-predestined sea.

'Did he like Stilton cheese?' he asked instead.

Her thin eyebrows rose and her voice was hard. 'I beg your pardon?'

He repeated the question.

'Yes, he did, but I find that offensively trivial, Mr Pitt. Some insane creature has attacked and murdered my husband in the most'—tears filled her eyes and she swallowed—'the most unspeakable manner, and you sit here in his house and ask if he cared for cheese!'

'It is not irrelevant, ma'am,' Pitt replied with an effort at patience. She could not help herself: Social values and dignity were her only defence against such enormous fears. 'There were crumbs of Stilton cheese on his clothes.'

'Oh.' She apologized stiffly. 'I beg your pardon. I suppose you know your trade. Yes, my husband was very fond of the table. He always ate well.'

'Did I understand you earlier to say that he did a certain amount of charity work?'

'He did a great deal of unprofitable work!' she replied with a sudden welling-up of resentment. 'He wasted most of his time on people who were—yes—unworthy of him. If you are looking for rivals in his profession, Mr Pitt, you are wasting your time. My husband had great abilities, but he did not ever realize them as he should have.' Her voice held years of disappointment, of opportunities glimpsed and lost.

'Nevertheless he was well respected, I believe.' Pitt was torn between his instinctive dislike of her and a sense of pity for her frustration. She had been tied to a man who had failed her and there had been no escape for her. Her dreams had been within his reach, and he had refused to pluck them.

She sighed. 'Oh, yes, in a certain fashion. He was very entertaining, you know. People liked him.' Her voice lifted a trifle in surprise; it was a fact that she did not understand, and perhaps did not consciously share. Her own disappointment was too deep to find his peccadilloes amusing. 'And occasionally he would make a brilliant diagnosis. That was his specialty, you know—diagnosis.'

Pitt reverted to the obvious. 'Can you think of anything at all, ma'am, that might help us—anyone who might have borne a grudge? An old patient, perhaps—someone who could not accept the death of a relative and blamed the doctor? Was there anything unusual in Dr Pinchin's behaviour lately, or any new acquaintance who was out of the ordinary?'

'My husband did not bring his less reputable friends to this house, Mr Pitt.' Her mouth tightened. 'There were certain persons he entertained elsewhere, as I am sure you will understand. And I noticed nothing odd in his behaviour—it was just as usual.' A look of unhappiness crossed her face, a mixture of disapproval of the dead man's habits and a sudden loneliness that he was gone. With all his failings and irritating ways, she had still grown used to him; he had been there for thirty years of her life. Now there was nothing.

For a moment Pitt felt unclouded pity for her, but he knew the gulf between them was too wide to bridge. His understanding would not ease her pain at all; on the contrary, to her it would be presumptuous.

He stood up. 'Thank you, ma'am, for your help. I hope I shall not have to disturb you again. I am sure Mr Mullen can see to everything else I need to know.'

'Good day, Mr Pitt.' She regarded him bleakly until he had reached the door. She then lifted the pot and poured herself another cup of tea, dabbing her napkin first to her mouth, then up to catch the tears running down her cheeks.

Pitt went out and closed the door with a faint click.

Mullen was waiting for him in the hallway. 'Is there anything else, sir?'

Pitt sighed. 'Yes, please. I would like you to show me the household accounts, and your cellar. I presume you have approved all the staff before they were hired, and checked their references?'

Mullen stiffened and his expression became chilly. 'Most certainly I have. May I ask what you expect to find, Mr Pitt? They are entirely in order, I assure you. And the staff are all above question in honesty and morals or they would not remain here! And as for any one of them being out at night, that is impossible.'

Pitt was sorry to have offended him. Actually, he had no suspicions of any of the servants. What he was looking for was evidence of Pinchin's standard of living, to judge his expenditures. Normally a man of his class would not go to the Acre, even for cheap entertainment. Was he a good deal less well-off than he appeared, or more well-off than his medical practice would account for? Was he spending money in brothels or gambling houses? Or was he earning it? He would not be the first outwardly respectable man to have a source of income in slum property.

'It is merely routine, Mr Mullen,' he said with a smile. 'Just as you check references, even though you believe them.'

Mullen relaxed a little. He respected professional thoroughness. 'Quite so, Mr Pitt. I am familiar with police procedure. If you will come this way...'

After his visit to the Pinchin household, Pitt spent the afternoon checking the Highgate medical practice and talking with shocked and extremely reticent colleagues. By the time he got home, at five past seven, he was tired, cold, and only a little wiser. If Pinchin owned property in the Devil's Acre, he had hidden all record of it—or any other business transactions outside those of his Highgate practice. His standard of living, however, did suggest he was enjoying an income rather larger than his medical abilities would account for. Inherited money? Savings? Gifts? Even a little juggling of the books? Or perhaps blackmail of patients with indiscretions that required medical help: social diseases, an unwanted child—the possibilities were legion.

Gracie met Pitt at the door and took his coat through to the scullery to dry out. ' 'Orrible wet night, sir,' she said, shaking the big coat like a blanket and nearly over-balancing with it. She scurried ahead of him, muttering to herself about the hours he was obliged to keep in all weathers. Not once did she meet his eyes. She was sorry for him, for some reason, and her rigid little back was full of disapproval.

It did not take him long to put two and two together when Charlotte was also sweetly attentive, and full of conversation. 'Have you been out?' he asked Charlotte.

'Only for a short while,' she said quite casually. 'I was home before it began to rain. It was really not unpleasant.'

'And no doubt you came back in the carriage,' he added.

She looked up quickly, a faint colour in her cheeks. 'Carriage?'

'Didn't you go to see Emily?'

There was reluctant admiration in her face. 'How did you know?'

'Gracie's back.'

'I beg your pardon?'

'Gracie's back. It is rigid with disapproval. Since I have only just come home, it cannot be anything I have done. It must be you. I imagine it was a visit to Emily to recount to her everything you know about the murders in the Devil's Acre—especially since one of them concerns the footman of a previous acquaintance. Now tell me, am I mistaken?'

'I—'

He waited.

'Of course we discussed it!' Her eyes were bright, the blood warm in her cheeks. 'But that is all—I swear! Anyway, what more could we do? We can hardly go to such a place. But we did wonder what on earth Dr Pinchin was doing there. There are much better places for picking up loose women, if that is what he wanted, you know?'

'Yes, I do know, thank you.'

Her eyes met his in a flash, then slid away into a professed candour again. 'Have you thought that perhaps he put up the money for Max, Thomas? You know, some unlikely-seeming people go into partnership with—'

'Yes, thank you,' he replied with a smile

bubbling up inside him. 'I thought of that, too.'

'Oh.' She looked disappointed.

He took her hand and pulled her toward him. 'Charlotte,' he said gently.

'What?'

'Mind your own business!'

CHAPTER 3

The following day, Pitt pursued the investigation in the next most obvious course. He took his oldest coat and a rather battered hat that normally not even he would have worn and set out in a drizzling rain for the Devil's Acre, to find Max's establishments—or at least one of them.

It was an area like many of the older slums of London, a curious mixture of societies that lived quite literally on top of each other. In the highest, handsomest houses with frontages on lighted thorough-fares lived successful merchants and men of private means. Below them, in smaller houses on lesser streets, were lodging-rooms for clerks and tradesmen. Beneath even these, squat and grimy, were the sagging tenements and cellars of the very poor, sometimes packed so full of humanity that two or three families shared one room. The stench of refuse and bodily waste was choking. Rats teemed everywhere, so that an untended baby might well be eaten alive. And more children died of starvation or disease than ever reached an age of six or seven years, when they might profitably join one of the schools for pick-pockets and apprentice thieves.

Among the warren of alleys and passage-ways were the sweatshops, the rooms where broken-down lawyers or clerks drafted false affidavits, account books, and receipts, where forgers practiced their art, and where receivers of stolen goods made bargains. And of course there were the gin mills, doss houses and brothels, and the police snouts.

Over it all loomed the shadow of the great towers of Westminster Abbey, coronation cathedral of kings, the tomb of Edward the Confessor before Norman William ever sailed from France to defeat the Saxon king and take England for himself. And beyond the Abbey was Big Ben, the Palace of Westminster, the Mother of Parliaments since the days of Simon de Montfort six hundred years ago.

There was no point in Pitt's hoping to receive answers to questions posed in this teeming rats' nest. The police were the natural enemy, and the swarming population knew an outsider as a dog knew one, by senses far subtler than mere sight. In the past he had made a few arrests here, but had also let a few slip by. He had friends—or, if not friends, at least those who knew what could be to their advantage.

Pitt followed grey alleys past youths idle and sullen, watching him with mean eyes. He hunched his shoulders, aping the furtive gait of the long-abused, but he did not look behind him. They would smell fear and be on him like a hunting pack. He walked as if he knew where he was going, as if the narrow passage—sometimes only wide enough to allow two men to pass each other sidewise—were as familiar to him as his home.

Beams creaked, wood rotted and settled. A dozen rats scattered as he approached, their feet scrabbling on the wet stones. Old men lay in doorways, perhaps in drunken stupor, or maybe they were dead.

It took Pitt half an hour before he found the man he was looking for, in a dilapidated attic where he did his work. Squeaker Harris, so named for his sharp, high-pitched voice. He was a little man with narrow eyes and a pointed nose—not unlike a rat himself, Pitt thought. All he lacked was the long, hairless tail. He was a scrivener, a forger of letters of recommendation, of papers of attorney.

'Wotcher want wiv me?' he demanded truculently. 'I ain't done nuffin', not as yer can prove!'

'Not trying to, Squeaker,' Pitt replied. 'Although I dare say I could if I put my mind to it.'

'Nah!' Squeaker dismissed the possibility, but there was anxiety in his quick little face. 'Nah—never!'

'We won't know, will we—if I don't try?' Pitt pointed out.

'So wotcher want, then? Yer never came ter Devil's Acre fer yer 'ealf!'

'Information of course.' Pitt looked at him with mild contempt. He should have known that; indeed the pretence was a waste of time.

'I dunno nuffin' abaht no crimes!' Squeaker warned.

74

'Of course not,' Pitt said dryly. 'You're an upright citizen, making a few pence writing letters for those who haven't the skill for themselves.'

'Vat's right—yer got it in one!' Squeaker nodded vigorously.

'But you know the Devil's Acre,' Pitt pursued.

'Course I do—I was bloody born 'ere!'

'Ever heard of a pimp named Max? And don't lie to me, Squeaker, or I'll arrest you for withholding information about a murder, and it'll be the long drop for you! This is a bad one.'

'Oh, my Gawd! Yer mean vat poor sod as was—oh, Gawd!' Squeaker paled under the dirt on his face. 'Oh, Gawd!' he said again.

'So?' Pitt prompted. 'What do you know about Max?'

'I dunno 'oo killed 'im, I swear to yer, Mr Pitt. Some kind o' maniac! 'Oo'd do vat ter any man? It ain't decent.'

'Of course you don't know who killed him,' Pitt conceded with a tolerant smile. 'Or you'd have told us all about it, naturally.'

'Natcherly,' Squeaker agreed, glancing away nervously. He thought Pitt was laughing at him, but he did not want to put it to the test. 'I swear,' he added for good measure.

'What about Max?' Pitt pressed. 'What was he like?'

'Good at it,' Squeaker said grudgingly. Pimping was a lot more profitable than petty forgery, as well as probably more fun. ' 'Ad a natcheral talent, 'e 'ad—fer vat sort o' fing!' He did not want to be too fulsome in his praise. After all, Max could not have made a good forgery to save himself. In fact, Squeaker was not sure if he could even write a legible hand! There was great skill in writing well, and it should not be undervalued.

Remembering the heavy, sensual face with its dark eyes, Pitt could well believe that Max had such a talent. 'Yes,' he said. 'So I heard. Had several houses, didn't he?'

Squeaker looked at him cautiously. 'Know vat, do yer?'

'I do. What sort of clients did he cater to?'

'Depends which 'ouse as yer talkin' abaht,' Squeaker said. 'If'n yer means ve one in Partridge Lane—well, anyone as 'ad ve price. Real scrubbers, vey are. But if'n yer means ve one up by George Street—well, nah, vat's diff'rent altergevver. Nah some o' vem 'as real class. An' I 'as 'eard say as 'e'll provide a gentleman wiv enough money ter spend wiv some ladies o' blood, as yer might say.' He leered knowingly, showing brown teeth. The idea obviously amused him, as a sort of obscene revenge upon the society that had excluded him completely.

'Ladies of blood, eh?' Pitt raised his eyebrows. That sounded interesting. He fixed Squeaker with a look of suspicion. 'Ladies of blood?' he repeated sceptically.

'Vat's wot I said—take it or leave it.' Squeaker knew he had Pitt's interest, and he enjoyed the sensation. 'Mebbe vat's w'ere yer murder comes from. Never mess wiv the Quality—golden rule. Vey ain't used ter bein' took and vey feels it very 'ard—can get real nasty. Stick to yer own—ven yer won't get someone as don't know ve rules, comin' all over spiteful and stickin' a shiv in yer gut. Although wot vey done ter Max was uncalled for, Mr Pitt—real uncalled for. I don't know wot you rozzers is lettin' the place come to!'

Pitt hid a smile. 'Disgusting,' he agreed. 'But a jealous man can get carried to extraordinary lengths if someone has taken his woman and then used her to sell to other men as a whore.'

Squeaker sighed. He had neither wife nor children, but he dreamed of them sometimes: a woman whose warmth would not have to be traded for or bought, someone who would become familiar with time, children who would treat him with respect—every man should have that, at least for a while.

'I reckon as yer right, Mr Pitt,' he said slowly. 'Never mess wiv a man's family—vat's anuvver rule as should be writ in gold. On the 'ole, I reckon as pimpin' ain't such an 'ealfy occupation after all. Women is a dangerous kind o' goods ter deal in—not ter mention a man's private needs, wot can be very odd in some o' them gents from up west, so I've 'eard say. Some 'o them stories yer wouldn't believe! Papers is much better fings ter sell. Knows w'ere yer is wiv papers. People don't lose veir 'eads over paper.'

Pitt did not bother to argue with him. 'And this more expensive house of Max's is in George Street?'

'Ain't vat wot I jus' said?' Squeaker

was patient, like a schoolmaster with an unnaturally dim pupil.

'Yes—thank you.' Pitt fished in his pocket and brought out a shilling. He gave it to Squeaker, whose grimy hand closed over it quickly. He raised it to his mouth and bit it sharply. It met with his satisfaction and he pushed it into his pocket.

'Fanks, Mr Pitt,' he said.

'Don't leave the Acre,' Pitt warned. 'If you've told me lies, I'll be back here to take that out of your skin!'

Squeaker was taken aback. 'I wouldn't tell yer no lies, Mr Pitt! Wouldn't be worf me w'ile, nah, would it? Yer'd only come back and ruin me business. Ain't good fer trade to 'ave crushers 'angin' around, beggin' yer pardon. Gives the 'ouse a bad name!'

Pitt snorted and went out of the ' 'ouse,' past the rotting wood in the yard, a pile of refuse, and two drunks in the gutter. He made his way rapidly through the rain to George Street. This was a distinctly more salubrious part of the Acre, only a few moments walk from the Houses of Parliament.

Max did indeed have an unusual skill. If

he had managed to acquire some 'ladies of blood,' as Squeaker put it, and three or four thoroughly handsome whores accomplished in their art, he would have made himself a very rich man in a few years.

Pitt found the house without much difficulty. A man asking for such a place was not unusual, and those willing to give directions were often compensated for their trouble by the proprietors of the establishments.

This particular house was inconspicuous, even a little grubby, on the outside. It could easily have been taken for another one of the numerous common lodging houses; anonymity was a necessary part of the trade.

Inside, however, the style changed. The entrance hallway was discreetly elegant. Pitt was reminded of Max's service in fine houses of men and women whose taste was nurtured by generations of money and breeding. These were people who knew the masters of painting and furniture design as instinctively as they knew how to construct a grammatical sentence, or to walk with head high and a very slight swagger to the hips.

Beyond the hallway in the main reception

room there was nothing opulent, nothing vulgar. Its sensuality was one of quiet colour, which belied the ease with which each piece of furniture and each painting complemented the others. The pleasure the room afforded was tactile as well: soft velvets, a carpet that made the feet tread silently, almost as if upon grass. Indeed, Max possessed a veritable art!

A man in livery came forward, affecting to be something between a footman and a butler. He was obviously in charge of who would be permitted to become a customer and who would be discreetly redirected elsewhere.

'Good afternoon, sir.' He eyed Pitt's clothes and with an almost imperceptible change of expression, determined that he was unlikely to be able to pay the house charges. But he was too skilled to dismiss him immediately. Gentlemen of the most distinguished rank and fortune were known to assume the oddest of disguises at times.

'Good afternoon.' Pitt understood the process exactly, and with a touch of amusement he played it all the way, using his most courteous manner. 'I came here by recommendation.' He made sure he stood perfectly straight-shouldered, as if his disastrous clothes were an attempt at passing for a native of the Acre—as indeed they were, but for an entirely different reason. 'I have heard from various of my friends'—could Squeaker Harris be termed a friend?—'that you have ladies of far greater quality than any of your competitors.'

The man's face relaxed. He decided Pitt was a gentleman, after all. His voice, not his clothes, betrayed the man: that beautiful diction, and the bearing.

'That is perfectly true, sir. What kind of quality had you in mind? We have both quality of experience and, if you prefer, quality of breeding—although that, of course, does require a little special arrangement.'

So business was proceeding as usual, in spite of Max's dramatic demise!

Pitt flared his nostrils a little and widened his eyes, looking very slightly down at the man. 'Quality of breeding,' he replied in a tone that suggested there could have been no other answer.

'Quite, sir,' the man replied. 'If you would care to make an appointment in advance, I will see that it is arranged. You understand, we can make less deference to individual tastes in such circumstances. But if you care to tell me what colouring, what figure, you prefer, we will endeavour to accommodate you.'

Yes, Max had had more than talent. He had had genius!

'Excellent,' Pitt answered easily. 'I like auburn colouring'—automatically he pictured Charlotte—'or, next to that, dark. And I do not care for fat women, nor yet too thin. Don't give me someone whose bones I can feel!'

'Quite, sir,' the man said again, bowing. 'An excellent taste, if I may say so.' He could have been a butler commenting upon a choice of wine for the table. 'If you will return in three days' time, we will provide you with something that will be to your satisfaction. Our financial settlement will be fifty guineas—payable in advance—upon your meeting the lady and believing her acceptable, of course.'

'Naturally,' Pitt replied. 'I must say, my friend was correct. You would appear to be by far the most superior establishment in the area.'

'We have no rival, sir,' the man said simply. 'Those like Mr Mercutt, who imagine they can imitate us, are quite

83

inferior—as perhaps you have already heard.'

'Mercutt?' Pitt repeated, frowning a little. 'I don't think I have heard the name?' He let his voice rise, inviting explanation.

'Ambrose Mercutt.' The man's eyebrows lifted fractionally in disdain. 'A most indifferent person, I assure you, sir, but with pretensions.' A duchess might have spoken of a social climber with just such a tone of weary condescension.

Pitt had the name he wanted. He had accomplished all he could here. The local station would know where to find Mr Mercutt.

'No.' He shook his head. 'I cannot think that anyone has mentioned his name to me. He cannot be of any account.' Better to leave the man flattered and secure. Comfortable people betray far more than those who are suspicious.

The man smiled with satisfaction. 'Quite, sir—of no account at all. If you care to return at about this time in the afternoon, in three days' time?'

Pitt inclined his head in agreement and took his leave, equally satisfied.

Inspector Parkins received Pitt with a look of expectant pleasure. The case of Max Burton had been handed over and Parkins was delighted to be rid of it. There were already more than enough unsolved crimes within his responsibility, and this particular one promised little joy.

'Ah! Mr Pitt, come in. Wretched day. What can I do for you?'

Pitt took off his coat and the appalling hat, then ran his fingers through his hair, making it look as if he had had a bad fright. He sat down in the chair opposite Parkins.

'Ambrose Mercutt?' he asked.

Parkins' face relaxed into a dry smile. 'Ambrose Mercutt,' he repeated. 'An elegant pimp with ambitions. You think he might have murdered Max out of a business rivalry?'

'Max was taking his trade.'

Parkins shrugged and raised his eyes. 'Do you know how many brothels there are in this area?' It was a rhetorical question.

Pitt took it literally. 'About eighty-five thousand prostitutes in London,' he answered.

Parkins put his hands up to his face. 'Oh, God—is it that many? I look at them

85

sometimes and wonder how they came to it. Stupid, isn't it? But there are a couple of thousand at least, here on my patch. We can't clean them out—and what good would it do anyway? They'd only start up somewhere else. We don't call it the oldest profession for nothing. And a lot of the patrons are men with money—and power. I dare say you know that as well as I do. A police inspector who made things embarrassing for them would have a good deal more courage than sense.'

Pitt knew it was all ugly and painfully true. 'So you didn't take a lot of interest in Max—or Ambrose Mercutt?'

Parkins pulled a face. 'We can't do everything. Better to concentrate on crimes where there are obvious victims and we can imprison someone, if we catch them—theft, forgery, robbery, assault. There are enough of them to use all our time.'

'Then what is the gossip about Ambrose Mercutt and Max?'

Parkins relaxed again, leaning back in his chair. 'Mercutt used to have the carriage trade till Max came along. But Max could provide a better class of women—I've heard even a few of distinct breeding. God knows what they're doing it for!' His face mirrored his complete mystification, an attempt to understand, and defeat. 'Yes, Mercutt had good reason to hate Max. But I wouldn't have thought he was the only one, by any means! Pimping is a very cutthroat business—' He stopped, remembering the literal use of the knife in the crimes.

'Where would Max get women like that?' Pitt spoke his thoughts aloud. 'Society is quite capable of providing its own diversions, if some of their women want a little adultery.'

Parkins looked at Pitt with interest. He had worked all his professional life in the Acre or areas like it: Whitechapel, Spitalfields, places where he never even spoke to 'the Quality.' 'Is that so?' Parkins glimpsed a world beyond his own.

Pitt tried very hard not to sound condescending. 'I've known a few cases that have shown it,' he answered with a small smile.

'Not women?' Parkins was shocked.

Pitt hesitated. Parkins worked in the Devil's Acre amid its filth and despair; most of its inhabitants were born to live hard and die young. We all need to believe in some idea, even if it is forever out of reach—dreams are still necessary.

'A few.' He spoke less than the truth. 'Only a few.'

Parkins seemed to relax, and the anxiety died out of his face. Perhaps he also knew it was fairyland he imagined, but he wanted it all the same. 'Do you want to know where to find Ambrose Mercutt?' he offered.

'Yes, please.' Pitt noted the address Parkins gave him, talked a little longer, then took his leave into the bitter evening. The sky had cleared and the east wind was so sharp on his face that it stung his skin.

The following day, he went first to his office to see if there was any further information, but there was nothing beyond the autopsy report on Hubert Pinchin, which told him only what he already knew. Then he went back to the Acre to find Ambrose Mercutt.

It proved a less easy task than he had first supposed. Ambrose supervised most of his business himself; at eleven o'clock in the morning he was not up, nor did he wish to receive visitors of any sort, least of all from the police. It was half an hour before

Pitt prevailed upon his manservant, and Ambrose was brought, protesting, into the pale-carpeted dining room, with imitation Sheraton furniture and erotic paintings from the new 'decadent' artists on the walls. He was lean and elegantly effete, clad in a silk dressing robe, his wavy hair falling over half his face, hiding rather wispy eyebrows and pale, puffy-lidded eyes.

Pitt could see instantly why Max had succeeded him as the proprietor for the carriage trade. Max had had a sensuality himself that would attract the women who worked for him, and a taste of his own to appreciate and select the best new whores for the trade—perhaps even teach them a little? Nature had given him an advantage that Ambrose, with all his intelligence, could not hope to emulate.

'I've never heard of you?' Ambrose said, his eyes wide, looking Pitt up and down. 'You must be new in the Acre. I can't imagine what you want here. I have some very good custom. You'd be foolish to make life—awkward—for me, Inspector.' He paused as if to see if Pitt had the mental agility to understand him.

Pitt smiled. 'I believe you do have some very good custom,' he agreed coolly. 'But perhaps not as much as you had before Max Burton moved into the trade?'

Ambrose was shaken. His hand moved down his body and tightened on his silk robe, pulling it a little further around himself. 'Is that what you're here about, Max's murder?'

So he was not going to pretend to be stupid. That was a relief. Pitt was not in the frame of mind to play games with him. 'Yes. I'm not interested in your other affairs. But Max took a lot of your business, and maybe some of your women as well—and don't waste time in denying it.'

Ambrose shrugged and turned away. 'It's a chancy trade. You do better one year, worse another—depends on your girls. Max was doing well now—his girls would have left in time. High-class women always do. Either they get bored, or settle their debts, or they marry someone and get out of it altogether. He wouldn't have lasted.'

Perhaps Ambrose had talked himself into believing this, but personally Pitt thought Max would have been well able to replace any women that left.

Ambrose must have sensed his doubts. He turned back and stared at Pitt defiantly.

90

'Ever wondered—Inspector'—his voice was very delicately sarcastic, as if the title were ill-deserved—'ever wondered just how Max got the quality of women he did? Women like his don't take to whoring in the Devil's Acre, you know, just for a little diversion! There's plenty of whoring to be had in their own circle, if that's all they want. Surprises you, that, does it?' He looked into Pitt's eyes and saw that it did not. His face hardened.

'If you want to find out who murdered Max and then castrated him, look among the husbands or lovers of some of the highborn women he's brought in here! Believe me, if I simply wanted a business rival removed, I should stick a knife into him, by all means, and then throw him into the river—or put him in one of the rat holes deep inside the Acre. I wouldn't cut him about and then leave him where he'd be found by you lot! No, Inspector'—again he hesitated fractionally, making the title an insult—'look at some man he cuckolded, or whose wife or daughter he's seduced into whoredom.'

Pitt led him further. 'And how would he seduce a wellborn woman into whoredom?' he asked with a trace of doubt. 'For that matter, where would he even meet one?'

'He used to be a footman somewhere. He probably knew other "menservants." ' Ambrose used the word to convey all his hatred and contempt for Max and his class in general. 'Probably blackmail. That's where your murderer is, believe me!'

'Perhaps,' Pitt conceded with an affectation of far more reluctance than he felt. Much as he disliked Ambrose, what he said made excellent sense. 'Then what about Dr Hubert Pinchin?'

Ambrose threw up his hands theatrically. 'God knows! Perhaps he was the one who did the blackmailing. Maybe he used his medical practice to find these women, or to discover their secrets. Maybe they were partners. How should I know? Do you want me to do your entire job for you?'

Pitt smiled and saw a trace of irritation on Ambrose's face; he had meant to offend, not amuse.

'I'm always glad of a little expert help,' Pitt replied softly. 'I've worked on a few murders, one sort and another. Arson, burglary—know a lot about fine art—but keeping a whorehouse is outside my experience.'

Ambrose drew a sharp breath to retort,

but he did not find the words before Pitt had turned and left the elegant room of pale décor and Ambrose himself standing in his silk robe in the middle of it.

Pitt went out into the rainy, grey-walled street. He felt a glow of satisfaction for at least having been thoroughly rude.

And there was also a strong possibility that Ambrose was right.

CHAPTER 4

Lady Augusta Balantyne was not looking forward to the morning. She had decided that she could no longer put off visiting her daughter Christina to discuss her behaviour in the frankest terms. Christina and Alan Ross would be at the family dinner party this evening, but what Augusta had to say required uninterrupted privacy. As in the past when dealing with Christina's indiscretions, Augusta intended to keep the entire matter from General Balantyne's knowledge. He might be an excellent military tactician when he had cannon and horses to dispose, but when the battle concerned emotions and the possibility of scandal, he was a babe in arms.

Over breakfast she maintained a civilized conversation about the usual trivialities. General Balantyne, of course, did not mention the murders in the Devil's Acre that filled the newspapers, in case he should distress her—not realizing that she had read them for herself. And she was perfectly happy to leave him in his ignorance, if it pleased him.

At ten o'clock Lady Augusta called the carriage and gave the coachman instructions to take her to her daughter's house. She was received with some surprise.

'Good morning, Mama!'

'Good morning, Christina.' She walked in, for once not bothering to notice if the flowers were fresh or if there were new ornaments—not even if Christina's gown was the very latest. She had already made her comments on extravagance; from now on it was Alan Ross's affair. Today something infinitely more serious filled her mind.

Christina still looked surprised. 'I have only just finished breakfast. Would you care for a dish of tea, Mama?'

'No, thank you. I do not wish to be

interrupted by servants coming and going, or the inconvenience of fiddling about with cups.'

Christina opened her mouth to say something, then decided against it. She sat down on the sofa and picked up a piece of embroidery. 'I hope you have not been obliged to cancel this evening's dinner?'

'I have footmen to send on errands like that,' Augusta said dryly. 'I wish to talk to you privately, and the opportunity will not present itself tonight.' She looked at her daughter's charming profile, her soft chin and wide, tilted eyes. How could anyone have such a passionate will and at the same time so little sense of survival? Augusta had tried all her life to impart to her her own understanding of the possible and the impossible, and she had failed. This was going to be unpleasant, but it was unavoidable.

'Will you please put that down—I wish for your attention! A situation has arisen which means that I can no longer allow you to continue with your present behaviour.'

Christina's blue eyes widened in surprise at the questioning of her conduct. She was a married woman and accountable to her husband, but certainly not to her mother!

'My behaviour, Mama?'

'Don't treat me as if I were foolish, Christina. I am perfectly aware that you have been amusing yourself in some most unsavoury places. I can understand boredom—'

'Can you?' Christina said scathingly. 'Have you really the faintest idea what it is like to be so bored you feel as if your whole life is sliding away and you might as well be asleep for all you do with it?'

'Of course I have. Do you imagine you are the only woman to find her husband tedious and her usual acquaintances infinitely predictable, till she could recite every word of their conversation before they begin?'

'But, Papa—' A shadow darkened Christina's face. Was it pain or merely irritation? 'At least he must have been exciting when he was young, when he was in the army, fighting?'

'My dear girl, how many times do you think I wish to hear the exact detail of the disposition of the guns at Balaclava—or anywhere else? He considered it disloyal to talk about other officers' faults or ambitions, and vulgar to discuss their love affairs in front of women. Good God! There were times when he bored me till if I had not been a lady I would have screamed at him and slapped his face out of sheer desire to jolt him out of his damned satisfaction! But it would have served no purpose at all. He would not have understood. He would merely have thought I was having hysterics, and ordered me rest and a soothing tisane. So I learned to adjust my expression to look interested and to occupy my mind with something else. A little self-discipline would improve you a great deal, and would provide a rather better understanding of what is really important to you to keep. Alan spoils you—'

'Spoils me? He provides everything I need and then treats me like a social entity, someone to be polite to!' Christina's face flushed with temper. 'He is so pious he is insufferable! He should have married a nun! Sometimes I wonder if he has any passion in him at all—real passion!'

Augusta felt a stab of pity and dismissed it. This was not the time. 'Do not confuse passion with mere excitement,' she said coolly. 'Excitement is like playing cards for matchsticks—win, lose, or draw, you

97

have nothing left at the end but a pile of splinters.'

Christina's face set, her chin hard. 'Don't patronize me! I shall do as I choose.'

Augusta changed her approach. 'Do you read the newspapers?'

'What of it? If Alan doesn't mind, it is none of your concern.'

'Then you cannot be unaware that there have been two particularly unpleasant murders in the Devil's Acre,' Augusta continued.

The colour faded from Christina's cheeks. Max Burton had been footman in the house before she had married Alan Ross. It hurt Augusta to have to recall anything of that painful affair, but Christina's present foolishness, and now her stubbornness in denying it, left her no alternative. 'One of the victims used to be employed as a servant in our house.'

'I know,' Christina said quietly. She took a shaky breath. 'It is extremely unpleasant.'

'The police are investigating both crimes.'

'Naturally. Although I cannot see what good it will do. Every so often, people like that are bound to get murdered. I don't suppose there is the slightest chance they will ever discover who did it, and why hardly matters. I really cannot believe they care—they have to go through the motions because it is expected of them.'

'Doubtless. But that is not the point. It is Inspector Pitt who will try—do you remember Pitt?'

Christina winced.

'There are houses in that quarter,' Augusta continued, 'where wealthy women occasionally find themselves some diversion. I dare say it offers them a certain thrill to enter into a world of filth and danger. Perhaps their own looks the sweeter after it?'

Christina's eyes were hard and angry, her skin tight across her cheekbones. 'I have no idea!'

Augusta sighed. 'Don't pretend to be stupid, Christina. And, above all, do not pretend that I am! Alan may prefer to affect ignorance of a great deal that you do—indeed, he appears to be remarkably patient. But he cannot ignore scandal—no one can. The Devil's Acre will come under very close scrutiny. These crimes have shocked people—and, since Pinchin was relatively respectable, frightened them as well. If you cannot control your taste for slumming, you must do it elsewhere.

Although you would be very wise not to do it at all. London is much smaller than you think—you cannot be anonymous for long. Your lady friends will not frequent these gambling houses or music halls, but their husbands might well. What is a dangerous adventure for you is merely a lark for them—'

'Hypocrites!' Christina spat out.

'My dear girl, stop behaving like a child. You are too old for it. Naïveté excusable at twenty is boring at twenty-five, and at thirty it becomes ridiculous. You stand in danger of losing your reputation. Take a great deal of thought as to what that means!'

'On the contrary, I am very popular and considered most entertaining!'

'So are buffoons and whores! Do you wish to be one of them?'

Christina's face was very white. 'I'm sorry you imagine I go to cheap music halls, Mama. I have never entered one in my life, so I cannot say what they offer. But if I wished to gamble, there are plenty of perfectly respectable houses where I could do so. And I do not need to find myself a lover—I have more offers than I can entertain!'

Augusta was unimpressed. She had seen Christina's wounded dignity before. 'Do you indeed? Are you telling me you have not been to the Devil's Acre?'

'I had no intention of discussing it with you at all!'

The matter was too urgent for Augusta to lose her temper. She did not wish to tell Christina that she had learned through an old servant's loyalty of her trips to the slums under the shadows of Westminster. It would jeopardize the servant's post—but, more practical than that, it would remove her own source of information, and with Christina so rash there was only Augusta to protect her.

'No doubt,' she said tartly. 'Which is why it is just as well I am aware of it for myself. You were seen. You must stop immediately.'

Christina was frightened now. Augusta had known her too long to be deceived by the arrogant stance, the squared shoulders under the thick satin. Good heavens—she was still so much of a child, as feckless as a summer day. So little thought of consequences. She saw what she wanted and reached for it. Where on earth had she come by such abandon? It was certainly not her father! He had never done anything emotionally prodigal in his life—would to God he had! And Augusta had always had enough strength of will at least to be discreet. She knew the line between pleasure and duty and would walk it with an acrobat's balance. Why was Christina such a fool?

'Really—you try my patience!' she said furiously. 'Sometimes you don't seem to have retained the wits you were born with!'

'If you've never had an affair worth a damn, then I'm sorry for you!' Christina was shouting now, pouring all her frustration, her hunger, and her pride into a burning contempt for what she considered a lesser woman. 'I went to the Acre to a house owned by a friend of mine. And yes, I did go there to meet a lover. But you won't tell Alan that because you want to ruin my marriage even less than I do! Alan Ross was your choice for me—'

'He was the best offer you had, my girl, and you were as happy to take it as I—at the time,' Augusta reminded her. 'Who is this lover?'

'At least be glad I am conducting it in a very private room, and not at someone else's house party, creeping in and out of bedrooms,' Christina snapped. 'Who he is is none of your business. But he is a gentleman—if that is your concern.'

'Then your taste is improving!' Augusta said cruelly, and rose to her feet. 'But from now on you will restrict it to your own home. Remember, Christina, Society does not forgive women, and it does not forget. A great deal of flirtation may be overlooked—even affairs if they are conducted discreetly enough. But slumming in the Devil's Acre halls will not. It is a betrayal of one's own class.' She moved to the door and opened it. There was no servant in the hall. 'Be careful, my dear. You cannot afford another mistake.'

'I have not made one!' Christina replied through her teeth. 'I thank you for your concern, but it was unnecessary.'

Augusta had chosen to make dinner a very formal affair. The servants were in full livery and all the best crystal was out. There were three Georgian silver candelabra and arrangements of flowers on the table that must have come from a dozen glasshouses. General Balantyne chose not even to imagine what they had cost.

Augusta herself wore black and white, favourites of hers, complimenting her dark hair with its streaks of silver and her still perfect white shoulders. General Balantyne was obliged to acknowledge with a little jolt of surprise that she looked magnificent. He could still see in her the beauty and the dignity that had delighted him as a young man. Of course it had been a very suitable marriage. He was of excellent family, with a long and spotless reputation. But all its titles were military ones, and there was not a great deal of money. Augusta's father, however, had been an earl; her title was her own for life, regardless of whom she married—unless, of course, she gained a better one! And there was not a little wealth in her dowry, and, later, in her inheritance.

All the same, her person and her qualities had enabled him to ask for her hand with considerable enthusiasm, and she had seemed happy to accept. The surprise was that her father had also been agreeable.

That brought the general's mind to his own daughter Christina, and to her marriage to Alan Ross. Of course that had been different. Christina was nothing like her mother, though as far as he could judge, she was even less like him. She had not Augusta's regal beauty, but she was dazzlingly pretty. And she had always had charm, allied with a considerable wit—a wit too often exercised at the expense of someone else, for his pleasure. But that was what made Society laugh. A harmless wit was for them a contradiction in terms.

He was not sure whether she had ever really loved Alan Ross or, indeed, if she was ready yet to love anyone. But she had certainly been determined to marry him, and that was something Augusta had refused to discuss. It all belonged to the shock and the weeks of fear and distress during the murders here in Callander Square three years ago.

The suspicion still filled him with unhappiness. He liked Alan Ross; he was an unusually quiet man. One moment the fine aquiline nose made him look strong, even arrogant. Then that peculiarly vulnerable mouth shattered the impression, leaving one with a sense only of the passions that might lie unreachable beneath. Balantyne had never quite known what Ross felt about Christina.

On the other hand, he had come to know his son a great deal better. Brandy had Augusta's dark good looks, but he was gentler. He had a well of laughter within him—one might even go so far as to say an appreciation of the absurd—and Balantyne envied it. There was random joy in such a quality he would dearly have loved to possess.

And Brandy had certainly shown a courage no one had expected when he had insisted on marrying Reggie Southeron's governess, Jemima! She was a charming girl, well mannered, and apparently more than adequately educated, though she was barely more than a superior servant till the marriage.

But they were obviously happy, and they had named their daughter after Balantyne's mother—a gesture he found remarkably pleasing. Yes, Brandy had made a good choice.

The dinner was served in seven courses, and naturally took a great deal of time. Augusta presided at the far end of the table, although Balantyne himself was nominally at the head. On the side nearest the windows, with their moss-green velvet curtain drawn to exclude the night and its driving sleet, Alan Ross sat with the candlelight gleaming on his fair hair. As usual, he spoke little. Jemima sat next to him. She was wearing pale green and white, the design of the fabric suggesting it would be like flowers to touch. She reminded Balantyne far more of spring or the gentle days of early summer than this icy January. Jemima always did; she made him think of daisies, and saplings bending in the wind. She was talking to Augusta, and on the far side Brandy was watching her, smiling.

Beside him Christina sat, immaculately dressed in a deep shade of gold, her dark hair gleaming. Balantyne could see why men found her beautiful, although her nose was a little small, her eyebrows winged instead of arched, and her lips too rounded for classical taste. But there was something individual about her, an impression of daring. She had a touch of Brandy's humour, but without his tolerance or his sense of the absurd.

The course was cleared away and the next one served.

'Do you remember that fellow Pitt?' Brandy asked, looking up from his plate. They were eating a whitefish curled and baked, covered with sauce and flaked almonds. Balantyne did not like it.

'No,' Augusta said coldly. 'The only Pitt I know of was the first Minister of England who introduced income tax during the Napoleonic Wars.'

Alan Ross hid a smile and Jemima bent her head. But the arch of her neck suggested to Balantyne that she was smiling also.

'The policeman who always looked as if he'd just come in out of a gale,' Brandy went on, oblivious of the chill. 'Three years ago.' Even he avoided mentioning the events of death so close to them then.

'Why on earth should I remember such a person?' Augusta inquired critically.

Brandy seemed impervious to the ice in her voice—or to the warning. 'He was rather memorable—'

'For goodness' sake!' Christina interrupted. 'He was a policeman! That is like saying one ought to remember other people's servants!'

Brandy ignored her also. 'He's in charge of this maniac case in the Devil's Acre,' he continued. 'Did you know that?'

Augusta's face froze, but before she could speak Christina turned on her brother, her voice unusually brittle. 'I think it is most coarse of you to bring up such a subject at table, Brandy. Indeed I cannot see the need to discuss it anywhere at all! And I would be obliged if while we are eating you could talk of something pleasant. For instance, did you know that Lady Summerville's eldest daughter is betrothed to Sir Frederick Byers?'

Augusta relaxed, the tension in her shoulders easing under the stretched silk of her gown. But she did not yet resume eating, as if she might be required at any moment to rescue the situation.

'I know Freddie Byers doesn't know it!' Brandy replied dryly. 'At least he didn't on Tuesday.'

Christina laughed, but without the usual full-throated delight.

'Oh, how marvellous! I wonder if we are to have a scandal? I can't bear Rose Summerville anyway. Did I tell you that story of when she was presented to the Princess of Wales, and what happened to her feathers?'

Balantyne could not think what on earth she meant. 'Feathers?' he repeated with disbelief.

'Oh, Papa!' Christina waved her small

hand, delicate, ringed with two beautiful diamonds. 'When one is presented at Court, one has to wear the Prince of Wales' feathers as a headdress. It is really dreadfully difficult to keep them standing up, especially if you have wispy hair like Rose.' She proceeded to tell the disaster so trenchantly that even though Balantyne found the whole social presentation of débutantes farcical, and more than a little cruel, he was obliged to smile.

He looked once at Jemima, who of course had never been anywhere near the Court. But her eyes were bright with laughter, even if her mouth showed some indecision on just how much pity she felt for the hapless girls herded like competing livestock one after another, dressed in hundreds of guineas' worth of gowns for their entrance into 'Society.' Honour demanded they find a suitable husband before the Season's end.

The dishes were cleared away and the next course served: chicken in aspic. The colour and texture of it reminded Balantyne of dead skin, and in a flash of memory the present footman's face was replaced by Max's as he bent forward to offer the silver dishes.

Suddenly he did not wish to eat. There was no more food on the table than usual, but it seemed too much. He thought of the cold body on the mortuary slab. That was meat, too: grey-white flesh, like fowl, all the red blood settled to the back and buttocks. And yet even robbed, emasculated, Max had not seemed anonymous in death, as most men he had seen. That heavy face was too similar to his memory of the man in life.

Augusta was staring at him. He could not possibly explain to her what was in his mind. Better force himself to eat, even if it stuck in his throat. He would be able to wash it down with the Chablis, and the physical discomfort was easier than the continuing constrictions of trying to explain.

'I rather liked Miss Ellison, too,' Brandy said, out of nowhere. 'She was one of the most individual women I have ever met.'

'Miss Ellison?' Augusta looked non-plussed. 'I don't think I know any Ellisons. When was she presented?'

'Never, I should think.' Brandy smiled broadly. 'She was the young woman who helped Papa put his papers in order when

111

he began writing his military history of the family.'

'For goodness' sake, why ever should we talk about her!' Christina shot him a contemptuous glance. 'She was the most ordinary creature. The only possible thing remarkable about her was a good head of hair. And even parlourmaids can have good hair!'

'My dear girl, parlourmaids have to have good hair,' Brandy answered scornfully. 'And all the other physical attributes as well. Any house with pretensions to quality chooses its parlourmaids for their looks. But you know that as well as I do.'

'Are we really to be reduced to discussing the appearance of parlourmaids?' Augusta's nostrils flared as if at some faintly unpleasant odour.

Balantyne was compelled to defend Charlotte—or was it his memory of her? A thing that mattered to him needed safeguarding. 'Miss Ellison was hardly a parlourmaid,' he said quickly. 'In fact, she was not a servant at all—'

'She certainly was not a lady!' Christina snapped back a shade too rapidly. 'I can tell the difference, even if Brandy cannot! Really, sometimes I think anything the least bit handsome in a skirt, and some men lose whatever judgment they once had!'

'Christina!' Augusta's voice was like ice cracking and her face was whiter than Balantyne could remember ever having seen it before. Was she so angry for him because his daughter had insulted him at his own table? Or was it for Jemima, who had once been so little more than a servant? Oddly, he would rather believe it was for Jemima.

He turned to stare at his daughter. 'One of the qualities of a lady, Christina,' he said quietly, 'is that she has good manners and does not, even accidentally, cause offence to others by her clumsiness.'

Christina sat perfectly still, her eyes glittering, her cheeks bloodless, fist clenched over her napkin.

'On the contrary, Papa, it is servants—and social climbers—who do not give offence, because they know they cannot afford to.'

There was a ruffle of embarrassment round the table. It was Alan Ross who spoke, laying his fork down beside his plate. He had good hands—strong, without excess of flesh.

'Servants do not give offence because they dare not, my dear,' he said quietly to his wife. 'A lady would not wish to. That is the difference. It is people who are obliged to no one, but have not the mastery of themselves, nor sufficient sensitivity to understand the feelings of others, who offend.'

'You have everything worked out so neatly, don't you, Alan!' She said it as though it were a challenge, even an insult, implying he had curtailed thought with some preconceived answer.

Balantyne felt a cold wave of unhappiness, and pushed his plate away from him. Alan Ross was dignified; he had a sense of decency. He did not deserve this ill-behaviour from his wife. Mere beauty was not nearly enough. One hungered for gentleness in a woman, no matter how splendid her wit or her face, or even her body. Christina had better learn that before it was too late and she forfeited Alan's affection beyond retrieval. He must have Augusta speak to her about it. Someone should warn her—

Brandy jarred him back to an even uglier subject. 'It was Max Burton, who used to be our footman, who was killed in the Devil's Acre, wasn't it?' He looked at them in turn.

His remark had the presumably desired effect of stopping the previous conversation utterly. Augusta's hands hung paralyzed over her plate. Christina dropped her knife. Alan Ross sat motionless.

A petal fell from one of the flowers onto the tablecloth, whiter, purer than the starched linen.

Christina swallowed. 'Really, Brandy, how on earth would we know? And, for that matter, why should we care? Max left here years ago, and it's all completely disgusting!'

'The Devil's Acre and its occupants are not of the least concern to us,' Augusta agreed huskily. 'And I refuse to have them or their obscenities discussed at my table.'

'I disagree, Mama.' Brandy was not impressed. 'As long as everybody refuses to talk about them—'

'I imagine half the city is talking of little else,' Augusta cut him off. 'There are plenty of people whose nature wallows in such things. I do not intend to be among them—and neither will you while you are in my house, Brandon!'

'I'm not thinking of the details.' Brandy leaned forward, his face earnest. 'I'm talking about the general social conditions in our slums. Apparently, Max was a pimp. He procured women for prostitution—'

'Brandon!'

He ignored the interruption. 'Do you know how many prostitutes there are in London, Mama?'

Balantyne looked across at Augusta's face and thought he would not forget her expression as long as he lived.

Her eyebrows rose and her eyes widened. 'Am I to assume, Brandon, that you do?' she inquired in a voice that could have chipped stone.

The colour came up Brandon's cheeks slightly, but his face set in the same defiance that echoed as far back as nursery days over such trivialities as rice pudding and taking naps. He swallowed. 'Eighty-five thousand.' To have added 'approximately' would have diminished the impact. 'And some of them are no more than ten or eleven years old!'

'Nonsense!' she snapped.

For the first time, Alan Ross joined in. 'I am sorry, Mama-in-law, but that is true. Several people of some reputation and quality have been espousing the cause of these people lately, and there has been

116

much investigation.'

'Don't be ridiculous!' Christina laughed, but it was a high sound, without happiness. 'Mama is perfectly correct. How could a person of any quality whatsoever take up such a cause? That's preposterous. It really is not worth discussing. We are descending to absurdity, and it is most unpleasant.'

Balantyne wondered at Christina's agreeing so readily with her mother; it was not like her. He was surprised to hear his own voice. 'Eighty-five thousand unfortunates in London!' He had unconsciously used the current euphemism for prostitution. It made the whole dark, amorphous misery seem less terrible; it allowed one to think that people were moved by compassion.

'Unfortunates!' Brandy's eyes were narrow with scorn. He ripped Balantyne's thought apart exactly as if he had read it from his mind. 'Don't make it sound as if we had some kind of pity for them, Papa. We don't even want to know about them! We've just said they are not suitable conversation for our table. We prefer to pretend they don't exist, or that they are all doing it quite happily and sinfully, because they want to—'

'Don't talk rubbish, Brandy!' Christina

snapped. 'You know nothing about it. And Mama is perfectly correct. It is most disagreeable, and I think you are ill-mannered to force it upon us. We have already made it as plain as we can that we don't care to learn of such coarse subjects! Jemima.' She stared across the table. 'I'm sure you don't wish to hear about prostitutes over your dinner, do you?'

Balantyne leaned forward, wanting to defend Jemima. She was peculiarly vulnerable. She was in love with Brandy—and she had married wildly above herself.

But Jemima smiled back at Christina, her grey eyes clear and level. 'I should find it extremely uncomfortable at any time,' she answered. 'But then, when I can regard other women's distress, either physical or moral, without feeling uncomfortable about it, then I am in need of a very sharp reminder of my responsibilities as a human being.'

There was a moment's silence.

Brandy's face broke into a dazzling smile and his hand moved for a moment as if he would reach across the table and touch her.

'How very pious,' Christina said with

delicate contempt. 'You sound as if you were still in the schoolroom. You really must learn not to be so unimaginative, my dear. It's such a bore! And, above everything else in the world, Society hates a bore!'

The colour drained out of Brandy's face. 'But it usually forgives a hypocrite, darling.' He turned on his sister. 'So you will remain a success, as long as you are careful not to become too obvious—which you are doing at the moment. A clumsy hypocrite is worse than a bore—it is insulting!'

'You know nothing about Society.' Christina's voice was brittle, her face hot. 'I was trying to be helpful. After all, Jemima is my sister-in-law. No one wishes to sound like a governess, even if one thinks like one! Good heavens, Brandy—we have all had more than enough of the schoolroom!'

'Of course we have.' Augusta came to life again at last. 'No one wishes to be instructed about social ills, Brandy. Take a seat in Parliament if you are interested in such things. Christina is right. But it is not poor Jemima who is a bore—she is merely being loyal to you, as a wife should be. It is you who are being extremely tedious. Now please either entertain us with something

119

pleasant or else hold your tongue and allow someone else to do so.'

She turned to Allan Ross, ignoring Balantyne at the end of the table. He was still unhappy, and sought the words to convey his sense that the subject could not so easily be dismissed. Its comfort or discomfort was irrelevant; it was its truth that mattered.

'Alan,' Augusta said with a slight smile. 'Christina tells me you have been to see the exhibition at the Royal Academy? Do tell us what was interesting? Did Sir John Millais show a picture this season?'

There was no alternative but to answer. Ross gave in gracefully, offering her a light and delicately humorous description of the paintings at the Academy.

Balantyne thought again how much he liked the man.

After the desert had been cleared away, Augusta rose and the ladies excused themselves to the withdrawing room, leaving the gentlemen free to smoke, if they chose, and to drink the port that the footman Stride brought in in a Waterford crystal decanter, with a silver neck and an exquisite fluted stopper. He left it on the table and retired discreetly.

Without knowing why he said it—the subject had been a ghost on the edge of his mind for days—Balantyne returned to Max and the Devil's Acre. 'It was our old footman who was murdered.' He filled his glass and picked it up, turning it, looking at the light on the ruby-reflecting facets. 'Pitt came here. He asked me to go and identify the body.'

Ross's face was blank. He was a very private man; it was not often easy to know what he thought or felt. Balantyne remembered Helena Droan, whom Ross had loved before Christina, and the painful idea occurred to him that possibly he had never entirely stopped loving her. It hurt him for both of them—for Ross himself and for Christina. Perhaps that was why she was so—so fragile at times, and so unkind. Jemima's happiness must be like caustic in the wound.

And yet the happiness of how many marriages is based on anything else than a certain sharing of time, of experience that welds a couple together simply because it is something held in common? The fortunate marriages mellow into a kind of friendship. Had Christina even tried

121

to win Alan Ross's love? She had all the wit and beauty it could have needed; the gentleness, the generosity of spirit were her duty to acquire, and then to show him. Again the thought intruded that he must have Augusta speak to her.

Brandy was staring at him. 'Pitt came here? Didn't they know who he was?'

Balantyne brought his mind back to Max. 'Apparently not. He was using several names, but Pitt recognized his face, or thought he did.'

They sat in silence. Perhaps in some obscure way they had half imagined it was not really the same man. Now it was different. It was undeniably a person they had known, had lived with and seen every day, even if as a servant he was merely a part of the household appurtenances, not an individual like themselves.

'Poor devil,' Brandy said at last.

'Do you think they'll ever find who did it?' Ross asked, turning to look at Balantyne. His expression was very intense. 'If he was trading in women, one has a certain understanding for whoever killed him. It has to be as low as a man can sink, this side of insanity.'

'The trade in children is the lowest,'

Brandy said quietly. 'Especially in boys.'

Ross winced. 'Oh, God!' he breathed out. 'I hadn't even thought of that. How criminally ignorant we are! I cannot imagine what brings a human being to do such things. And yet there must be thousands who do, here in my own city. And I may pass them in the street every day of my life.'

'In boys,' Balantyne repeated, not entirely as a question. After thirty years in the army, he could not help being aware of the appetites and aberrations of men far from home, under pressure of war. Presumably such hungers were latent before loneliness and the absence of women brought them to the point of physical indulgence. But he had not thought of anyone earning a living by selling the bodies of children for such acts. It was beyond his capacity to comprehend the mind of such a person.

'Did Max deal in boys?' he asked.

'Women, I think,' Brandy replied. 'At least that's what the newspapers said. But perhaps they would have avoided mentioning it if he had used boys. People don't want to know about the trade in children. Adult women we can blame, say they are immoral, and anything that happens to them is beyond society's responsibility. Prostitution is as old as mankind, and will probably last as long. We can wink at that—even well-bred women affect not to know. That way they are not required to react. Ignorance is a most effective shield.'

Balantyne suddenly thought how little he really knew Brandy. There was anger in him, and bitterness he had never recognized before. Years had slipped by, and because Balantyne himself felt that he had barely changed, he assumed that Brandy had not changed either. The difference between forty-five and fifty was nothing; the difference from twenty-three to twenty-eight could be all the world.

He looked at his son, at the line of his brow and nose, utterly different from Alan Ross: very dark, smooth straight lines, and that stubborn, emotional mouth. One imagines vaguely that one's son will be like oneself. But had Brandy ever been much like him? Thinking about it now—perhaps not?

'Are we as shallow as that?' he said aloud.

'Defensive,' Brandy answered. 'Self-preserving.'

Alan Ross ran his hand over his hair. 'Most of us avoid looking at the unbearable,' he said so quietly they could only just hear him. 'Especially when there is nothing we can do about it. You can't blame a woman who doesn't choose to know that her husband uses a prostitute—particularly if that prostitute is a child. To accept that the child is also a boy would force her to leave him. We all know that divorce ruins a woman. Even to quite moderate society she ceases to exist. She would be an object of intolerable pity, not to mention the obscene imaginations and suggestions of the less charitable. No.' He shook his head in a fierce little gesture. 'Her only option is to connive at his secrecy, and never in any circumstances allow herself to kill the last precious doubt. There is nothing else she can afford to do.'

For once, Brandy was silenced.

Balantyne stared at the flame of a candelabra. He tried to imagine what it might be like, trapped in such a relationship, suspecting and yet knowing you dare not acknowledge such a truth. In fact, for your own survival, and perhaps the survival of your children, you must be the most ardent accomplice in hiding it. It had never occurred to him that Augusta was anything but a virtuous and satisfied wife. Was that insufferably complacent of him—blindly, stupidly insensitive? Or was it simply a measure of his trust in her, even perhaps a kind of happiness? He had never used a prostitute in his life, even in his early army days. There had been the occasional lapse, of course, before he was married—but for mutual pleasure, never for money. But after that he had not ever questioned his moral duty to abstinence when either he or Augusta were away from home or indisposed. Augusta was not a passionate woman; perhaps decency precluded it? And he had long ago disciplined himself to master his own body and its demands upon him; such control was part of the mind of a soldier. Exhaustion, pain and loneliness must be governed.

Alan Ross sat back. 'I'm sorry,' he said, running his hand over his hair again. 'It was not a suitable subject to discuss. I have spoiled your dinner.'

'No.' Balantyne swallowed and dragged his thoughts back. 'What you said is true,' he corrected quickly. 'The situation is hideous. But you cannot blame people for not acknowledging what can only destroy them. God knows—a man who procures prostitutes is barely fit to live. But murder cannot be the answer. And this mutilation is barbaric.'

'Have you ever been to the Devil's Acre, Papa?' Brandy spoke without fire now, his face sombre. 'Or any of our other slums?'

Balantyne knew what he was thinking. In the fight for survival in grinding, hopeless poverty, what else could people be but barbaric? Memories of army camps came back to him, of the Crimea, of Scutari, of sudden and violent death—of what men do in towns during the weeks and the nights waiting for battle. Any day their bodies could be mangled, faceless under the sun of Africa or frozen in the Himalayan snows. If he did not really know Brandy, neither did Brandy know him.

'I've been thirty years in the army, Brandy,' he replied. 'I know what can happen to people. Is that an answer?'

'No.' Brandy drank the last of his port. 'Only I don't find it acceptable to avoid the question anymore.'

Balantyne stood up. 'We had better

rejoin the ladies in the withdrawing room before they realize we have been discussing this subject again.'

Alan Ross rose also. 'I know a member of Parliament I'd like to see. Do you wish to come, Brandy? We might be of assistance to him. I hear he has some sort of bill to put before the House.'

'What about?' Brandy followed them.

'Child prostitution, of course,' Ross replied, opening the door. 'But don't mention it in front of Christina, if you don't mind. I think the subject is one that distresses her.'

Balantyne was pleased. He had thought from her remarks that she merely considered the matter in ill taste rather than painful. This was entirely different. He was ashamed for having misjudged her. But there was nothing he could say; to apologize would only betray the thought.

Just before midnight, when the others had gone, Balantyne followed Augusta slowly up the stairs. 'You know, I like Alan Ross better each time I see him. Christina is very fortunate,' he remarked.

She turned and looked at him coldly. 'And what do you mean by that?'

'Precisely what I said—that with the best intention, one may still find that a person is not what one had hoped. Alan Ross is even more than we might have presumed on our early acquaintance.'

'Not on mine,' she answered firmly. 'Do you imagine I would have permitted my daughter to marry a man of whose worth I was not sure?'

He was surprisingly stung, and spoke the truth without thinking. 'It is difficult to know how much choice we had in the matter with Christina.'

Augusta's eyes were as unfamiliar as those of some stranger he had accidentally jostled in the street. The sense of comfort he had felt at the dinner table among the wineglasses vanished like an illusion.

'I have every choice,' she said cuttingly. 'I see to it that I do. Do you imagine that I am incompetent?'

That was one thought that had never crossed his mind since the day he had first met her, at her coming-out ball. She had been formally composed even then. Her lack of nervousness, the fact that she neither flirted nor giggled, was among the things that had attracted him. The memory was of too long ago. He tried to recapture the feeling he had had then—the excitement, the sense of anticipation—and it eluded him. Vaguely it hurt. The qualities that had delighted him then were now frightening, like a closed door.

'Don't be ridiculous!' He was wounded into a defence of himself, affecting the arrogance that had once sat on him so easily. 'I am as well acquainted with Christina as you are.' A lie of majestic proportions. 'She is excessively strong-willed. And even you, my dear Augusta, are capable of the occasional error.'

She was tired; her face hardened, finally shutting him out. She turned and continued her way up the stairs. Her back was straight, but she climbed with an effort.

'Naturally,' she said. 'And so are you, Brandon. I wish you would refrain from discussing at the table such disagreeable subjects as slums and their various unfortunates—especially when we have guests. It is ill-mannered and can only lead to embarrassment. I would have expected you to see that for yourself! A social conscience is a worthy thing, but there are appropriate times and places for exercising it. In view of the fact that

that wretched footman once served in this house, I would be obliged if you would refrain from mentioning him again. I do not wish the entire staff sent into hysterics, or the next thing we know, half of them will be giving notice—and it is hard enough to keep good servants these days as it is!' She reached the landing and turned for her bedroom. 'Good night, Brandon.'

There was nothing else for him to do but reply, and to go on along to his own room. He closed the door and stood still. The room felt unfamiliar, though every furnishing, every book and memento had been his for years.

Balantyne was met the following morning in the hall by Stride, his face white, hands knotted in front of him instead of by his sides as usual. There were no members of the female staff to be seen. For an instant, it flashed across Balantyne's mind that Augusta was right. All the maids had given notice and fled in the night, afraid that they were employed under the same roof as some creature like Max, and that they might be spirited off to a life of whoredom at any moment.

Stride was waiting, his eyes bleak.

131

'What is it?' Balantyne demanded. 'What has happened?'

'The newspapers, sir—'

Was that all! Balantyne was furious with relief. 'God damn it, man so they're late! If they haven't come in an hour, send someone out for them!' He turned to brush past him and go in to breakfast.

Stride stood firm. 'No, sir. I fear I have not made myself clear. The newspapers are here—it is what they contain, sir. There has been another murder in the Devil's Acre, sir, this one far worse.'

Balantyne could not conceive of anything worse than the mutilation of Hubert Pinchin. His mind fumbled in horror, and failed.

'He was not so badly—' Stride hesitated and swallowed. 'So injured, sir.'

Balantyne was confused, and relieved. 'Not so badly? I thought you said worse?'

Stride's voice dropped. 'It was Sir Bertram Astley, sir. He was found outside a house of pleasure, for male persons only.'

'For male—? Good God! You mean a homosexual brothel?'

Stride winced; he was not accustomed to such vulgar frankness. 'Yes, sir.'

'Bertie Astley...' Balantyne felt a little sick. Suddenly the smell of kedgeree drifting from the silver serving dish on the breakfast-room sideboard was nauseating.

'Would you like a brandy in the library, sir?' Stride offered.

'Yes, please.' Bless the man. Balantyne had never appreciated him fully before. 'Yes, I would.' He started gratefully toward the library.

'What would you like me to tell her Ladyship, sir?'

Balantyne stopped. He would like to have protected her from knowing at all. It was so ugly; she should not have to learn about such things.

'Tell her there has been another murder.' Reality would be forced upon her anyway; he could not shield her from that. But better she become acquainted with it by the decent words of someone like Stride, rather than the anonymous sensationalism of the newspaper or someone's unthinking tattle. 'You had better tell her it was Sir Bertram Astley, but do not say where he was found.'

'Quite so, sir. Unfortunately, Sir Bertram's death will become common knowledge quite soon,' Stride said.

'Yes.' Balantyne could think of nothing more to say. 'Yes. Thank you, Stride.'

He even went into the library and found the brandy already there, on a salver beside the newspaper. He poured himself a stiff tot and then sat down to read.

The corpse of Sir Bertram Astley had been found on the doorstep of a house of dubious repute in the Devil's Acre. How idiotically they phrased it! The cause of death was a deep stab wound in the back, but he had also been slashed across the groin and the pit of the stomach. They did not mention the more private organs, but the implication was obvious, inexplicably the more grotesque for its omission. Apparently the murderer had intended to mutilate him as he had the previous victims, but had been frightened away before he could do more than vent his insane hatred in a single violent sweep of the knife. Inspector Thomas Pitt was in charge of this case, as he was of the two others.

Balantyne put down the paper and finished the brandy in a single, burning gulp.

CHAPTER 5

Pitt had been called for in the pre-dawn darkness by a white-faced sergeant in a hansom cab. The man fumbled with his hat and clung to it with numb fingers as he tried to convey the urgency of his message without articulating the horror he had seen.

Pitt understood. There had been another murder. Only a very grave discovery would bring the sergeant to his door at such an hour.

'It's mortal cold outside, sir,' the sergeant offered, intending to be helpful.

'Thank you.' Pitt put on his jacket and then a voluminous coat that made him look as if a stiff wind might fill him out like a sail. He accepted a muffler from the sergeant's outstretched hand, wound it around his neck, jammed on his hat, squashing his hair over his ears, and opened the front door. It was, as the sergeant had said, mortal cold.

They sat together in the hansom while it jolted over the uneven cobbles toward the Devil's Acre.

'Well?' Pitt asked.

The sergeant shook his head. 'Bad one,' he said sadly. 'Sir Bertram Astley. Cut about—but not—well, not actually in pieces, as you might say.'

'Not mutilated like the others?'

'No—rather looked like our maniac was interrupted. Bit o' late business, maybe.' He shook his head again. 'I dunno!'

Pitt was confused. 'Bit of late business—what do you mean?'

'Some'd say as that's the worst part, sir. I dunno 'oo's goin' to tell 'is family! 'E was found in the doorway of a brothel—for male persons only.'

'Oh, God!' Pitt suddenly knew why the sergeant felt so awkward, why it was all so difficult to put into words. How do you tell people like the Astleys that the scion of their house has been murdered and indecently wounded in the doorway of a male brothel? Now he understood the reason for the pity in the sergeant's face, the unnecessary warning that it was cold outside.

But before all that he must see the corpse, and the place where they had found him.

'Sorry, sir.' The sergeant put on his hat

136

and banged it with the flat of his hand.

'Who discovered him, and when?' Pitt asked.

'Constable Dabb, sir. I left 'im there in charge to see that nothin' was moved. Bright lad. Saw 'im—Sir Bertram, that is—about quarter past four, or a few moments after. 'Eard Big Ben, 'e did. Body was lyin' in the doorway. So Constable Dabb goes over to look at wot 'e's doin' there, like. Then o' course 'e sees as 'e's dead. We gets a fair few dead uns in the Acre and all around there, so 'e don't take all that much notice, not like to send for me, till 'is coat falls open and poor Dabb sees wot's bin done to 'is—wot's bin done to 'im. Then, o' course, 'e sends for us—'otfoot! And we sends for you.'

'How did you know who he was?' How long could a dead man lie in the Devil's Acre and not be robbed of everything but his clothes?

The sergeant understood. 'No money, o' course, but still got 'is cards and a few letters and the like. Anyway, don't know what the doc'll say yet, but 'e won't 'ave bin there that long, not more'n an hour. Trade comin' and goin' 'd 'ave fallen over 'im otherwise. Course they finish on the early side. Daylight, an' they all want to be w'ere they ain't ashamed to be seen. Back at their own tables, most like, to lead family prayers!' The contempt in his voice was as thick and pungent as tar, although Pitt was not sure whether it was for their use of the place itself or for their hypocrisy in hiding it. Another time, perhaps, he would ask.

The hansom jarred to a stop and they both climbed down. They were on the southern edge of the Acre, hard by the river, its damp breath swirling up over the rime of ice hardening on the pavement since the rain had stopped. Above and beyond them in the clogging darkness loomed the Gothic towers of the Houses of Parliament.

A young constable with a lantern was standing guard over a body crumpled in a doorway, all of it but the face covered by a heavy overcoat. Decency had prompted the constable to hide the face with his own cape, and he stood shivering beside it. A strange reverence, Pitt thought, that makes us take off our own clothing and stand chilled to the bone in order to clothe the dead already touched with the final coldness of the grave.

'Mornin', sir,' the constable said respect-fully. 'Mornin', Mr Pitt.'

Such is fame.

'Good morning, Constable Dabb,' he said, returning the compliment. It was a mean street, smelling of dirt and refuse. There were other derelicts asleep in the doorways opposite. Glanced at in the grey light, they did not look significantly different from the corpse of Bertram Astley. 'How did you know he was dead?' he asked, wondering what had made the constable stop and examine this particular body.

Constable Dabb straightened a little. 'West side of the street, sir,' he replied.

'West side?'

'Wind's from the east, sir. And bin rainin', too. Nobody, even a drunk, is goin' to sleep in the wet when there's shelter twenty feet away on the other side.'

Pitt gave him a smile of appreciation, then picked up the cape and handed it back to him. He bent over the corpse. Bertram Astley had been a handsome man: regular features, good nose, fair hair and side whiskers, and very slightly darker moustache. His eyes were closed, and it was impossible to guess what virility he might have possessed in life.

Pitt looked down and opened the coat where Constable Dabb's sense of decency had compelled him to close it over the wound. This one was peremptory, a single slash, not deep. There was not a great deal of blood. He lifted the shoulders enough to see the back. The coat was cut and there was a long, dark stain a little to the left of the spine. This was the death wound, the same as the others. He let the body ease back to its position.

'Have you sent for the surgeon?' he asked.

'Yes, sir.' Of course he had; his professional pride would not permit him to forget such a primary task.

Pitt looked around the street. There was nothing else unusual. It was narrow, lined with houses that sagged as timbers rotted and plaster grew mold and bulged, crumbling away. Drains overflowed. Would anyone have noticed a man carrying a corpse, or two people fighting? He doubted it. If there had been a witness entering or leaving the brothel, would they ever be found—or speak if they were? Hardly. Homosexuality was a crime carrying a long penalty of imprisonment, and social ruin for life. Of course to practice it discreetly was common enough, but to force people to admit they were aware of it was utterly different.

'See what else you can do here,' he instructed. 'Do you have the address of the family?'

'Yes, sir.' The sergeant handed it to him on a slip torn from his notebook.

Pitt sighed. 'Then I'd better go and tell them before the newspapers have time to print a late extra. No one should learn of this sort of thing from a paper.'

'No, sir. I'm afraid there was reporters 'ere over an hour ago. I don't know 'ow they 'eard—'

It was not worth discussing. There were eyes and ears everywhere—people accustomed to death, and keen for a sixpence to let some newshound be the first to run to Fleet Street with material for glaring headlines.

Pitt climbed back into the hansom and gave the driver the address of the Astleys' London house.

There was faint light in the sky when he stepped out and dismissed the cab. He had no idea how long he would be.

The street was almost deserted. A kitchenmaid carried out rubbish; a bootboy

141

slammed a back door. Only the servants' quarters were alive. He climbed the steps to the front door and knocked. A footman, looking surprised, answered. Pitt did not give him time to make judgments.

'Good morning,' he said firmly. 'I am from the police. I am afraid I have very serious news to deliver. Will you please conduct me to a suitable place, and inform the head of the family? And you had better bring brandy, or whatever you consider best for the treatment of shock.'

The footman was stunned. He made no protest as Pitt stepped in past him and closed the door.

'Sir Bertram—' he began.

'Is not at home. I know,' Pitt interrupted quietly. 'I am afraid he is dead.'

'Oh.' The footman attempted to collect himself, but the situation was beyond him. 'I had—' He swallowed. 'I had better fetch Mr Hodge, the butler—and Mr Beau, Sir Bertram's brother.' And before Pitt could speak, the footman flung open the door of the cold morning room where a maid had cleaned the grate but not yet lit the fire. 'Sir.' He left Pitt to fend for himself, and disappeared toward the back of the dark hallway, the green baize door, and safety.

Pitt stared around the room. It was full of rich furniture, much of it exotic: lacquered Japanese tables, inlaid ebony, intaglio. French watercolours on the wall. The Astleys lacked neither taste nor money to indulge themselves, and their choice was exceedingly catholic.

An elderly butler came in, sober-faced, a silver tray with brandy and French lead-crystal glasses in his hand.

'Is Frederick correct, sir, that Sir Bertram has met with an accident and is dead?'

There was no purpose in lying; the butler would be the one who would have to control the staff and see that during the first days' distress of the family all the necessary duties of the household were continued. 'I am sorry, it was not an accident. Sir Bertram was murdered.'

'Oh dear.' Hodge set the brandy down sharply on the table. 'Oh dear.'

He had not managed to think of anything else to say when a few moments later a young man opened the door and stood staring. He was still dressed in night attire and robe. His fair hair was damp from his morning ablutions, but he was not yet shaved. There was a marked resemblance between his features and those of the dead

143

man: the same good nose and broad brow. But this face, even in the tight expectancy of fear was animated; there were lines of humour about the mouth, and the eyes were wide and blue.

He closed the door. 'What is it?'

Pitt realized how fortunate he had been with Mullen and Valeria Pinchin. He thought he had remembered how hard it was, but the impact was there all over again.

'I am sorry, sir,' he replied very quietly. It was easier to say it all at once, more merciful than spinning it out a detail at a time. 'I have to tell you that we have just discovered the body of your brother Sir Bertram, in the Devil's Acre. I am afraid he has been murdered, in a similar manner to Dr Hubert Pinchin, although he was far less mutilated—' He stopped; there seemed nothing more to say. 'I'm sorry, sir,' he repeated.

Beau Astley stood perfectly still for several seconds, then straightened his shoulders and walked over to the table. Hodge offered him the brandy, but he ignored it. 'In the Devil's Acre?'

Was it worse to ask now, in the numbness of shock, or later, when the anaesthesia had worn off and the wound was raw and inescapable? Either way, there was only one answer Pitt could act on.

'Do you know what Sir Bertram might have been doing in that area?'

Beau Astley looked up. Then at last he took Hodge's brandy and drank it in two gulps. He poured himself two more fingers, and drank it also.

'I suppose there is no point in lying, Inspector. Bertie gambled occasionally, not much, and I don't think he ever lost. In fact, I think he won most of the time. Usually he went to one or other of the gentleman's clubs. But once in a while he liked to go slumming somewhere like Whitechapel, or the Acre. Can't think why—disgusting places!' He paused, as if the incomprehensibility of it might yet make it untrue.

Pitt was surprised; in his state of shock Beau Astley was so jarred out of his normal composure that he seemed not even to resent a policeman in his own morning room, asking him personal questions about his family. There was no condescension in his voice.

'And Sir Bertram went gambling yesterday evening?' Pitt pursued.

Beau reached for a chair and Hodge pulled it in position for him immediately. He sat down. Hodge retreated silently and closed the door behind him.

'No.' Beau put his head in his hands and stared at the table. 'No, that's it. He went to call upon May. He was invited there to dinner.'

'May?'

'Oh, of course, you wouldn't know. Miss Woolmer, she and Bertie were to be betrothed—at least I think so. Oh, God! I'd better go and tell her. I can't let her find out from the police, or some idiotic gossip.' He looked up without hope. 'I suppose there's no chance of keeping it out of the newspapers? My father is dead—but Mother lives in Gloucestershire. I'll have to write...' His voice trailed off.

'I'm sorry, the newspapers had already been there by the time I was called myself.' Pitt replied. 'In an area like that, sixpence is a lot of money.' He thought he did not need to explain further.

'Of course.' Beau was suddenly terribly tired, his face leached of the animation that had been there only minutes before. 'Do you mind if I get dressed and go to Miss Woolmer immediately? I don't want her to hear it from anyone else.'

'No, sir, that would be by far the best thing,' Pitt said. He watched as Beau stood up. He must tell him the rest; it would be common knowledge by late morning. 'I—I'm afraid there is one more thing, sir. He was found in a most'—he searched for the right word—'a most unfortunate place.'

'You said. The Devil's Acre.'

'Yes, sir—but in the doorway of a brothel, for men only.'

Beau's face tightened in an attempt at a smile. He was past any further shock. 'Surely brothels are, Inspector?'

Pitt hated telling him; already he liked the man. 'No,' he said very quietly. 'In most brothels the staff are female...' He let it hang.

Beau's dark blue eyes widened. 'That's ridiculous...Bertie wasn't—'

'No,' Pitt said quickly. 'He was near—I expect that was merely where his attacker caught up with him. But I had to warn you—the newspapers will possibly mention it.'

Beau ran his hand through the hair that was falling forward over his brow. 'Yes, I suppose they will. They can't leave the

Prince of Wales alone, so they certainly won't have any compunction about Bertie. If you'll excuse me, I'll go and get dressed. Hodge will get you a brandy, or something.' He was gone before Pitt could thank him.

Pitt decided to ask for hot tea, and perhaps a slice of toast. The thought was enough to make him even more conscious of the cold void inside him. To look at a corpse was grim, but the dead were beyond feeling. It was telling the living that hurt Pitt, and made him feel guilty and helpless. He was the bringer of pain, the onlooker, shielded from everything but its mirror image.

He would take his tea in the kitchen. There was nothing else he could ask Beau Astley at the moment, but there might be something to be learned in the servants' quarters, even inadvertently. Then later, when the first news had been broken, he would have to see Miss May Woolmer, who apparently had been the last person they knew of to talk with Bertram Astley before he left for the Devil's Acre.

During that brief respite in the kitchen's warmth, nursing a mug of tea, Pitt learned a great deal of detail from Hodge, the footman, the valet, and from several of the maids. Later he had an excellent luncheon with the entire staff, very sober, at their long table. Housemaids were sniffing, footmen silent, cook and kitchenmaid red-nosed.

But none of it, as far as he could judge, amounted to anything other than the outline of an ordinary young man of title, of very much more than adequate means and extremely pleasing looks. His character had not been unusual: a little selfish, as one might expect in an elder son who had known from birth that he had the exclusive right of inheritance. But if he had practiced either malice or outward greed, it appeared his household had been blind to it. His personal habits had been typical: a little high-spirited gambling now and then—but who did not, if he could afford it? Occasionally he drank rather too much, but he was neither quarrelsome nor licentious. None of the maids had complained, and he was not niggardly with the expenses of the house. Altogether he was a fine gentleman.

A little after two o'clock, Pitt was permitted into the Woolmer house, again reluctantly and only in order to keep him from being observed importuning on the doorstep by inquisitive neighbours. No one wished it known that there were police in the house, whatever the reason!

'Miss Woolmer will be unable to see you,' the footman said coolly. 'She has received news of a bereavement, and is indisposed.'

'I am aware of the bereavement,' Pitt answered. 'Unfortunately, because Sir Bertram apparently dined here yesterday, I am obliged to ask Miss Woolmer what she may know of his frame of mind, any remark he may have made as to his intentions...'

The man stared at him, abhorring his crassness. 'I'm sure if Miss Woolmer knows anything of value to you she will be happy to inform you when she is recovered,' he said coldly.

All day Pitt had felt nothing but grief; now at last he found release for it in anger. 'I am afraid the pursuit of murder cannot wait upon the convenience of Miss Woolmer,' he retorted. 'There is an insane creature loose in the Devil's Acre. Three people have been murdered and mutilated already, and if we do not catch him, there is no reason to doubt there will be a fourth and a fifth. There is no time to wait upon indisposition! Will you please inform Miss Woolmer that I regret the necessity of disturbing her at such a time,' Pitt continued, 'but she may be able to give me information that will assist us to arrest whoever killed Sir Bertram.'

The footman's face was white. 'Yes—if it is unavoidable,' he conceded grudgingly. He left Pitt alone and went down the hall searching in his mind for words to relay the order.

More than half an hour passed before Pitt was shown into the withdrawing room, a place crowded with pictures, ornaments, lace, crochetwork, and embroidery. A brilliant fire burned and all the lamps were lit. Of course the curtains were lowered, as suited a house suffering a violent bereavement.

May Woolmer was a remarkably handsome girl with a fine figure, now draped in elegant grief on a chaise longue. She was dressed in dove grey—neither too colourful for such a delicate moment nor yet an ostentatious display of her feelings. Her hair was thick and shining like honey, and her features were regular. She stared at Pitt with her large, wide-spaced eyes, and held a handkerchief in one white hand.

Mrs Woolmer stood behind her like a sentry, her large bosom encased in beaded purple, suitable for half mourning, very appropriate in such awkward circumstances. Her hair was as fair as her daughter's but faded in patches, and her face was heavier, her chin too soft, her throat thick. Without question, she was grossly offended, and Pitt was the obvious target for her wrath. He was here, and she assumed he was without defence. She glared at him.

'I cannot imagine why you feel it necessary to intrude upon our distress,' she said icily. 'I trust you have sufficient good taste to be brief.'

Pitt wanted to be equally rude in return, to tell her what he believed good taste really was: a matter of self-mastery, of consideration so that you did not avoidably discomfort others, least of all those unable to retaliate. 'I shall try to, ma'am,' he said simply. 'Mr Beau Astley tells me that Sir Bertram expected to dine here yesterday evening. Did he in fact do so?'

They did not invite him to sit down, and Mrs Woolmer still remained standing, on guard. 'Yes he did,' she answered bluntly.

'What time did he leave?'

'A little after eleven. I cannot tell you precisely.'

'Was he in good health, and good spirits?' It was almost a meaningless question. If they had had a furious quarrel, neither of these women would be in the least likely to tell him.

'Excellent,' Mrs Woolmer lifted her chin. 'Sir Bertram was always most happy here. He was devoted to my daughter. In fact, he had approached me with a view to asking for her hand.' She took a breath, and a shadow of indecision flickered across her face.

Was that a lie that no one could now disprove? No—Beau Astley had said much the same. Then why the doubt? Had there been some ill-feeling last night, a change of mind?

'I am most distressed for you, ma'am,' he said automatically. 'Did Sir Bertram say anything about where he intended to go after he left here?'

Her eyebrows went up. 'Why—home, I assume!'

'I can't understand it.' May spoke for the first time. She had a pleasant voice, a little soft, but agreeably low. 'I simply cannot understand it at all.'

'Of course you can't!' Mrs Woolmer said irritably. 'It is incomprehensible to any person of decency. One may only assume he was kidnapped. That is the course you should follow, Mr—' She disregarded his name, hunching one shoulder to indicate its unimportance. 'Poor Sir Bertram must have been abducted. Then when the perpetrators of this crime became aware of whom they had taken, they were afraid—'

'Perhaps Bertie fought them?' May suggested. Tears came to her eyes. 'How brave of him! He would!'

Mrs Woolmer liked that explanation. 'It is perfectly dastardly! That is what must have occurred. I am sure of it. I don't know why we pay the police, when they allow such things to happen!'

Pitt had already questioned the Astley coachman over luncheon. 'Sir Bertram did not leave in his own carriage?' he said aloud.

'I beg your pardon?' Mrs Woolmer had expected an apology or an attempt at defence, not this extraordinary question.

'No,' May answered for her. 'He dismissed his own brougham, and then had Willis call him a hansom. We offered to have our carriage take him, but he would not hear of it. He was most considerate.' She dabbed at her cheek with her handkerchief. 'Most.'

'If only we had been more persuasive, he might not have been abducted!' Mrs Woolmer still directed the accusation at Pitt; it was the police who were at fault. People of quality should not have to protect themselves from blackguards in the streets.

It was possible that Astley had been abducted, but extremely unlikely. Still, if the Woolmers did not know of his habit of occasionally slumming in the Devil's Acre, there was no point in telling them now. They would probably not believe him anyway. And perhaps this anger was their way of encountering grief; it was not uncommon. In illness it was the doctor who could not save who received the blame; in crime it was the police.

Pitt looked at them; May still adhered to the rules for a young lady's behaviour. None of the awkwardness of real grief showed yet. Her feet were tucked carefully on the chaise longue, her skirt draped in the most modestly becoming folds. Her hands were twisted a little in her lap, but they were still beautiful; the lines were composed, serene. She could have sat just so for a neoclassical painter, had they removed three-quarters of the decoration from the tables and the pianoforte behind her.

Mrs Woolmer was bracing herself like Britannia to repel the foe. They were both gathering their thoughts out of the confusion, and would betray nothing yet. There was no point in pressing them. They had not really understood. In time, it would come—perhaps a memory of some word or gesture that mattered.

'He left in a hansom about eleven,' he repeated. 'And, as far as you know, he was in good health and spirits, and intended returning directly home.'

'Precisely,' Mrs Woolmer agreed. 'I do not know what else you imagined we could tell you.'

'Only the time, ma'am, and the means of transport. And that as far as you know, he had no intention of calling upon anyone else.'

She blew down her nose with a little snort, reminding him of a dray horse. 'Then if that is all, perhaps you would be kind enough to take your leave, and

156

permit us to be alone.'

He went outside, past the footman and down the step into the street. He started to walk east again, facing into the wind. He wondered what May Woolmer was like when her mother was not present. Had Bertram Astley loved her? She was undoubtedly handsome, and well mannered enough to make any gentleman a wife acceptable to Society. Did she also have wit and courage, the honesty to laugh at herself and to praise others without grudge? Was she gentle? Or had Bertie Astley even considered such things? Perhaps beauty and a temperate disposition were enough. They were for most men.

And what was it he had seen in Beau Astley's face at the instant thought of May, even in the moment of his own bereavement? Had that been love also?

He would have to remember next time he saw him that he was now Sir Beau! And presumably a considerably wealthier man. After the appropriate interval, would he step into his brother's shoes and marry May Woolmer as well? It was not unlikely that Mrs Woolmer would do her best to see that he did. There were not so many eligible young men around with titles and money, and it was late in the year—the next Season was almost on them.

Pitt pulled his coat collar up; the east wind had a breath of sleet in it. He hated the thought of examining the private failures and weaknesses of the Astleys' lives.

In the morning he was sent for by his superior.

Dudley Athelstan was standing in his office. His suit fit him as immaculately as the tailor's art could contrive, but his tie was askew and his collar seemed too tight for him. The morning's newspapers lay spread over his great desk.

'Pitt! Pitt, come in. We've got to do something about this—it's appalling! Commissioner's been to see me about it, came here himself. Next thing I'll be getting letters from the Prime Minister!'

'Over three murders in a slum?' Pitt looked at the chaos on the desk and at Athelstan's flushed face. 'There'll be a new society scandal for them to talk about in a day or two, and they'll forget it.'

'You swear that?' Athelstan's eyes bulged and he threw his hands up. 'You'll arrange one, will you? Great heaven, man, have

158

you got any idea what this latest murder has done? Decent men are terrified to—' He stopped abruptly.

'To go into the Devil's Acre?' Pitt finished for him, smiling.

Athelstan grunted. 'It's all very well for you to be pious, Pitt. You don't have to explain yourself to these people—thank God!—or we'd have the whole police force thrown out on its ear! Some very influential men find the odd entertainment in establishments like Max Burton's. They accept the risk of being overcharged, even robbed outright in the street, or the occasional roughing up. But being murdered and emasculated! God—it doesn't bear thinking of! And the scandal, the shame!'

'Perhaps it's an ardent reformer trying to put the whorehouses out of business,' Pitt said, his tongue in his cheek.

'Damn your impertinence,' Athelstan replied without heat. 'This is no time for levity, Pitt.' He ran his fingers inside his collar to ease it. 'I've got to get this solved and the maniac responsible in Bedlam, where he belongs. And I don't care if he's a demented clergyman trying to clear up hell single-handed, or a greedy pimp who thinks he can carve himself an empire. What have you got so far?'

'Very little, sir—'

'Don't make excuses, damn it! Facts, witnesses—what do we know?'

Pitt repeated the few medical facts.

'That's not much use!' Athelstan said desperately.

'No witnesses,' Pitt added.

'None at all?'

Pitt shrugged with a faint smile. 'Did you expect any? Do any of your outraged correspondents say they were there?'

Athelstan gave him a filthy look. 'What about other pimps—whores, vagrants—anyone?'

'No.'

Athelstand shut his eyes. 'Damn! Damn! Damn! We've got to get this tidied up, Pitt.' He put his hands to his face. 'Can you imagine what they'll do to us if the next victim is one of the nobility, or a member of Parliament? They'll crucify us!'

'What do they expect us to do? Patrol the streets of the Acre where the whorehouses are?'

'Don't be idiotic. They want us to get rid of this lunatic and get things back

160

to normal.' He stared at Pitt, his eyes pleading. 'And we've got to do it! Find your snouts, your informers—use money if necessary. Not much, mind! Don't lose your head! Someone'll talk, someone knows. Look for motives, rivalries, jealousy. See who was losing money. My advice is find who killed the pimp Max, and the rest will follow. What is the connection between Max and this Dr Pinchin?'

'We haven't found one yet.' Pitt, aware of his failure, felt his face tighten.

'Well, get out there and look for it!' Athelstan clenched his fist. 'And for God's sake find it, Pitt! Lock someone up. We've got to stop this—this—' His hand knocked the nearest newspaper onto the floor, exposing a pile of letters on embossed notepaper. 'They're panicking! Important people are very upset!'

Pitt shoved his hands into his pockets. 'Yes—I'm sure they are.'

'Well, get on with it!' Athelstan shouted in exasperation. 'Get out there and do something!'

'Yes, sir.'

Accordingly, Pitt went back to the Devil's Acre to question Ambrose Mercutt more precisely over his rivalry with Max. He found him dressed in a scarlet robe with a velvet collar and cuffs, and in a remarkably ill humour.

'I don't know what on earth you expect of me!' he said exasperatedly. 'I've no idea who killed the wretched man! I've already told you everything I can think of. Good heavens, he had enough enemies!'

'You seem to be the most obvious among them, Mr Mercutt.' Pitt was armed with the additional research of two more constables, and was in no frame of mind to be patronized by an effete pimp dressed in a red robe at ten o'clock in the morning. 'Max Burton had taken a considerable amount of your custom, and at least four of your best whores. He was a very great threat to your livelihood.'

'Nonsense!' With a wave of his long fingers, Ambrose dismissed the idea as ludicrous. 'I told you before, women come and go. And in time they'd have left Burton and gone to someone else anyway. It was nothing out of the ordinary. If you were remotely competent at your job, Inspector, you would start looking at some of those married women he used! Try Louisa Crabbe! I'll wager you haven't

162

even thought of that, have you?' His eyes gleamed with malicious satisfaction as he saw Pitt's surprise. 'No—I thought not! I wonder what Albert Crabbe thought of Max? I'll wager he'd have been delighted to cut him to pieces in the most disgustingly intimate way!' He screwed up his face. Such vulgarity was offensive. He made a more than comfortable living out of the physical appetites of others, but he found such things distasteful himself. He sat down and crossed his legs.

The thought flickered through Pitt's mind that Louisa Crabbe was an invention, but Ambrose's face was too secure, too satisfied.

'Indeed,' Pitt said with as little expression as he could. 'And where do I find this Albert Crabbe?'

Ambrose smiled. 'My dear Inspector, are you completely incapable? How in God's name do I know? Look through Max's books—there's bound to be some record of how he contacted her. He suited the women to the client, you know. This is not a merely haphazard business. One has to have a certain flair! We at this end of the market are not common, take-your-chance whorehouses!'

'Thank you,' Pitt said sarcastically. 'I confess I had not fully appreciated your entrepreneurial art.'

'What?'

Pitt did not bother to explain. He felt a flicker of satisfaction, but it was a poor victory, and he knew it. The aftertaste was thin.

'I imagine Louisa Crabbe was not the only one—simply the only one whose name you care to give me,' Pitt said.

'I told you, Inspector, Max Burton was of no importance to me.' Ambrose's face was smooth again, unconcerned. 'I didn't bother to keep up with his comings and goings. Why should I? I have a steady clientele and I do very nicely. Naturally there were those he hurt in the way of taking their business. If I were you, I'd ask the Daltons. They're in the cheap end of the trade. I dare say they had cause to be upset with Max.'

Pitt could go back to the police station and find out about the Daltons, but he could not be bothered to pretend. His pride was not worth it. 'Where are they?' he asked.

A smile of superiority touched Ambrose's mouth. 'Crossgate Street. Really, Inspector, what would you do without me?'

'Ask someone else,' Pitt replied. 'Don't tempt me to think. If the Devil's Acre were not such a cesspit, I'd be inclined to work for one whorehouse the fewer.' He glanced round the pale room. 'But what difference would it make? Have you ever read of the labours of Hercules?'

Ambrose knew he was being insulted both directly and obscurely. He resented the one he did not understand the more.

'No, perhaps not,' Pitt answered his own question. 'Look up the Augean Stables sometime. We might consider diverting the Thames!'

'I haven't the slightest idea what you're talking about!' Ambrose snapped. 'Hadn't you better get on with your job? It doesn't strike me you've made so much progress that you can afford to stand around here wasting your time—and mine!'

It was hurtfully true. And with Hubert Pinchin and Bertie Astley also dead, the motive for the murder of Max was becoming less and less important anyway.

'Was Sir Bertram Astley ever a customer of yours?' Pitt asked as a parting shot from the doorway.

165

Ambrose raised his thready eyebrows. 'Really, Inspector, do you imagine I ask gentlemen for their names? Don't be naïve!'

'No, I didn't imagine you asked them, Ambrose,' Pitt replied levelly. 'But I most certainly imagined you knew!'

Ambrose smiled. In an obscure way it was an admission of his competence, of his professional skill. Indecision wavered for a moment in his face, then disappeared. 'No,' he said at last. 'Not Bertram Astley—nor Dr Pinchin either.' His smile widened. 'Sorry.'

Pitt believed him. The indecision he judged not to be whether to admit to it but whether to brag a little and pad out the importance of his clientele—and by implication the fact that he had nothing to fear from Max.

'No.' Pitt glanced around the room again and allowed a faint curl to his lip. 'No—I imagine not.' He closed the door on Ambrose's hot eyes and the flare of sudden anger on his face.

Crossgate Street was dirty and cold, but Pitt had no difficulty locating the Daltons' establishment. It was large and seemed to be cheerful, full of gaudy red and pink furnishings, and there was a fire in the main receiving room, even though it was the middle of the afternoon. Apparently the Daltons catered to clients around the clock. The place did not have the stale, acrid smell of a public house in off business hours; it seemed they kept maids, like any domestic establishment.

He was met by a plump round-faced girl, ordinary enough, with a country-fresh complexion. Pitt felt a twinge of pity that she should be engaged in such an occupation. Still, she was far better off in a bawdy house such as this, with a roof over her head and regular meals, than many another woman who walked the streets looking for any man who would buy her body for the price of a day's food for her child, or a piece of clothing for its back.

He saved her the indignity of importuning him. 'I'm here from the police,' he said immediately. 'I want to speak to Mr Dalton. He may be able to help me with some information.'

'Mr.—oh!' Comprehension and amusement flooded her face. 'You mean Miss Dalton. Would that be Miss Mary or Miss Victoria, sir? Although I'm not rightly sure as they'll want to be seein' the police!'

'Miss—' It had not occurred to him that the Daltons would be women, although there was no reason why not. There was an air of femininity about the place, a simple sensuality that was less self-conscious and infinitely less effete than the house of either Max or Ambrose Mercutt. Somehow he found it less offensive, although he could not think why.

'Either Miss Dalton will do,' he answered. 'And I am sorry, but I insist upon seeing them. It is a matter of murder. If they make it necessary, I shall return with other officers, and things may become unpleasant. I cannot imagine that anyone will wish that. It is bad for business.'

The girl looked startled. His manner was courteous, his voice so very civilized, and yet what he said jarred. 'If you'll wait here—' She scuttled away, and immediately Pitt was sorry. He had had no need to be so harsh, but it was impossible to undo it now.

Barely moments later, a slightly older woman appeared, perhaps in her early thirties, buxomly built, with a blunt, handsome face and a dusting of freckles on her skin. She looked like a competent parlourmaid on her day off. Her dress was high to her neck and of plain lavender colour; there was no paint on her face that Pitt could see.

'I am Victoria Dalton,' she said civilly. 'Violet says you are from the police and you wish to speak to me. Would you like to come into the parlour at the back? Violet will bring us tea.'

Feeling ludicrous, as if he had made a wild error of judgment, Pitt silently followed her trim back as she walked out of the big red and pink hall, with its sofas and cushions, along a corridor and into a small, more intimate room where there was another fire burning. From somewhere upstairs he heard the peal of woman's laughter, followed by a shriek of delight and a fit of giggles. He did not hear any man. Apparently it was two women recounting exploits to each other—not a matter of trade.

Victoria Dalton sat down on a large green sofa and invited Pitt to make himself comfortable on a similar one opposite her. She folded her hands in her lap and stared at him pleasantly.

'Well, what is it you wish of us?'

He was a little taken aback; she was so

composed, so totally different from Max, or Ambrose Mercutt. This place was like a middle-class house, comfortable, with an air of family about it. He felt impelled to use euphemisms, which was ridiculous.

'I am investigating a murder, ma'am,' he began, not as he had intended. Somehow she had put him out of ease. 'In fact, three murders.'

'How unpleasant.' She spoke as if he had remarked upon the weather.

She continued to regard him candidly, like an obedient child, waiting for him to continue. It was disconcerting. Either she had not fully understood him, or else death was so commonplace it held no power to shock her. Meeting her steady grey eyes, he believed it was the latter.

The maid brought the tea and left it on a tray for them. Victoria Dalton poured and handed him a cup. He accepted it with thanks.

He began again. 'The first victim was Max Burton. He kept a house in George Street. Perhaps you know of him?'

'Of course,' she said. 'We knew he had been murdered.'

'He was good at his business?' Why was he finding it so hard to question her? Was it because she gave him no openings and, unlike Ambrose Mercutt, was not defensive?

'Oh, yes,' she answered. 'He had a remarkable talent.' For the first time, her face showed some expression, one of anger. Her full lips turned down at the corners, but Pitt had the odd conviction that it was a reflection of disapproval, not any sense of personal injury.

'Ambrose Mercutt says he used a number of wellborn women in his George Street establishment.' Pitt went on.

She gave a slight smile. 'Yes, Ambrose Mercutt would tell you that.'

'Is it true?'

'Oh, yes. Max was very clever. He was very attractive to women, you know. And there is a certain class of women, wellborn, idle, married for convenience to some bloodless man—probably a great deal older than themselves, poor in the bedroom, without appetite or imagination—and they become bored. Max appealed to them. They began by having an affair with him; then he introduced them to the top end of the trade. He could get a high price for whores like that.' She discussed it as any merchant might speak of her goods, a

171

marketing process.

'Did he take any of your custom?' he asked equally bluntly.

She was quite sober. 'Not much. We provide skill rather than novelty. Most of these wellborn women have more sense of adventure, more'—she frowned a little—'more need to fill their boredom than patience or knowledge how to please. A good whore has humour and generosity, and doesn't ask questions.' She smiled bleakly. 'As well as a good deal of practice.'

She was so used to the idea that it was ordinary to her.

The traffic in womanhood was her daily life, and it did not move her emotions. To know her business was necessary for survival.

'What about Ambrose Mercutt?' He changed direction.

'Oh, yes, Ambrose was suffering,' she said. 'He caters to the same trade: gentlemen with jaded tastes who want something novel, something to stimulate their imagination, and are prepared to pay for it.' Now there was real contempt in her face. Her eyes narrowed and there was a sudden brilliant glitter in them that could even have been hatred, but for whom he had no idea. Perhaps for those rich, spoiled women with money and time to dabble in whoredom for entertainment—her women did it to live. Perhaps for Ambrose because he pandered to them. Or maybe for the men who made it all worthwhile by paying.

Or was it hatred for Max because he had taken her trade after all? Or something he had not even considered yet? Could she even have been attracted to Max herself? It was conceivable, she was young, the curves of her mouth were soft and rich. Was Max's killing simply the rage of a woman rejected?

Considered in that light, though, Hubert Pinchin's death made no sense.

'Where did he meet these highborn women?' he asked instead. 'Not here in the Acre?'

The emotion died from her face. Her eyes were calm again, like grey water with flecks of slate in them. 'Oh, no, he went to some of the dining places and theatres where such women go,' she replied. 'He had been a footman in a big house—he knew how to behave. He was very striking to look at and he had good clothes.

He had an art to sense when a woman was dissatisfied, and he knew which ones had the nerve or the desperation to do something about it.'

Once again, Pitt was forced to acknowledge that Max had had a talent of massive proportions, and had exercised it to the full. But if it was immense, it was also dangerous.

What happened when these women grew bored, or frightened? Society would turn a blind eye to a great deal, but whoring for money in the Devil's Acre was grossly beyond its capacity to ignore. There was an almost infinite difference between what a man might do and get away with—as long as he was discreet—and what a woman, any woman, might be forgiven. Sexual appetite was part of a man's nature, abhorred by the sanctimonious but accepted—even made the butt of sly jokes—and given a certain reluctant admiration by most.

But, by convention, men chose to believe that women were different. Only harlots took pleasure in the bedroom. To sell one's body was sin unto damnation. And when these women of Max's saw their safety—their marriages—imperiled, what did they do? Did Max allow them to leave quietly, as secretly as they had come, and then obliterate their names from his memory? Or did he keep an eternal whip held over them?

The reasons for murder were legion!

Victoria Dalton was still regarding him soberly. He had no idea how much of his thought she had guessed.

'Have you ever heard of a Dr Hubert Pinchin?' he asked her.

'He was murdered also, wasn't he.' It was a statement, not a question. 'That was some distance from here. No, I don't think I knew anything about him.' She hesitated. 'Not under that name, anyway. People here don't always give their own names, you know.' She kept all but a shadow of her contempt out of her voice.

'He was stocky, running to paunch,' Pitt said, starting to described Pinchin as he had seen him dead in the slaughterhouse yard, yet trying to re-create him alive in his mind's eye. 'He had thinning grey-brown hair, a broad, rather squashy nose, mouth apparently good-humoured, small eyes, and a plum-coloured complexion. He wore baggy clothes. He liked Stilton cheese and good wine.'

She smiled. 'There are a lot of gentlemen in London like that, and a great many of them, with unfriendly wives of forbidding virtue, find their way here at some time or another.'

That described Valeria Pinchin remarkably well. It would not be surprising if Hubert Pinchin had found his way to Victoria Dalton's house, a place of considerable laughter and purchased pleasure, fat pillows, soft bosoms, lush hips, and obliging habits.

'Yes, I imagine so,' he said unhappily. 'What about Sir Bertram Astley—young, fair, good-looking, quite tall?' He had forgotten to ascertain the colour of his eyes, but the description was useless anyway. There must be several hundred young men in London, even with breeding and money, who would answer it.

'Not by name,' she answered patiently. 'And we do not pry. It's bad for business.'

That was unarguable.

It began to look more and more as if it were a random lunatic with some passionate hatred of masculinity, perhaps some man injured or impotent himself, tormented by it until his mind had turned. That was an unsatisfactory answer. But so far he had discovered no connection, however tenuous, between Max, Dr Pinchin, and Sir Bertram Astley.

Perhaps if he pursued Max's conquests something would emerge, some woman known to all of them—perhaps used by all of them. Yes...a revenge-crazed husband was not impossible. Or even if the woman herself had been blackmailed, she might have hired some ruffian to blot out all traces of her aberration. There were plenty in the Devil's Acre who would do such a thing for a small fee, small compared to the ruin that might face her. And if she spoke to the ruffian anonymously, well cloaked and hooded, she might be safe enough afterward.

But why the terrible mutilation? His stomach tightened and he felt sick again at the memory of Pinchin with his dismembered genitals. Perhaps it was a husband who had done it, after all. Or a father. There was too much hate involved for something as cold as money.

The speculation was useless until he had more information. He stood up.

'Thank you, Miss Dalton, you have been most helpful.' Why was he being so polite, almost deferential to this woman? She was a bawdy-house keeper, like Ambrose Mercutt and Max himself. Maybe it was a mark of his own worth, and had nothing to do with her. 'If I can think of anything else I need to ask, I shall come back.'

She stood also. 'Of course. Good day, Mr Pitt.'

The maid showed him out into the grimy street, the already darkening afternoon. The stink of sewage came up from the river, and the long moan of a foghorn sounded as barges, gunwale deep, made their way toward the Pool of London and the busiest docks in the world.

Perhaps it was not even the same murderer in all three cases. They had been given wide publicity. Maybe one at least was a copycat crime. What about Beau Astley, with his brother's title, fortune—and possibly even May Woolmer—to inherit?

Why should he be surprised to find the Devil's work here in the Devil's Acre?

CHAPTER 6

The murder of Bertram Astley was on the front pages of all the newspapers. The public was outraged. Under the shrill cries of horror, of the offence to decency, beneath even the compassion, there was a hard, real feeling of fear, close and personal. If a man like Astley could be so obscenely murdered for no apparent reason, who was safe in the streets?

Of course it was not said openly. There were letters to the editor requiring more action from the police, more efficiency, men of better discipline and intelligence. There was a demand to know whose errors were being hidden by this silence. Was there corruption in high places that these monstrous crimes were still unsolved? One elderly gentleman even suggested that the Devil's Acre be burned to the ground and all its denizens transported to Australia forthwith.

Charlotte put down the paper and tried to clear the echoes of hysteria from her mind, to think what kind of man Bertram Astley might have been. Everything she had read was filtered by the rosy gloss of emotion that allowed no evil thought of the dead. Simplicity is so much easier, grand sweeps of feeling that are full of dramatic blacks and whites: Max was evil, Astley an innocent victim, the police either fiddled, or, worse, were corrupt. Either way, society itself was in peril.

And Pitt was working from before dawn till long after dark. When he came home, more often than not he was too tired to speak. But where did one even begin to look for a random lunatic?

She must help. Of course she could not tell him; he had specifically forbidden her to meddle in this affair. But that was before Bertram Astley, when it had involved only people quite outside her social knowledge. Now things were different. Surely Emily would know the Astleys, or someone of their acquaintance through whom an introduction might be scraped. She would have to be very discreet; if Pitt found out before she achieved something significantly helpful, he would be furious.

'Gracie,' she called cheerfully. Gracie must not even guess. With the best will in the world, the girl was totally transparent.

'Yes, ma'am?' Gracie's head appeared around the door, her eyebrows raised. Her glance fell to the newspaper. 'Ooo—isn't it terrible, ma'am, there's bin another one! A real gentleman this time, with a proper title an' all! I don't know wot the world's comin' to, I don't.'

'Well, perhaps that's just as well,' Charlotte said briskly. 'I never did approve much of "second sight." Smacks of superstition to me, and only causes a lot of trouble.'

Gracie was nonplussed, as she was intended to be. 'Ma'am?'

'Don't dwell on it, Gracie.' Charlotte stood up. 'It's all miles from here, and doesn't have anything to do with anyone we know.' She passed her the paper. 'Here, use it to light the fire in the parlour later.'

'But there's the master, ma'am!' Gracie protested.

'Pardon?'

' 'E 'as to do with it, poor man! 'E looked proper froze yesterday night w'en 'e came 'ome, an' I think 'e still don't know as 'oo done it any more'n we do! Beggin' your pardon, ma'am, if I'm bein' impertinent.' A trace of anxiety passed over her face. 'But I reckon as 'e's chasin' the forces o' evil!'

'Stuff and nonsense! It's a lunatic. Now stop thinking about it, put the newspaper on the back of the fire, and get on with your work. I'm going to order myself a new dress. I'm going for a fitting this morning.'

'Ooh!' Gracie's eyes lit up immediately. A new dress was more fun than a murder, second hand. 'What colour, ma'am? Are you going to 'ave it that new line down the front that's in the pictures in the London *Illustrated*?'

'It's too fashionable.' Charlotte bought what she could afford. 'I don't like following everyone else as if I were a sheep without a mind of my own.'

'Quite right, ma'am,' Gracie said. She also had an excellent mind for the practical. 'Get a good colour, I always says, and the rest'll take care of itself, as long as you smiles at people, polite like, but not so friendly as to lead 'em on.'

'Excellent advice.' Charlotte nodded. 'But I shall take a little look and see what other people are wearing all the same, so I may not be back for luncheon.'

'Yes, ma'am. Never hurry a new dress.'

Charlotte arrived at Emily's house to find her sister out at the dressmaker's herself, and was obliged to wait nearly an hour for her to return.

'How on earth can you go visiting seamstresses on a morning like this?' she demanded as soon as Emily was in the room. 'For goodness' sake, don't you read the newspapers?'

Emily stopped short; then her face tightened. 'You mean about Bertie Astley? Charlotte, there is nothing we can do! Thomas already told you not to meddle.'

'That was before, when it only concerned pimps and that odd doctor. Now it has struck one of our own social circle!'

'You mean *my* social circle!' Emily closed the door and came over to stand in front of the fire. 'Actually I don't know the Astleys, but I don't see what good it would do if I did.'

'Oh, don't be so stupid!' Charlotte lost her patience. 'What do you suppose Bertie Astley was doing in the Devil's Acre in the middle of the night?'

'Visiting a house of pleasure.'

'You mean a whorehouse!'

Emily winced. 'Don't be so coarse, Charlotte. You are beginning to lose your refinement. Thomas is right. You shouldn't meddle in this affair—it is not our sort of case at all.'

'Not even if Bertie Astley knew Max, and they were involved in something together—with Dr Pinchin?' Charlotte dangled the most tempting bait she could think of: a really first-class scandal.

Emily was silent for a moment. Fashion could become extremely tedious, removed from anything that really mattered. Who cared whether someone had a subtler colour or a lower neckline? Even gossip at this time of the year was distinctly jaded.

'That would be different,' she said. 'And very serious. It would mean it was not a lunatic at all, but someone perfectly sane, and very dreadful.'

'Quite.'

Emily shivered as her ideas changed altogether. 'Where should we start?'

That was less easy. The practical possibilities open to them were very few. 'The Astleys,' Charlotte decided after a moment. 'There isn't anywhere else. We might be able to discover exactly why he was in the Acre, and if he knew either Max or Dr Pinchin.'

'What does Thomas say?'

Charlotte was perfectly honest. 'He is too tired to say anything much. He hardly ever tells me about the case, just the odd word. There's been a lot of public outcry, and the police are being accused of inefficiency, even corruption.'

That removed the last shred of reluctant conscience from Emily's mind. 'Then we must help. I don't know the Astleys personally, but I do know he was paying considerable attention to May Woolmer. Everyone has been wondering if she would catch him. She is this Season's newest beauty. Not my taste, actually. Very handsome, I suppose, in a creamy sort of way, like an extremely well-bred dairymaid, and about as interesting.'

'Oh dear!' Charlotte pictured something in frills, carrying a bucket.

'Oh, there's nothing whatsoever wrong with her.' Emily backtracked a step or two. 'But that in itself is bound to grow tiresome in time. She is as predictable as a jug of milk.'

'Whatever did Bertie Astley want to marry her for? Has she money? Or influence?' Charlotte inquired hopefully.

'None at all. But her manners are perfect, and she is certainly extremely agreeable. And all that rich white flesh is attractive to some men.'

Considering Emily's slender shoulders and slight bosom, Charlotte forbore from making comment on the subject. Instead she recalled a fragment of a remark Pitt had made when he was too tired to guard his tongue. 'Thomas says that Max even had women of good breeding and family working for him sometimes.'

'Good God!' Emily's chin dropped in incredulity. 'You mean for money —with...Oh, no!'

'Apparently.'

Amazement superseded disbelief, and then a reluctant thrill of horror. 'Charlotte, are you sure?'

'I'm sure that's what Thomas said.'

'But whatever kind of well-bred woman would need money so badly she could think of...I simply cannot imagine it!'

'Not out of need. Married women, out of boredom, or frustration—the way men gamble with more money than they can afford to lose, or drive crazy races with a four-in-hand and get themselves half killed when they turn over.'

'Did he keep books—Max?'

'I don't know, and I haven't thought it wise to ask Thomas yet. But, Emily, if we really tried, surely we could discover who some of these women might be? Perhaps one of them killed Max because he was blackmailing her, wouldn't let her go. That would be a real reason worth killing for.'

Emily pursed her mouth doubtfully. 'But what about Dr Pinchin?'

'Brothels must need doctors sometimes, mustn't they? Maybe he was in partnership with Max. Perhaps he put up the money, or found the women through his practice. He would be in a position to know.'

'And Bertie Astley?'

'Maybe he was a customer and recognized her. That would account for why he was not so badly—hurt—'

'That doesn't make sense. If it was her husband who killed them, he would hate Bertie just as much!'

'Well, maybe it wasn't. But someone did!'

'Charlotte, we shouldn't—' Emily let out a long breath. 'I've met May Woolmer two or three times. We could go and convey our condolences to her. I've got black accessories you can borrow. We've got to start somewhere. We'll go this afternoon. What are you going to tell Thomas? You're a terrible liar—you always say too much and end up by giving yourself away.'

'I told Gracie I was going to the dressmaker.'

Emily grunted and gave her a suspicious look. 'Then I suppose I had better give you a dress—for your alibi!'

'Thank you,' Charlotte said graciously. 'That is very generous of you. I'd like a red one.'

'Would you indeed!'

Mrs Woolmer turned over the gold-embossed card and examined it carefully. It was of excellent quality, discreet. And there was no denying the title, Viscountess Ashworth.

'Who is she, Mama?' May enquired hopefully. She was finding this state of limbo exceedingly tiresome. No one yet seemed sure whether Bertie had been the victim or an offender who deserved whatever end he met. May herself, therefore, could not be sure what attitude to adopt, and meeting people in the meantime was testing all her abilities.

On the other hand, not meeting people was like being imprisoned.

'I have no idea,' Mrs Woolmer replied with a frown between her carefully plucked brows. She was wearing purple again, a good choice for those who were not quite certain whether they were in mourning or not. May wore black because she looked utterly dazzling in it; she glowed like warm alabaster in sunlight.

The parlourmaid dropped a curtsy. 'If you please, ma'am, she is most soberly dressed, ma'am, an' she came in a carriage with a coat of arms on the side, and two footmen, ma'am, in livery. An' she 'as 'er sister with 'er, very proper like. An' she looks like she would be a lady, too, but she didn't give me any card.'

Mrs Woolmer made a rapid decision. Social behaviour must be judged to a nicety if one were to climb to the heights. Nature had given her one great advantage in the most beautiful daughter of the Season. It would be ungracious to squander it with a clumsy gesture now.

She smiled at the maid. 'Please invite Lady Ashworth and her sister to come in, Marigold, and then tell cook to prepare refreshments—tea, and the best cakes and delicacies—and bring them to us.'

'Yes, ma'am.' Marigold withdrew to do as she was bidden.

As soon as Emily and Charlotte came in, Mrs Woolmer was reassured. Obviously the Viscountess Ashworth was a lady; one had but to observe the quality and discretion of her clothes. Only the nobility mixed good taste with the spending of money in quite such a way.

May was also delighted. They were young enough to gossip a little, and perhaps before too long even extend her an invitation. A private dinner would not be unseemly; after all, she had not actually been betrothed to Bertie! The more she thought about it, the more she considered it would be best to maintain a gentle and dignified silence upon the whole affair. Let people interpret that as they wished; to say nothing was always safer than to commit oneself. And a great many men preferred women without too many opinions of their own. And—rather more to the point in the marriage stakes—their mothers always approved. Silence and a sweet smile were taken as signs of an obedient nature, a thing much to be desired in a daughter-in-law.

Lady Ashworth was dressed in the height

of fashion, in a subdued colour that made her look all the more elegant. Her sister was far less fashionable, but undeniably handsome. Indeed her face was quite individual; there was a warmth in it May found herself drawn to.

'My dear.' Lady Ashworth came forward, her hands outstretched, and took May's before she could readily think of anything to say. 'I am so sorry. I had to come and assure you of my sympathy in your distress.'

May had been distressed, but not as Lady Ashworth supposed. She had not been especially fond of Bertie. In fact, she greatly preferred Beau Astley; he was better-looking and a good deal more fun. But one had to be practical. He had been a younger son with very few prospects, and he would have had even fewer when Bertie married and there was a new mistress in Astley House.

She re-collected herself and smiled sadly. 'Thank you, Lady Ashworth, that is most sensitive of you. I can still hardly believe that anyone I knew could meet with such a dreadful fate.'

Mrs Woolmer cast her a warning glance. She must not say anything to link herself irretrievably with the Astleys. They might turn out to have possessed heaven knew what disgusting habits! For all the newspapers' genteelisms, one knew where he had been found. But May was perfectly aware of all the pitfalls and had no intention of falling into any of them.

Lady Ashworth introduced her sister Mrs Pitt, and the ladies accepted seats graciously. 'Life can give us some cruel surprises,' Emily observed, her expression one of wise sorrow. 'They can be very hard to bear.' She lowered her head, apparently overcome with her own thoughts.

May felt compelled to say something; good manners demanded it. 'Indeed. I—I realize now how little I knew him. I had never imagined such a...' She stopped because there was no satisfactory conclusion to that sentence. She looked frankly at Lady Ashworth's sister Mrs Pitt. 'I believe I must be most lamentably innocent. I fear the less charitable might be laughing at me already.'

'The envious,' Mrs Pitt corrected generously. 'And they will always be there. The only way to avoid them is to fail where they may see it and be satisfied. I assure you, no person of worth will feel anything but understanding for you. It is a situation in which any woman might find herself.'

May had a fluttering, nervous feeling that Mrs Pitt was referring to her indecision about Beau Astley with a very acute perception, and not at all to her grief for Bertie. It was uncomfortable to have her motives so thoroughly perceived. She looked at Lady Ashworth and saw the same frank understanding in her clear blue eyes. She decided at once to enlist them as allies. May was blessed with one virtue of perspicacity; she knew precisely whom she could deceive and whom she could not.

She let out a sigh and smiled disarmingly. 'What a relief it is to know someone who really does understand. So many people speak kindly, but they think only of a natural grief at losing a friend.'

Mrs Woolmer fidgeted, twisting her hands in her lap. She did not like the turn of this conversation, but could not think how to alter it without displaying marked discourtesy.

'Quite.' Lady Ashworth agreed with a little nod, continuing May's thought. 'One imagines one knows people, and then something like this occurs! But what can one do? If one is introduced by respectable acquaintances, that is all anyone requires. My husband and I were astonished.' She took a deep breath. 'Of course I do not know Sir Beau at all—'

But May was not to be so easily trapped.

'He appears to be extremely pleasant,' she replied without emotion. She forced Beau's face from her mind—the laughter, the soft voice, memories of dancing, lights, music, whirling feet, his arms about her. 'Sir Bertram always behaved himself impeccably in my company,' she finished levelly.

'Of course!' Mrs Woolmer said, a shade too quickly.

'I'm sure.' Lady Ashworth brushed her fingers delicately over her skirt. 'But if you will forgive me saying so, my dear, men have been known to behave very rashly indeed when they fall in love. And even brothers have learned to hate one another over a beautiful woman.'

'Oh!' Mrs Woolmer's hand flew to her mouth and stifled an exclamation in language far less than genteel.

May felt distinctly uncomfortable. Of course she was aware that many men had desired her. Surely that was what the Season was for? But so far she had considered the emotions superficial, all a part of the exquisite charade where the winners retired with agreeable husbands and with futures assured both socially and financially. The losers retreated to consider next year's tactics. May had always known her strengths and her weaknesses, and how best to deploy them. She had every intention of being a winner, and envy was to be expected—but not hatred, and certainly not the kind of passion that breeds murder.

'I think you flatter me, Lady Ashworth,' she said carefully. 'I have given no one cause for such feelings.' Perhaps it would be better to change the subject, turn Lady Ashworth's curious eye onto something even more shocking. 'I do not have the amorous skill of many of the ladies with'—she gave a tiny smile—'shall we say "experience"? I am loath to repeat rumour, but it is so persistent that in all common sense I cannot believe it is entirely false. There are some ladies of perfectly good family who behave like women of pleasure. No doubt they have the art to inflame the sort of dreadful emotions you are speaking of.'

It burst like a bombshell, as was intended.

'Nonsense!' Mrs Woolmer choked on her indrawn breath. 'You cannot possibly know of such a thing! Women of pleasure indeed! I will thank you to hold your tongue.'

Lady Ashworth's head came up, her eyes wide. But surprisingly it was Mrs Pitt who came to May's rescue. 'It is most distressing,' she agreed, dropping her voice to a confidential tone. 'But I also have heard of such things. And I have to admit that my source was irreproachable. It makes me wonder how ever to judge where to pursue acquaintances, and where one dare not! I am sure you must have had the same doubts as I. I feel guilty even for suspecting people who are probably as innocent as the day, and yet I would be appalled to find myself, through good nature and an excess of gullibility, in a situation from which I could not retreat with my reputation unblemished—not to think of things far worse!'

Lady Ashworth seemed to be in the grip of some over-powering emotion. She coughed furiously and covered her face with her handkerchief. Her shoulders shook. Her skin was pink to the very roots of her hair. Fortunately, at that moment the maid returned with tea and other refreshments, and they were able to revive Lady Ashworth. Her face was flushed but she was apparently otherwise in control of herself.

But Mrs Pitt was quite right. One simply could not afford to associate with women who were even suspected of such behaviour. May racked her thoughts to know which of her acquaintances might be involved. Several names came to mind, and she determined to avoid them on every possible occasion. Perhaps she should, in all kindness, warn Mrs Pitt?

'Are you acquainted with Lavinia Hawkesley?' she inquired.

Lady Ashworth's eyes widened. There was no need for indelicate explanations. May blandly mentioned a few other names, and then they discussed fashion and current romances for a pleasant half hour, all undershot with a frisson of scandal. Mrs Woolmer tried to guide the conversation toward the Ashworths' acquaintance with eligible young men, and met with no success whatsoever.

At four o'clock, the parlourmaid opened

the door and asked if the ladies would receive Mr Alan Ross, who had called to offer his family's sympathies.

Lady Ashworth jumped to her feet, seizing Mrs Pitt by the hand. 'Come, Charlotte, we really must not monopolize the whole afternoon.' She turned to May. 'I fear we have enjoyed your company so much we have forgotten our manners. If you will permit us to take our leave before Mr Ross arrives, we will not make him feel uncomfortable by appearing to avoid him.'

Mrs Woolmer was startled. 'Of course, if—if that is what you wish. Marigold, have Mr Ross wait in the morning room for a moment, if you please.'

Marigold closed the door behind her.

Lady Ashworth bent to May with a confidential whisper. 'My sister and I were once acquainted with Mr Ross's family during a period of tragedy which must be most distressing to him. I think it would be a kindness, my dear, if you were not to mention our names to him. I'm sure you understand?'

May did not understand at all, but she was perfectly capable of taking a hint. 'Of course. You will merely be two ladies who have called by in friendship. I appreciate your sensitivity, and I hope I shall have the good fortune to meet you again in more fortunate circumstances.'

'I am sure of it,' Lady Ashworth said confidently, with the slightest of nods.

May understood; it was all she wished.

Outside in the street, Charlotte turned on Emily. 'What are you thinking of? Surely it would have been to our advantage to meet with Alan Ross again? Max may have used his old connections to find these women!'

'I know that!' Emily exclaimed. 'But not in there. He won't be long—we can wait out here for him.'

'It's freezing! Why on earth should we stand around here? He'll know we are forcing an acquaintance if—'

'Oh, don't be so silly. William!' She waved her hand at the coachman. 'Find something wrong with one of the horses —keep yourself occupied until Mr Ross comes out of the house.'

'Yes, m'lady.' William obediently bent and ran his hand down the near horse's leg, and began to examine it.

Charlotte shivered as the wind cut through her coat. 'Why on earth couldn't we simply have stayed in there and met him?' she demanded, glaring at Emily.

'I always thought General Balantyne was very fond of you.' Emily appeared to ignore the remark.

Charlotte had liked to think so, too. The memory brought a pleasant glow, a tinge of excitement. She did not argue.

'Christina moves in just the right circle to know the sort of women who might be used by Max,' Emily continued. 'She could be of great assistance.'

'Christina Ross wouldn't assist us across the street if we were blind!' Charlotte remembered Callander Square vividly. 'The most likely assistance she could give me would be into the nearest ditch!'

'Which is why we must pursue the general instead,' Emily said impatiently. 'If you conduct yourself properly, he will help you to anything you like! Now be quiet. Mr Ross is coming out. I knew he wouldn't be long.'

As Alan Ross approached, Emily smiled dazzlingly at him.

He smiled back and raised his hat a little uncertainly. Then his eyes moved to Charlotte and his face eased in recognition.

'Miss Ellison? How charming to see you

again. I hope you are well. Do you have trouble with your carriage? May I take you somewhere?'

'Thank you, I am sure it is nothing serious,' Charlotte answered quickly. 'Do you recall Mr Ross, Emily? My sister, Lady Ashworth—' She wanted to tell him delicately that she was Mrs Pitt. During the Callander Square murders, she had found a position in the Balantyne house by pretending she was a single woman in need of respectable work. 'Mr Ross—'

Emily cut in, offering her hand to Alan Ross. 'Of course I remember Mr Ross. Please give my best wishes to Mrs Ross. I confess it is quite some time since I have seen her. One becomes so busy with people one is obliged by courtesy to visit that one misses those one is genuinely fond of. She is such an entertaining person. I look forward to meeting her again.'

Emily detested Christina and always had. Her smile did not waver a fraction. 'And Charlotte has spoken of her frequently. We really must call upon her. I hope she will forgive us for our neglect.'

'I am sure she will be delighted to see you.' He gave the only possible answer he could.

Emily smiled as if equally charmed by the prospect. 'Then please tell her that Lady Ashworth and Miss Ellison will call upon her next Tuesday, if she receives upon that day?'

'I am sure she will. But why do you not come to dine? That would be far pleasanter. It will be only a small gathering, but if Lord Ashworth is not engaged—?'

'I am sure he is not.' Emily accepted with alacrity. She would make sure that George was not. Other engagements would have to be dispensed with.

He bowed slightly. 'Then I shall see that invitations are sent. If you are sure I can be of no assistance?' He looked at William, now standing to attention by the horse's head.

'I am sure we shall be perfectly all right,' Emily said.

'Then I bid you good day, Lady Ashworth, Miss Ellison.' He met Charlotte's eyes for a moment, smiled, then turned and walked back along the pavement to his own carriage.

Emily accepted William's assistance into the carriage, and Charlotte followed after her, landing in a bundle.

'What on earth is the matter with you?'

she said furiously. 'Why did you let him go on thinking I am Miss Ellison? I hardly need a job in Christina's household!'

Emily yanked her skirt free from where Charlotte was sitting on it. 'We'll hardly be in a position to discover much if they know you are married to a policeman!' she pointed out. 'Let alone the very policeman who is investigating the murders. Added to which, it will do no harm for the general to see you as still unmarried.'

'What are you—' Charlotte began, then stopped short. There was considerable good sense in what Emily was saying. People like Christina Balantyne did not dine with policeman's wives! If they knew she and Emily were bent on inquiring into murder, they would never even get through the front door.

After all, they had a certain moral duty to discover as much as they could—it was every person's duty. And, in truth, they had proved unusually skilled in the past!

'Yes,' she said meekly. 'Yes, I suppose you are quite right, Emily.'

If she and Emily were to investigate effectively, they must have all the knowledge available. But to get it from Pitt was no easy matter. So far, he had spoken of no further discovery. It seemed he was trudging day after day through the squalor of the Acre, pursuing a word here, a suggestion there. But if he was any nearer finding a connection between Max, Dr Pinchin, and Bertie Astley, he had not told Charlotte of it.

'Thomas?' she began softly.

He opened his eyes and looked at her. It was late; he was half asleep by the fire in the parlour. She had chosen her time with care, and tried to sound casual. 'Have you learned anything more about Max?'

'I know everything there is to know about Max,' he replied, sliding a little farther down in his chair, looking at her through his eyelashes. 'Except who his clients were, who his women were, and who killed him.'

'Oh.' She was not sure how to pursue it. 'That means he kept no sort of record. Or else it was taken?'

'He was killed in the street,' he pointed out. 'Unless it was his house manager who did it, there would be no chance to look for papers. Anyway, according to all I can find out, there were none. He kept names in his head, and all business was strictly cash.'

No records! 'Then how could he blackmail anyone?' she asked curiously.

'I don't know that he did.' He moved his feet off the fender; it was getting too hot. 'But he might have had knowledge enough to ruin anyone's reputation. Proof is not necessary. Word of mouth in the right place, substantiated by a few names and places, would do excellently. Suspicion alone can destroy. But the motive could just as easily have been professional rivalry. He was taking other people's business. Either way, it is none of your affair. This isn't a case where an amateur can help.'

She met his gaze and suddenly felt a great deal less sure of herself. 'Oh, yes, of course,' she said. After all, she was not really investigating! It was only a matter of keeping her ears open for any odd piece of information that might prove relevant. 'But it is only natural I should be interested, isn't it?' she said reasonably.

Charlotte was something less than honest over the dinner invitation to the Rosses' on Tuesday. Pitt was working, as she had trusted he would be. She mentioned that they had been invited to dine with Emily and George, and would he mind very much if she went, even though he was unable to? She knew he would not refuse her. After all, he had not been able to take her anywhere himself, or even to offer her much companionship, since the case began. And so far as it went, what she said was true; she would be with Emily and George! Even if it was not in their home, as she allowed Pitt to presume.

Emily lent her a gown, as usual, and Charlotte dressed for the occasion at Paragon Walk, with Emily's maid to dress her hair. She felt not the least qualm about that, for the whole idea had been engineered by Emily's connivance, with Alan Ross!

The gown was of apricot silk, with the most delicate lace a shade or two deeper, and appeared to be quite new. In fact, it crossed her mind to wonder if Emily had obtained it for the purpose. It was a colour Emily herself should never have worn, with her fair hair and clear blue eyes. The shade was ideal for a warmer complexion and darker, heavier hair with gleams of red in it.

She felt a sudden gratitude for Emily's generosity, both in providing the gown, which flattered her so much, and for doing it in such a discreet manner. She decided to say nothing, and thus let the gift reach the fullest measure. Instead she swept down the stairs from the spare dressing room like a duchess entering her own ballroom, and swirled to a grand curtsy in the hallway at Emily's feet. The sense of excitement inside her was as vivid as the light on the chandeliers.

'Your dress is perfect,' she said, rising with a little less grace than she had intended. 'I feel fit to dazzle everyone and make Christina quite sickly with envy! Thank you very much.'

Emily was in the palest aquamarine, with diamonds at her ears and throat sparkling like sunlight upon clear water. They were as different as could be, which of course had been the intention—although possibly Emily had not expected Charlotte to look quite so splendid. But if she hadn't, she rapidly adjusted her thought, and smiled back with unclouded approval.

'Now, just remember not to say anything too candid,' she warned. 'Society adores mirrors to its face and its attire, but has no love whatsoever for a reflection of its morals or its soul. I shall be obliged if you bear that in mind before you express your opinions!'

'Yes, Emily.' She did owe her something for the dress.

Emily had obviously taken some care in forewarning George of the purpose of their visit. He had agreed to accompany them, and to refrain from enlightening their hosts about Charlotte's marriage and thus her current social status, although Charlotte did not know if Emily had also told him the reason for this!

Christina Ross received them distinctly coolly. Obviously the invitation had come from her husband, and she had been obliged to go along with it, since it could hardly be withdrawn. 'How kind of you to come, Lord Ashworth, Lady Ashworth,' she said, with a very small smile.

George bowed and passed some civil remark, vaguely complimentary.

'And Miss Ellison.' Christina's eyes swept over Charlotte's gown with slight surprise. She allowed it to show, as a delicate insult to what she considered to be Charlotte's station, and therefore the unsuitability of the gown—let alone how she might have come by it! 'I hope you are in good health?' There was a lift in her voice, which was wasted. Charlotte too obviously glowed with an abundance of well-being of every sort.

Christina abandoned the inquiry without waiting for an answer, and indicated where they were welcome to seat themselves.

George did not believe that they should interfere with the solving of the crimes, and he had in fact barely known Bertie Astley. But he was generally good-natured, as long as he was not unduly criticized or robbed of his habitual pleasures. Emily had proved an excellent wife. She was neither extravagant nor indiscreet, she rarely lost her temper, she never sulked or rebuffed him, and she was far too subtle in her dealings with him to need to nag.

He was aware, in afterthought, of having changed one or two of his amusements—maybe even three or four—in order to please her. But it had proved less painful than he had anticipated, and one had to be prepared to make some adjustments. He therefore did not really object to humouring her with regard to cultivating Christina Ross, if she felt it was useful. Of course he knew quite well it was absolutely pointless, but if it entertained her, what matter? And he could see no reason why it should not be pleasant.

Charlotte he had never understood, nor had he tried to. He liked her well enough; in fact, to be honest, he even liked Pitt!

Accordingly, he put himself out to be charming to Christina and, without any great effort, was devastatingly effective. His face was handsome, especially his eyes, and generations of privilege and money had given him an assurance so easy it required no attention at all. He could sit and stare at Christina with appreciation, and flatter her merely by giving her his undivided concern.

There was little enough time, and Emily wasted none of it, but began immediately on the subject that had brought her. 'It is so pleasant to see you again,' she said to Alan Ross, with a smile. 'George was delighted when I gave him your invitation. We spend so much time with those in society who are not of the most attractive. I confess, I am not as clever at judging people as I had imagined I was. I have been somewhat naïve, and have found myself in the company of persons I would not have chosen had I been wiser. But one so often learns these things too late. Even now I do not fully understand.' She dropped her voice as if imparting a confidence. 'But I have heard whispers that some ladies of what one would have thought to be impeccable family have been behaving in ways too appalling to speak of!'

'Indeed?' A shadow crossed Alan Ross's face, so brief Charlotte was not sure if she had imagined it, but it left her with an impression of pain. Had the unintended clumsiness of Emily's remark disturbed some memory of the past? The murder in Callander Square?

'Emily,' she said quickly. 'Perhaps it is a subject indelicate to discuss!'

Emily gave her a blue stare of amazement, then turned back quickly to Alan Ross. 'I do hope I have not offended you by speaking my feelings too candidly?' She looked wounded, anxious, but underneath the wide swirls of her skirt she gave Charlotte a sharp kick. Charlotte winced, but was obliged to keep her face expressionless.

'Of course not!' Ross said with a slight movement of his hand, the smallest gesture of dismissal—it was too trivial to require more. 'I quite agree with you. There is only one thing more boring and more unpleasant than debauchery, and that

211

is to hear of it interminably and at second hand.' He smiled very slightly, and Charlotte could only guess at the thoughts that had prompted the remark.

'How I agree with you!' Emily's foot gave Charlotte a warning tap—painful, since it caught exactly the spot where she had landed the first kick. 'I find it most embarrassing when women speak of such things. I hardly know what to say.'

Charlotte moved her feet discreetly out of Emily's reach. 'And that is a mark of how deeply she is affected,' she put in. 'It quite robs her of a response—and what a remarkable instance that is you may judge!'

Emily's foot came out sharply and met only piles of skirt. She looked at Charlotte with acute suspicion out of the corner of her eye. Charlotte smiled ravishingly at Alan Ross.

At that moment the door opened and the footman ushered in General Balantyne and Lady Augusta. George and Alan Ross both rose to their feet, and the rest of the party remained perfectly still. Balantyne stared at Charlotte until she could feel the colour burn in her face. She wished desperately that Emily had not lied and introduced her as Miss Ellison.

Christina broke the pattern. She stood up and sailed forward, arms stretched in a theatrical gesture stopping just short of embracing her father. 'Papa, how delightful to see you!' She half turned and held out a cool cheek to Lady Augusta. 'Mama! You know Lord Ashworth, of course.'

Formal acknowledgments were made, George bowing gracefully.

'And Lady Ashworth.' Her voice dropped to a tone distinctly chillier.

Emily had risen, as was fitting for a younger woman to an elder when they both possessed titles. Again the acknowledgments were made.

Christina turned at last to Charlotte, also, of course, now standing. 'And perhaps you recall Miss Ellison, who was so kind as to assist Papa with some clerical work a few years ago?'

'Indeed.' Augusta did not wish to be reminded of that time, or of anything to do with it. 'Good evening, Miss Ellison.' Her incomprehension that Charlotte should be included in the company at all clearly showed.

'Good evening, Lady Augusta.' Suddenly, Charlotte's guilt vanished, and she stared back as coldly as she imagined Augusta herself might have if confronted with a débutante who did not know her place.

There was a faint tinge of colour on the general's high cheekbones. 'Good evening, Miss Ellison.' He caught something in his throat and coughed. 'How pleasant to see you again. I was thinking of you only the other day—' He stopped. 'That is—a certain event brought you to mind.'

'I have remembered you often.' Charlotte wanted to rescue him, and what she said was almost true. She never heard or read of any military event without in one way or other associating it with him.

Christina's raised eyebrows showed her amazement. 'Oh dear! I had no notion we had become so fixed in your mind, Miss Ellison—or perhaps you are referring only to Papa?'

Charlotte wanted to hurt her. 'The circumstances of our meeting were not common enough in my life for me to forget anything of them,' she said, meeting Christina's eyes icily. She saw Christina pale at the memory of murder. 'But of course I learned to admire the general very much as I became acquainted with his memoirs. I am sure, knowing him so much better, you must share my regard.'

Christina's face tightened. 'Naturally—but then he is my father! That is an entirely different thing—Miss Ellison.'

The colour deepened in Balantyne's face, but he seemed to find nothing to say.

'You never read your father's military papers, my dear.' It was Alan Ross who rescued them. 'A daughter's affection is quite a different emotion from the respect of someone quite impartial.'

The pink drained out of Balantyne's cheeks and he turned away quickly. 'Of course it is,' he said with some tartness. 'I cannot imagine you meant that as it sounded, Christina. Miss Ellison was merely being courteous.' He did not look at Charlotte, but settled himself talking instead to George.

Emily engaged herself with Christina, leaving Charlotte to try to balance an awkward conversation with Alan Ross and Lady Augusta. She was immensely relieved when dinner was announced.

The table was rich, and Charlotte noticed Emily looking it over and probably adding up what she judged it to have cost. Emily knew the quality of crystal, silver, and napery to a nicety, and she was also precisely aware of what a cook was worth. Charlotte caught her eye a few moments after they had sat down, and from the slight incline of one fair brow, she gathered that in Emily's opinion Christina was being extravagant.

The first course was served, and the general conversation turned to the kind of polite trivia appropriate to the importance of taking the first edge from appetite, and at the same time maintaining a degree of elegance. Charlotte took no part in it; she was not acquainted with the people referred to, and could not comment upon the likelihood of one person marrying another, or what a disaster it would or would not be.

She found her gaze straying towards General Balantyne, the only other person uninvolved, either from ignorance or lack of interest. She was a little discomforted to find him watching her, in spite of the fact that Christina was speaking with great animation.

There was a ripple of laughter around the table, and suddenly Christina became aware that her wit had left two of the company untouched. She looked directly at Charlotte, pulling a little face.

'Oh, I am so sorry, Miss Ellison. Of course I forgot you cannot know Miss Fairgood, or the Duke's grandson. How very unkind of me. You must feel so left out. Do please forgive me!'

Nothing she might have said would be better calculated to make Charlotte's exclusion more obvious. The conversation was tedious and Charlotte had not cared before, but now she felt her face burning with self-consciousness. She remained silent, because if she spoke she would be rude and thus give Christina yet another victory.

'I do not know Miss Fairgood either.' Balantyne picked up his glass. 'I cannot say that I have been aware of the loss. And I am as indifferent as Miss Ellison as to whom the Duke's grandson should marry. However,' he turned to Charlotte, 'I have recently come upon some letters of a soldier who served in the Peninsular War. I think you might find them interesting, and most encouraging when one realizes how far we have progressed since then. I remember your admiration for Miss Nightingale's work in organizing care for the wounded in the Crimea.'

Charlotte did not have to feign interest. 'Letters?' she said eagerly. 'Oh, that is so much more exciting than a history book.' Without a thought for Emily's strategy, she leaned forward a little. 'I should be so pleased if I might see them. It would be like—like holding a piece of the real past in my hands, not merely somebody else's judgment of it! What do you know of him—the soldier who wrote the letters, I mean?'

The stern lines of Balantyne's face softened and some reserve within him released itself. He put the glass down. He ignored the formality of saying that of course she might see the letters, as if that should be assumed and need not be put into words between them.

'He was a person of considerable intelligence,' he said intently. 'It seemed he served as an enlisted man instead of as an officer by his own choice, and he was obviously well able to read and to write. His observations are most sensitive, and betray a compassion I admit I find very moving.'

'It is hardly an uplifting conversation for the dinner table.' Augusta looked at them with disfavour. 'I cannot imagine that we wish to know of the sufferings of some pathetic common soldier in—wherever it was!'

'The Spanish peninsula,' Balantyne explained, but she ignored him.

'I should think they are quite as uplifting as the matrimonial aspirations of Miss Fairgood,' Alan Ross said dryly.

'To whom, for goodness sake?' Christina asked caustically.

'To me,' Ross replied. 'To your father, and—unless she is being more courteous than others have been so far this evening—to Miss Ellison.'

Charlotte caught his eye, and looked down quickly at her plate. 'I am afraid I cannot claim credit for such delicacy, Mr Ross,' she said, forcing her face to remain modestly composed. 'I am most genuinely interested.'

'How quaint,' Christina muttered. 'Lady Ashworth, you were saying that you have lately made the closer acquaintance of Lavinia Hawkesley. Don't you find her quite the most entertaining creature? Although I am not at all sure how much she has any intention of being!'

'I fancy the poor soul is bored to weeping,' Emily replied with a furious glance at Charlotte. 'And I cannot say that I entirely blame her. Sir James is a man fit to bore anyone. He must be thirty years older than she is, at the very least.'

'But extremely wealthy,' Christina pointed out. 'And with any decency at all, he will die before another ten years are past.'

'Oh!' Emily rolled her eyes heavenward. 'But what can she possibly do for another ten years?'

A small smile flickered across Christina's face. 'She is not without imagination—'

'And that is her misfortune!' Augusta interrupted sharply. 'She would be much better off if she had none at all. And whatever your fancy begets, Christina, it would be more discreet if you were not to speak of it. We do not wish to be the prognosticators of other people's misdeeds.'

Christina took a deep breath. That was obviously precisely what she had wished to be, but curiously she did not argue. In fact, Charlotte thought she saw a momentary pallor, a tightening of her face, but whether it was pity or temper she could not judge.

'I suppose she might occupy herself in some charitable work,' George suggested hopefully. 'Emily frequently tells me how much there is to be done.'

'And that is it!' Christina was suddenly

savage. 'When a gentleman is bored, he may gamble at his club at dice or cards, go to the races, or drive his own pair if he wishes! He may go shooting or play billiards, or go to theatres—and worse places—but if a lady is bored she is expected to occupy herself with charitable work—going round and visiting the hungry or the dirty, muttering soothing words at them and encouraging them to be virtuous!'

There was too much truth in her outburst for Charlotte to argue, and yet she found herself unable even to begin to tell Christina Ross of the sense of purpose and satisfaction she herself found from working to bring about parliamentary reform. There was a reality about it, an urgency to life, that would have made games, or even sports, seem divorced from the world and unbearably trivial.

She leaned forward, searching for a way to express her feelings. Everyone was staring at her, but nothing adequate came to her mind.

'If you are about to expound on the delights of Papa's military histories, Miss Ellison, please do not bother,' Christina said freezingly. 'I do not wish to know about cholera in Sebastopol, or how many wretched souls died in the charge of the Light Brigade. The whole thing seems to me to be an idiot game played by men who should be locked away in Bedlam where they can harm no one but themselves...and perhaps each other!'

For the only time in her life to that moment, Charlotte felt a rush of sympathy for Christina. 'Can you think of a way in which we might enforce that in law, Mrs Ross?' she said enthusiastically. 'Think of all the young men who might not die, if we did!'

Christina looked at her with a curious little frown. She had not expected agreement from anyone, least of all from Charlotte. She had begun by intending only to be rude. 'You surprise me,' she said candidly. 'I thought you were a great admirer of the military.'

'I hate bland vanity,' Charlotte answered. 'And I deplore stupidity. The fact that they occur in the army more dangerously than anywhere else, except perhaps in Parliament, does not make my respect for courage of the soldier any less.'

'In Parliament?' Augusta was incredulous.

'Really, my dear Miss Ellison! Whatever can you mean?'

'A fool in Parliament can oppress millions,' Balantyne offered. 'And God knows there are enough of them! And vain ones, too.' He looked at Charlotte with complete frankness, as if he had temporarily forgotten she was a woman. 'I have not heard so much sense put so succinctly in years,' he added with a slight drawing together of his brows. 'I had a feeling you were about to say something else when Christina brought back the subject of the army. Please tell me what it was?'

'I—' Charlotte was acutely conscious of his eyes upon her. They were brighter, clearer blue than she had remembered. And she was increasingly aware of his power, the will that had enabled him to command men in danger and fear of death. She abandoned the effort to phrase her feelings politely.

'I was going to say that when I have time to spare, I involve myself in an attempt to have some of the laws upon child prostitution reformed, so that they would be a great deal more rigid than at present, and it would be a very grave offence either to use children oneself or to traffic in the use of them, whether they are boys or girls.'

Alan Ross turned to face her, his eyes keen.

'Really?' Augusta's expression was one of complete incomprehension. 'I would not have imagined one could have any success in such a venture without considerable knowledge upon the subject, Miss Ellison.'

'Of course not.' Charlotte accepted the challenge and stared back at her unflinchingly. 'It is necessary to acquire it, or one can have no influence at all.'

'How extremely distasteful,' Augusta said, closing the subject.

'Of course it is distasteful.' Alan Ross refused to be silenced. 'I think that is what Brandy was saying the other evening—you remember Brandy, Miss Ellison? But then if those of us who are able to reach the ears of Parliament do not care about such ills, who will effect any change?'

'The church,' Augusta said finally. 'And I am quite sure they will do a better job of it than we will by indulging in wild and unprofitable speculation over the dinner table. Brandon, will you be so good as to pass me the mustard? Christina, you had better have a word with your cook—this sauce is totally insipid. It is no better than cotton wool! Do you not think so, Miss Ellison?'

'It is mild,' Charlotte replied with a slight smile. 'But I do not find it disagreeable.'

'How odd.' Augusta turned over her fork. 'I would have expected mustard to be much more to your taste!'

After the meal was finished, the butler brought in the port. Augusta, Christina, Emily, and Charlotte excused themselves to the withdrawing room to leave the gentlemen to drink, and to smoke if they wished. It was the part of the evening Charlotte had looked forward to least. She was sharply aware of Christina's dislike, and now also of Augusta's disapproval. And above either of these unpleasant feelings, she felt acutely nervous about what Emily might do. She had come for the sole purpose of pursuing the names and characteristics of Christina's less reputable friends, with a view to discovering if any of them might have been seduced by Max. Please heaven she was at least subtle about it—if one could conceivably be subtle about such a thing.

Emily gave her a warning look before they sat down. 'You know, I do so agree with you,' she said to Christina with an air of conspiracy. 'I long to do something a little more adventurous than calling upon people one already knows positively everything about—and making polite and tedious conversation. Or else doing "good works," I am sure they are very worthy, and I admire those who can enjoy them. But I confess I do not.'

'If you attend church occasionally, and look after the families of your servants, that is all that is required of you,' Augusta pointed out. 'Other good works of visiting, and so on, are only necessary for single ladies who have nothing else to do. It keeps them occupied and makes them useful. Heaven knows there are enough of them—one must not usurp their function!'

They all seemed for the moment to have forgotten that, as far as they knew, Charlotte fell into that category.

'I think perhaps I shall take to riding in the park,' Emily mused. 'One might meet all manner of interesting people there—or so I have heard.'

'Indeed,' Christina said. 'I know exactly

what you mean. But believe me, there are things which one may do that have far more spirit of adventure, and are a great deal more entertaining, than writing letters or making social calls upon people who are inexpressibly dull. It is not really improper, if one does not go alone, for one to visit—'

'Do you paint Miss Ellison?' Augusta cut across Christina in a loud, penetrating voice. 'Or play the pianoforte? Or perhaps you sing?'

'I paint,' Charlotte replied immediately.

'How pleasant for you.' Christina's opinion of painting was implicit in her tone. Single women who could think of nothing more exciting to do than sit about with brushes and bits of wet paper were too pathetic to waste emotion upon. She turned back to Emily. 'I have quite decided that I shall ride in the Row every morning that the wish takes me and the weather is agreeable! I am sure that with a spirited animal one might have a great deal of pleasure.'

'With a spirited animal, my girl, one may very well land flat on one's face in the mud!' Augusta snapped. 'And I would have you remember it, and not behave as if taking a fall were a light thing!'

Christina's face drained of all colour. She stared straight ahead, looking neither at Augusta nor at Emily. If she had any rebuttal, it was stillborn inside her.

Charlotte tried desperately to think of something to say to cover the silence, but everything trivial and polite seemed grotesque after the sudden reality of emotion, even though she did not understand it or its cause. If Christina had injured herself, perhaps in some recklessness on horseback, it was a most indelicate subject to refer to. It did flicker wildly into her mind that perhaps that was the reason she appeared as yet to have no family. The uprush of pity was painful; she did not wish to feel anything for Christina but dislike.

'Emily plays the piano,' Charlotte said emptily, merely to change the subject and dismiss her thoughts.

'I beg your pardon?' Augusta swallowed. There were very fine lines on her throat that Charlotte had not noticed before.

'Emily plays the piano,' Charlotte repeated with increasing embarrassment. Now she felt ridiculous.

'Indeed? And you did not learn?'

'No. I preferred to paint, and Papa did not insist.'

'How wise of him. It is a waste of time to force a child who has no talent.'

There was no civil answer to that. Charlotte suddenly ceased to feel guilty about the softness she had seen in the general's face, or the quick honesty in his eyes when he had forgotten the niceties of the table and simply spoken to her as a friend with whom he might speak of things that mattered, things of the mind and the emotions.

Indeed, when the gentlemen rejoined them shortly afterward, she was perfectly happy to find herself almost immediately engaged in a long discussion with him about the retreat from Moscow. She did not need to make the least pretence to follow his every word and share his fascination with the wide sweep of history as the tide of Europe turned, or the wound of pity for the solitary deaths of men in the bitter snows of Russia.

When they rose to leave, it was the general's face that was in her mind, not Christina's. It was only afterward, when Emily spoke to her on the way home, that any sense of guilt returned.

'Really, Charlotte, I asked you to engage the general's sympathy so that we might learn something of use to us—not enchant the man out of his wits!' she said acidly. 'I really do think you might learn to control yourself. That apricot gown has gone to your head!'

Charlotte blushed in the darkness, but fortunately neither Emily nor George could see her. 'Well, there was little point in my trying to pursue Christina's more flighty acquaintances!' she said sharply. 'You all had me marked as a poor little creature who sits at home painting when I am not going out doing good works among the unfortunates!'

'I quite understand your disliking Christina.' Emily changed tactics and assumed elaborate patience instead. 'I do myself—and she was certainly very rude to you. But that is not the point! We were there to pursue the investigation, not to enjoy ourselves!'

Charlotte had no answer for that. She had learned nothing whatsoever, and, if she were even remotely honest, she had enjoyed herself indecently much. At least she had at times; there were moments that had been perfectly ghastly. She had forgotten how very crushing Society could be.

'Did you learn anything?' she asked.

'I have no idea,' Emily replied in the darkness. 'Perhaps.'

CHAPTER 7

Emily had thought about all the murders and the many different tragedies that might lie behind them. She was perfectly aware that a great many marriages were made quite as much for practical reasons as for romantic ones, attempts either to improve positions in Society or to maintain ones that were endangered. Sometimes such alliances worked out quite as well as those embarked upon in the heat of infatuation, but where the difference of age or temperament was too great, they became prisonlike.

She also knew the morally numbing effect of boredom. That she did not suffer from it herself was due to her periodic adventures into the stimulating, frightening, and turbulent world of criminal tragedy. But the long, arid intervals of social trivia in the meantime were the more pronounced because of the contrast. It was a world enclosed upon itself, where the most superficial flirtations assumed the proportions of great love, mere insults in etiquette or precedence became wounds, and matters of dress—the cut, the colour, the trimming—were noticed and discussed as if they were of immense importance.

As Christina Ross had said, idle men might occupy themselves with all manner of sport, healthy or otherwise, even finding excitement in risking money or broken limbs. Industrious or morally minded men might seek power in Parliament or trade, or might travel abroad upon missions to benighted nations somewhere, or join the army, or follow the White Nile to discover its source in the heart of the Dark Continent!

But a woman had only the outlet of charitable works. Her home was cared for by servants, her children by a nursery maid, a nanny, and then a governess. For those who were neither artistic nor gifted with any particular intelligence, there was little else but to entertain and be entertained. Small wonder that spirited young women, like some of Christina's set, trapped in marriages without passion, laughter, or even companionship, could be lured away by someone as raw and dangerous as Max Burton.

And of course Emily had never hidden from herself the other side of the argument, the fact that a number of men do not find all their appetites satisfied at home. Many abstained for one reason or another, but of course there were those who did not. One did not discuss 'houses of pleasure'—or the 'fallen doves' who occupied them. God!—that was a euphemism she hated! And only with the most intimate friends did one speak of the various affairs that were conducted at country houses over long shooting weekends, in croquet games on summer lawns, at great balls in the hunting season, or any other of a dozen times and places. None of which was to excuse it, but to understand it.

Therefore, in considering murder, Emily took into account the names and situations, such as she knew them, of Christina's social circle and those who might conceivably have been involved with Max. There were about seven or eight she found likely, and another half dozen possible, though she believed they lacked the courage, or the indifference to values of modesty or loyalty, to have taken such a step. But if nothing better presented itself, she would bear in mind to suggest their names to Pitt, so that he might discover where their husbands had been at the relevant times.

And there was always the possibility of an unfortunate recognition to consider—a little betrayal—or blackmail. What of a man who took his pleasures in a whorehouse and found he had bought his own wife! The permutations were legion, all of them painful and desperately foolish.

It could be that one such woman had been used by Max, that one of her customers had been Bertie Astley and, for some reason, a fear or hatred had arisen that resulted in the murder not only of Max but of Astley also. How Hubert Pinchin was involved, however, she did not yet have any suggestion.

The other most obvious possibility was even less pleasant to her: that Beau Astley had read of the startling murders of Max and Dr Pinchin, and had seized the opportunity to imitate these crimes and get rid of his elder brother. It would not be the first murder to ape another—and so saddle a man guilty of two murders with

234

the blame for one more.

Beau Astley had enough to gain for his brother's death, that was certain. But how much had he wanted it? Was he in financial straits, or did he manage very well upon whatever resources he had? Was he in love with May Woolmer? In fact, what kind of a person was he in general?

At the breakfast table, Emily sipped her tea. George was not at his best. He was hiding behind the newspaper, not to read it but to avoid having to think of something to say.

'I called upon poor May Woolmer recently,' Emily remarked cheerfully.

'Did you?' George's voice was absent-minded, and Emily realized he had forgotten who May Woolmer was.

'She is still in mourning, of course,' she continued. An outright request for information would be unlikely to produce it. George did not like curiosity—it was vulgar, and likely to offend people. He did not care if people took offence, when it was unwarranted, but he disliked the thought of being oafish, or anything that might appear ignorant of courtesy. He knew very well the value of acceptance.

'I beg your pardon?' He had not been paying attention, and now put the paper down reluctantly as he realized that she had no intention of allowing the matter to drop.

'She is still in mourning for Bertie Astley,' Emily repeated.

His face cleared a little. 'Oh, yes, she would be. Pity about that. Nice enough fellow.'

'Oh, George!' She contrived to look shocked.

'What?' He clearly failed to understand. It was a harmless remark, and surely Astley had been perfectly amiable.

'George!' She let her voice slide down, and lowered her eyes. 'I do know where he was found, you know!'

'What?'

She wished she could blush to order. Some women could, and it was a most useful accomplishment. She avoided looking at him, in case he read curiosity in her eyes instead of modest horror.

'He was found on the doorstep of a house of pleasure.' She voiced the euphemism as if it came to her tongue with some embarrassment. 'Where the "occupants" are men as well!'

'Oh, God! How did you know that?' This time he needed no pretence whatever to show interest. His face was startled, his dark eyes very wide. 'Emily?'

For a moment Emily could think of nothing to say. The conversation had taken a turn she should have foreseen, but had not. Should she admit to having read the newspapers? Or should she blame Charlotte? No, that was not a good idea—it might have unfortunate repercussions. George might even take it into his head that she should not associate with Charlotte quite so much, especially during the investigation of scandalous murders like these.

She had a sudden inspiration. 'May told me. Goodness knows where she heard it. But you know how these whispers spread. Why? Is it not true, after all?' She met his eyes squarely and with total innocence this time. She had no qualms about deceiving George in trivial matters—it was for his own good. She was never less than honest in things of importance, like loyalty, or money. But sometimes George needed a little managing.

His shoulders eased and he sat back in his chair again, but his expression was still

237

full of confusion. Two things troubled him: the extremely unsavoury facts concerning Bertie Astley, and quite how much of them it was proper to tell Emily.

She understood him very well, and rescued the situation before she lost the initiative and was obliged to begin all over again. 'Perhaps I should call upon May and reassure her?' she suggested. 'If it is only a malicious invention—'

'Oh, no!' He was unhappy, but quite decided. 'I am afraid you cannot do that—it is perfectly true.'

Emily looked suitably downcast, as though she had actually entertained a hope that it was not. 'George? Was Sir Bertram—I mean, did he have...a peculiar nature?'

'Good God, no! That is what is so damned odd! I simply don't understand it.' He pulled a face, in rare outspokenness. 'Although I suppose we seldom know people as well as we imagine. Perhaps he was...and no one knew it.'

Emily put her hand out across the table and clasped his. 'Don't think it, George,' she said gently. 'Is it not far more likely that some other suitor of May Woolmer's was so crazed he simply took the opportunity to rid himself of a rival and slander him horribly at the same time? That way he could be rid of him both literally and in memory. After all, how could May cherish the thought of a man who practised such indecencies!'

He considered it for a moment, closing his hand over hers. There were times when he was really extremely fond of her. One thing about Emily: even after five years of marriage, she was never a bore.

'I doubt it,' he said at last. 'She is a handsome creature, certainly, but I cannot imagine anyone getting so infatuated with her as to do that. She hasn't the—the fire. And she has very little money, you know.'

'I thought Beau Astley was exceedingly attracted to her,' she suggested.

'Beau?' He looked incredulous.

'Is he not?' Now she was confused also.

'I think he likes her very well, yes, but he has other interests, and he's hardly the sort to kill his own brother!'

'There is the title and the money,' she pointed out.

'Do you know Beau Astley?'

'No,' she said hopefully. At last they had

come to the point. 'What sort of a man is he?'

'Agreeable—rather more than poor Bertie, actually. And generous,' he said with conviction. 'I really think I should go and see him.' He let the newspaper slide to the floor and stood up. 'I always liked Beau. Poor fellow's probably feeling terrible. Mourning is such a tedious business—it makes you feel infinitely worse. No matter how grieved you are, you don't want to sit around in a house full of gaslights and black crêpe, with servants speaking in whispers and maids who sniffle every time they see you. I'll go and offer him a little companionship.'

'What a good idea,' she agreed earnestly. 'I am sure he will be very grateful for it. It is most sensitive of you.' How could she persuade him, without arousing suspicion, to question Beau Astley a little? 'He may very well be longing to unburden himself to someone, a good friend he can trust,' she said, watching George's face. 'After all, a great many disturbing and unhappy thoughts must have troubled him as to what can possibly have happened. And he cannot be unaware of other people's speculations. I am sure if I were in his situation I should long for someone to confide in!'

If it occurred to him that she had any ulterior motive, he did not show it in his face. At least, she did not think his flicker of a smile was for that reason...Was it?

'Indeed,' he answered soberly. 'Sometimes it is a great relief to talk—in confidence!'

Was George perhaps more astute than she had supposed? And enamoured of the idea of a little detective work of his own? Surely not! Watching his elegant back as he went out the door, she felt a sharp tingle of pleasant surprise.

Three days later Emily had contrived to take Charlotte with herself and George to a small private ball, where she had ascertained in advance that the Balantynes were to be present, as well as Alan Ross and Christina. What excuse Charlotte offered to Pitt was her own affair.

Emily was not sure quite what knowledge she hoped to acquire, but she was not innocent of the general habits of the gentlemen of Society. She had learned to accept the extraordinary feat of mental and ethical agility that enabled a man to indulge his physical appetites in the expensive brothels near the Haymarket all night, and then to come home and preside over his family at a silent and obedient breakfast table, where his wish was enough to produce a flurry of eagerness and his word held the force of law. She had chosen to live in Society and enjoy its privileges. Therefore, though she did not admire its hypocrisy, she did not rebel against it.

Emily had no liking at all for Christina Ross, but she could very well believe that Christina had sympathy for the few women who dared to break from social confines and play men at their own game, even to the point of risking everything for a wild masquerade at a house such as Max's in the Devil's Acre. Emily thought it was excessively foolish! Only a woman with no brains at all would wager so much for such a tawdry return—and she despised such idiocy.

But she was aware that boredom occasionally drove out all intelligence, even the sense of self-preservation. She had seen overwrought women imagine themselves in love and rush headlong, like lemmings, to their own destruction. Usually they were young, a first passion. But perhaps it was only the outside that changed with age: habits learned, a little camouflage for vulnerabilty. The desperation inside might be the same at any time. So by chance among Christina Ross's acquaintances tonight might there not be at least one of Max's women?

She wished Charlotte to come also for her added ability to observe. Charlotte was very naïve on certain points, but on others she was surprisingly acute. Added to which, Christina disliked her, seemed in some way to be almost jealous. And in the heat of strong emotion people were inclined to betray themselves. Charlotte could be extremely handsome when she was enjoying herself, giving someone all her attention—as she did, for some quite unaccountable reason, to General Balantyne. If anything might cause Christina to lose her self-mastery, her judgment, it would be Charlotte flirting with the general—and even perhaps with Alan Ross.

Accordingly, Emily, George, and Charlotte arrived at Lord and Lady Easterby's ball for their eldest daughter. They were just late enough still to be civil and yet also to cause a pleasing stir of appreciation among the guests already thronging the hall.

Emily was dressed in her favourite delicate water green, which flattered her fair skin; the gentle curls of her hair caught the light like an aureole. She looked like the spirit of an elusive early English summer, when the blossom is still clean and the air dappled with cool and shifting light.

She had taken great care over Charlotte. She had considered deeply what would attract the general most, and would therefore irritate Christina. Thus Charlotte swept into the ballroom in a swirl of vibrant and luminous gentian blue that was delicate on her throat and made her hair gleam with the shadowed lustre of old copper. She was like a tropical night when the gold of the sun has gone but the warmth of the earth still lingers. If she had even the faintest idea what Emily's intentions were, she showed no sign of it whatever. Which was as well, because Emily doubted Charlotte's conscience would have allowed her to go along with such a plan—however much she liked the idea—had she perceived it. And she was useless at flirting if she tried! But it was a long time since Charlotte had had the chance to dress exquisitely, to be extravagant, to dance all night. She was not even aware of her own hunger for the excitement of it.

They were received with a flutter of attention. George's title and the fact that Charlotte was a new face, and therefore mysterious, would have been sufficient, whatever their appearance. That the sisters looked ravishing was cause for a deluge of speculation and rumour enough to keep conversations alive for a month.

So much the better; it would add to the heat of the evening—Christina would not take well to being outshone. Emily wondered for a prickling moment if perhaps she had miscalculated and the results would be less informative and more purely unpleasant than she had intended; then she dismissed the idea. It was too late to alter things now anyhow.

She sailed forward with a radiant smile to greet Lady Augusta Balantyne, who was standing stiff and very regal, composing her face into an answering social charm.

'Good evening, Lady Ashworth,' Augusta said coolly. 'Lord Ashworth. How pleasant to see you again. Good evening, Miss Ellison.'

Emily was suddenly aware of being ashamed. She looked at Augusta, her shoulders tight, the fine tendons in her neck standing out under her ruby necklace, the weight of stones cold and heavy in their blood colour. Was Augusta really so afraid of Charlotte? Was it possible that she loved her husband? That this softness about his mouth as he greeted Charlotte, the slightly straighter shoulders, was deeper than a flirtation with an agreeable woman? Something that touched the emotions that endure, that hurt and disturb, and leave a loneliness behind that is never filled by any other affection—and Augusta knew it?

The ballroom glittered and people laughed around them, but for a moment Emily was unaware of it. Chandeliers full of tinkling facets filled the ceilings; violin strings scraped briefly, then found the full, rich tone; footmen moved with elegance while balancing glasses of champagne and fruit punch.

All she had intended was to scratch the veneer of Christina's temper, and perhaps to learn in a moment of carelessness a little of what she knew about the society women who might have frequented Max's brothel. The last thing Emily wanted was to cause a real and permanent injury. Please heaven Charlotte knew what she was doing!

Her thoughts were interrupted by the necessities of polite conversation. She attended with only half her mind, making some silly observations about who might or might not win a horse race in the summer—she was not even sure if it was the Derby or the Oaks. Certainly the Prince of Wales' name was mentioned.

It was some thirty minutes or so before the subject exhausted itself, and Alan Ross asked Emily if she would honour him with the next dance. It was an odd exercise, to be so close to a person, sharing a movement, at times touching each other, and yet hardly speaking at all; they came together and swirled apart so briefly that any exchange of meaning was impossible.

She watched his face. He was not as handsome as George, but there was a sensitivity about him that became more and more attractive as she knew him better. The events in Callander Square flashed back into her memory and she wondered how deeply he had been hurt. It had been no secret that he had loved Helena Doran. Was that wound still raw? Was that the pain inside him that honed fine his cheeks and the lines of his mouth?

That could be a very good reason for

247

Christina's sharpness, for her apparent need to hurt Charlotte. Charlotte would remember about Helena, and was now overstepping the lines of accepted flirtation with the general by making a friend of him. It was understandable, if a little crude, to entertain a relationship simply on the fullness of a bosom or the curve of a hip. But to engage the mind, the compassion, and the imagination was beyond the rules.

What rules did Christina observe? What did she even know?

Emily glanced around the room as she turned in Alan Ross's arms and, over his shoulder, saw Christina clinging close to a cavalry officer in resplendent uniform. She was laughing up into his eyes and she looked brilliantly alive. The officer was obviously enthralled.

Emily looked back at Alan Ross. He must have seen it; he had faced that way only the moment before, but there was no change in his expression. Either he was so used to it that he had learned to mask his emotions, or else he no longer cared.

The thought after that was obvious, and yet it was so unpleasant that for an instant Emily lost her footing and was clumsy. At another time she would have been mortified, but consumed as she was by the new thought, the triviality of mere physical gaucheness seemed quite banal.

Was Christina herself one of Max's women? Alan Ross was neither old nor in the slightest way boring. But perhaps his very charm, the unattainability of the inner man, was a far sharper goad to other conquests, no matter how shallow, than any boredom could be?

Suddenly Emily's animosity toward Christina turned to pity. She still could not like her, but she was forced to care. She was dancing close to Alan Ross; she could feel the cloth of his coat under her glove, and she was moving in perfect time with his body. Although they were barely touching, there was a union. Did he know about Christina, or guess? Was it his outraged vanity, suppressed for so long, that had finally murdered and mutilated Max?

It was ridiculous! Here she was, dressed in pale green silk, dancing to violins under all these lights, in and out of the arms of a man she spoke to as a friend, and her mind was following him down filthy alleys to a confrontation with a footman turned whoremonger, to commit a murder of hatred and obscene revenge for the degradation of his wife.

How could two such disparate worlds exist so closely side-by-side—or even within each other? How far away was the Devil's Acre—three miles, five miles? How far away was it in thought?

How many of these men here, with their spotless white shirts and precise manners, went on the nights it suited them to drink and fumble and copulate in the beds of some laughing whore in a house like Max's?

The dance came to an end. She spoke some formal words to Alan Ross, and wondered if he had had even the faintest idea what she was thinking. Or if his own mind had been as far from her as hers was from this twinkling ballroom.

Lady Augusta was talking to a young man with blond whiskers. Charlotte had been dancing with Brandy Balantyne, but now the general stepped forward and offered her his arm, not to dance but to accompany him away somewhere in the direction of the enormous conservatory. His broad shoulders were very straight, but his head was bent toward her, full of attention, and he was talking. Damn Charlotte! Sometimes she was so intensely stupid Emily could have slapped her! Could she not see the man was falling in love? He was fifty, lonely, intelligent, emotionally inarticulate—and idiotically, desperately vulnerable.

But Emily could hardly stride after Charlotte now and pry her loose and kick some sense into her. And, worst of all, when she realized what she had done she would be filled with pain—because she really had not the faintest idea! She simply liked the man enormously, and was unsophisticated enough to show it in the way that was natural to her—the giving of friendship.

George was at Emily's side, saying something to her.

'I beg your pardon?' she said absently.

'Balantyne,' he repeated. 'Really quite odd, for a man of his breeding.'

Emily might have her own private opinions about Charlotte, and at the moment they were a good deal less than charitable. But she was not about to accept criticism of her from anyone else, even George.

'I cannot imagine what you are talking about,' she said stiffly. 'But if you choose to apologize, I shall accept.'

He was nonplussed. 'I thought you were interested in social reform?' he said with a little shake of his head. 'It was you who brought up the whole subject in the first place—and Charlotte, of course.'

Now she was confused. She stared back at him impatiently; he did not seem to be making any sense.

'What is the matter with you—do you feel faint?' he said at last. Then a flash of suspicion crossed his face. 'Emily! What are you doing?'

It was very seldom that George questioned her affairs, but she had always contrived to provide herself with satisfactory answers beforehand. And if they were less than the truth, she was usually positive beyond any doubt that he would never discover it. This was too short notice to invent a successful lie. Evasion was all that was left.

'I'm sorry,' she said demurely. 'I was watching Charlotte and General Balantyne. I fear she is not aware of quite what she is doing. I thought you were speaking of that. Now, of course, I realize you were not.'

'I thought that was what you intended,' he said sincerely. 'You gave her the dress. You might have foreseen she would look well in it.'

It was too close to the truth for comfort, and Emily felt guilt sweep over her again. She had planned it, even if it had now gone beyond her control.

'I did not intend her to flirt like a fool!' she snapped at him.

'I think she does it rather well.' He sounded surprised himself. He had known Charlotte since the days before she married Pitt. She had been her mother's despair then, because she simply would not conduct herself with the required charm and the mixture of frankness and deceit, excitement and humour that make for a successful flirtation. But time and confidence had effected a considerable change in her. And she was not flirting in the usual sense; the invitation she extended tacitly to Balantyne was not for a little game of dalliance, but for a very real friendship, where pain and pleasure last, and something of the inner self is given away.

Emily had a sudden feeling that she was going to need George. 'What were you saying about social reform?' she inquired.

Maybe he sensed her unhappiness, or possibly he was only exercising good manners. 'Brandy Balantyne was talking about social reform,' he answered agreeably. 'These disgusting events in the Devil's Acre seem to have affected him quite surprisingly. I think he really intends to do something about it!'

She spoke spontaneously. 'George, what kind of men go to the Devil's Acre, to houses like Max's?'

'Really, Emily...I hardly think...' To her astonishment, he looked awkward, as though in spite of his more rational self, he still found the subject embarrassing in front of her.

She gave him a wide stare. 'Do you go, George?'

'No, I do not!' He was genuinely shocked. 'If I were going to do anything of that sort, I should at least go to the Haymarket, or the—Well, I certainly would not go to the Devil's Acre.'

'And what would you think of me, if I did?' she asked.

'Don't be absurd.' He did not even consider it seriously.

'There must be women there,' she pointed out, 'or there would be no brothels.' She momentarily forgot to use the euphemism for such establishments.

'Of course there are women there,

Emily,' he said with exaggerated patience. 'But they are of a different sort. They are not—well—they are not women that one would—would do anything but...'

'Fornicate with,' she finished incisively. Another euphemism was abandoned.

'Quite.' He was a little pink in the face, but she preferred to think it was due to a general discomfort for his own sex at large, rather than any personal guilt. She was perfectly aware that his conduct had not always been exemplary, but she was wise enough not to inquire into it. Such curiosity would bring nothing but unhappiness. To the best of her belief, he had been loyal since their marriage, and that was all she could reasonably ask.

She smiled at him with quite honest warmth. 'But Bertram Astley did.'

The shadow returned to his eyes and he looked confused. 'Odd,' he muttered. 'I don't think you should inquire into that, Emily. It's really very sordid. I don't mind your taking an interest in Charlotte's investigations when they are moderately respectable—if you absolutely must.' He was aware of the limitations of the authority he could exercise without unpleasantness, and he hated unpleasantness. 'But I think

255

you should not seek to know about certain aberrations. It will only distress you.'

Suddenly she was overwhelmingly fond of him. His concern was quite genuine; he knew the world she was beginning to examine, knew the frailties and the twisted hungers. He did not want her to be touched by it, and hurt.

She put her hand on his arm and moved a little closer. She had no intention whatsoever of doing as he suggested. She was far tougher than he supposed, but it was very pleasant indeed that he imagined her so tender, so untouched. It was an idiotic notion, but just for a little while, perhaps till the end of the evening when the laughter and the lights died down, she would pretend to be the innocent creature he thought she was.

Perhaps in the hard light of truth of Astley's and Max's death, and because of his fears for Alan Ross whom he liked, he, too, needed to pretend for a while.

Alan Ross did not enjoy the ball; the lights and the music gave him no pleasure. All he could see was Christina's laughing face staring up at one man after another as she danced closely and easily in their arms.

He turned and saw Augusta staring in the same direction. She was quite still. Her hand was resting on the balustrade of the staircase, and it was gripping so hard the fingers were crooked and clenched inside her lace gloves.

Ross's eyes travelled past the bracelets on her wrists, over her white shoulders to her face. He had never realized she was capable of such emotion. He did not understand what it was—desperation, fear, a tenderness that made her angry?

Beyond the dancers in their flower colours was the conservatory door where General Balantyne stood leaning forward a little, his face soft as he spoke to Charlotte Ellison. Ross's eyes were drawn to her because she was beautiful. She had not the flawless loveliness of the young girls, or the chiselled bones of classic beauty, but a sheer intensity of life. Even across the swirl of the room he could feel her emotions. And next to her, so close that his hand brushed her arm, Balantyne was oblivious of all the world.

Was that what Augusta saw that wounded her and caused the confusion he had seen?

He looked again. No—her head was

turned the other way now, and she could not possibly see the general. She was still looking at Christina, at the foot of the curved stairway leading to the gallery, her mulberry-coloured taffeta skirt billowing, gleaming where the light caught it, her cheeks flushed. The man beside her put his arm around her waist and whispered something so close to her ear she must have felt his breath on her skin.

Alan Ross decided that moment that the next evening Christina went out alone in the carriage, whomever she was going to visit, he would follow her and know for himself the truth. However painful, the truth must be better than the hideous thoughts that were crowding his imagination now.

His opportunity came almost before he was ready for it. It was the following day, shortly after dinner, Christina excused herself, saying she had developed a headache and would take a short drive to get a breath of fresh air. She had been in the house all day and felt the atmosphere too close. She might call upon Lavinia Hawkesley, who had been indisposed lately, and Ross was not to wait up for her.

He opened his mouth to protest; then, with cold fear inside him, he realized she had offered the perfect opportunity. 'Very well, if you think she is well enough to receive,' he agreed, with only the smallest shake in his voice.

'Oh, I'm sure,' she said cheerfully. 'She is probably bored stiff, poor soul, if she has been alone all day and confined to the house. I expect she will be delighted with an hour or two's company. Do not wait up for me.'

'No,' he said, turning away from her. 'No. Good night, Christina.'

'Good night.' She picked up the ruched skirt of her dinner dress and swept out. How different she was from the girl he had thought her! They were strangers, without humour and without trust.

Five minutes later, when he heard the front door close, he stood up and went to the cloakroom where his heavy coat was hanging and put it on. He added a muffler and a hat, then went out into the icy street after her. It was not difficult to follow the carriage; it could not go quickly on the rime-encrusted cobbles, and at a brisk walk he kept within twenty feet of it. No one paid him the least attention.

He had gone over a mile when he saw the carriage draw to a halt outside a large house. Christina got out of the carriage and went into the house. From the opposite pavement he could not distinguish the number, but he knew Lavinia Hawkesley lived in this area.

So Christina had come, precisely as she had said, for a simple call upon a woman friend. He was standing here shaking with cold for no reason at all. It was stupid—and pathetic! The carriage was moving away. It was turning and coming back, not round to the mews. Christina must have dismissed it. Was she proposing to remain here all night? Or simply to use the Hawkesley coach to come home?

Alan Ross was left to wait like a loiterer on the corner and decide whether to go home himself, soak the chill out of his bones in hot water, and go to bed, or to remain here until Christina came out and to follow her again. But that would be ridiculous; the whole idea had been futile, an aberration of his normal sanity. Christina was frequently selfish, but she was innocent of anything worse than indiscretion—a spoiled and pretty woman's exercise of power, the hunger to be the centre of attention, always lavishly admired.

The door of the house opened, a stream of light fell on the path, and Christina and Lavinia Hawklesley came out. The door closed behind them and they set off down the street on foot.

Where in heaven's name were they going? Ross went after them. When they came to the main road and stopped a hansom cab, he hailed one as soon after as he was able, and ordered the cabbie to follow them.

The journey was farther than he expected. Again and again they turned corners until he lost sense of direction, except that he thought they were coming closer to the river and the heart of the city. The way was narrower, the lights farther between. A dim halo of mist reflected the glow and the damp air smelled stale. High above loomed a great shadow against the sky. His throat tightened and suddenly he found it hard to breathe.

The Acre—the Devil's Acre! Why in God's name was Christina coming here? His mind was whirling, thoughts like a dark snowstorm battering him and melting into each other. There was no bearable answer.

The cab ahead stopped and one of the women alighted. She was small, slight, head high and feet quick on the stones. Christina.

Ross opened his cab door, thrust a coin into the driver's hands, and stumbled out onto the dim pavement, trying to discern the outline of the house Christina had by now entered. It was high, standing straight, windows glimmering in the faint gaslight—a merchant's house?

The other cab with Lavinia Hawkesley in it had disappeared. Wherever she was going, it was still farther into the labyrinth of the Acre.

For the first time, he looked around at the rest of the street. He had been so absorbed in watching the women he had not thought of anything else, but now he saw a group of four or five men about thirty yards to the left, and on the far side another three lounging in an alley entrance. He turned. There were more to the right, watching him.

He could not stay here; he was dressed conspicuously, and his coat alone would be worth attacking for. He might fight off one man, even armed, but not half a dozen.

He started to walk toward the door

through which Christina had disappeared. After all, his purpose in following her had been to learn where she was going, and why. The door was closed; if he gained entrance and faced Christina, what could he say? Did he even want her to know he had committed this foolish act of following her here? What could he do about it anyway? Confine her to the house? Withdraw all marital affection from her? Or put her away as a—a what? What was it that she was doing here?

The wild flights of imagining were worse than knowing; he understood himself well enough not to think he could dismiss it and ever again have an unclouded moment. And perhaps he was unjust to her? Perhaps she was innocent of the things now in his mind.

There was a noise behind him in the street. A violent shiver of fear ran through him like a drench of cold water. Had the victims of the Devil's Acre murderer been strangers like himself—men unwanted here, and hacked to pieces for their intrusion? His hand lifted the knocker and crashed it down violently.

Seconds dragged by. There was the sound of shuffling feet in the street, and the trickle of water. Ross slammed the knocker again and again, then twisted his head to look behind him. Two of the men were closer and still moving toward him. He had nothing to fight them with but his hands; he had not even brought a stick.

Sweat broke out on his body. It crossed his mind to go out toward them, to start the fight himself so at least it would be quick. He would not think of the mutilation afterward.

Suddenly the door opened; he lost his balance and stumbled in.

'Yes, sir?'

Ross collected his wits and peered at the man holding a candle in the dark hallway. He was shabby; his belly protruded over his trousers, his slippers were loose-soled and fraying. He was a big man, and he stood between Ross and the stairs that led upward.

'Yes, sir?' he said again quietly.

Ross said the first thing that came into his head. 'I want to rent a room.'

The man looked him up and down with narrow eyes. 'All by yerself, are yer?'

'None of your business.' Ross gulped. 'Do you have rooms? I saw a young woman come in a few minutes ago, and she most assuredly does not live here!'

'None o' your business.' The man mimicked his tone with perfect contempt. 'People rahnd 'ere keeps their noses in their own muck'eaps and don't go lookin' frough nobody else's, mister. That way vey don't get nuffin cut orf, like! Nasty fings can 'appen to vem as can't keep veir eyes and veir marvs to veirselves.'

Ross felt the cold run through him. For a moment, half his brain had forgotten murder. He tried to sound calm, sure of himself. His throat was dry, his voice higher than usual.

'I don't care in the slightest what she came for,' he said, trying to put a sneer in his voice. 'Whom she meets is of no possible interest to me. I merely wish to come to a similar arrangement myself.'

'Well, vat'll be kind o' difficult, mister, seein' as she comes ter see the gent wot owns 'ole row o' ahses!' He gave a harsh laugh and spat on the floor. 'Nah as 'is bruvver's bin snuffed, like! Reckon as ve Acre's slasher done 'im a good turn!'

Ross froze.

'Wot's ve matter wiv yer? Scared? 'Fraid ve slasher's after you too, eh? Mebbe 'e is an' all!' He sniggered. 'Mebbe yer'd better scarper w'ile yer still got all yer parts—yer dirty little git!' His voice was filled with disgust, and Ross felt his face sting as the hot blood burned up inside him. This creature thought he had come sneaking here to satisfy some appetite that—

Ross straightened up, muscles tight, chin high. Then he remembered the men outside in the street. He crumpled again. He could not afford pride, and he most certainly dare not appear inquisitive.

'Have you rooms or have you not?' he asked quietly.

' 'Ave you money?' The man held out a dirty finger and thumb and rubbed them together.

'Of course I have! How much?'

' 'Ow long?'

'All night, of course! Do you think I want to be shuffled in and out with someone waiting on my heels and looking at his watch?'

'All by yerself?' The man's eyebrows rose. 'W'y don'tcher lock yer door an' do it at 'ome? Wotever it is as takes yer fancy—'

Ross dearly wanted to hit him. He resisted the temptation for a moment; then anger, fear, and the scalding wound

266

of Christina's betrayal exploded inside him. He struck the man hard with a closed fist, sending him hurtling back, head cracking against the wall. He slithered down into a heap on the floor and lay still.

Ross turned and pulled the door open and stepped out into the street. Whoever was there, he had to face them. He had made it impossible to stay here. This time he did not hesitate. His heart was racing, his fists already clenched ready to strike anyone who had the recklessness to molest him. He walked quickly, bumping into a beggar on the corner and knocking him sidewise. The man swore and Ross passed on oblivious. He knew the direction of Westminster, and he was making for well-lit streets and safety.

Footsteps echoed behind him and he increased his pace. It must be only a few hundred yards now. There were people huddled in doorways, both men and women. Someone giggled in the dark. There was a slap of flesh. A pile of refuse fell over with a scatter of rats. He ran.

It was late in the afternoon two days later when the maid came into his study and told Ross that a Mr Pitt was here and would like to speak with him.

Pitt? He knew no one called Pitt. 'Are you sure?'

'Yes, sir.' The maid looked doubtful. 'He is a very odd person, sir. Beggin' your pardon, but he was most insistent. Wouldn't give no reason, sir, but says as you know 'im.'

'He must be mistaken.'

' 'E won't go away, sir. Shall I get Donald to put 'im out, sir? I daresn't tell 'im meself. 'E's sort o'—well, 'is clothes is all any'ow, like they wasn't properly 'is to begin with, if you know what I mean. But 'e speaks like a gentleman, real proper—'

Suddenly, Ross remembered. 'Oh, God! Yes, send him in. I do know him.'

'Yes, sir.' She forgot her curtsy and scurried out, overwhelmed with relief.

A moment later, Pitt came in, smiling casually as if he had been invited. 'Good morning, Mr Ross. Nasty weather.'

'Horrible,' Ross agreed. 'What can I do for you, Mr Pitt?'

Pitt sat down as if the offer had been one of natural hospitality. He pulled himself a little closer to the fire. He must already have given the maid whatever outer clothing he had, because he now wore only dark trousers, a clean but rather voluminous shirt, and a jacket whose pockets appeared to be stuffed with objects of awkward sizes. The whole thing hung crooked and looked to be fastened on uneven buttons.

'Thank you.' He rubbed his hands and held them out to the flames. 'A lot of police work is very tedious.'

'I'm sure it must be.' Ross was really not interested. He was unable to be sorry for the man.

'Endless questioning of not very pleasant people,' Pitt went on. 'And of course we have certain acquaintances who keep us informed if anything unusual happens.'

'Quite. But I'm afraid I am not one of them. I know nothing that could be of use to you. I'm sorry.'

Pitt turned to look up at him. He had remarkable eyes; the light shone through them like a shaft of sun through seawater.

'I was referring to quite a different sort of person, Mr Ross. Like the old fellow that told me today of a gentleman looking for rooms in Drake Street, in the Devil's Acre, a couple of nights ago. Lot of gentlemen do, for reasons of their own. However this particular one, well dressed, well spoken, just like most, got very upset when his reasons were commented on. And that's most unusual. Most gentlemen using such places are only too glad to be as discreet as possible.'

He appeared to be waiting for an answer. Ross felt suddenly stiff, as if he had walked miles and slept ill. 'I suppose they are,' he said awkwardly. His memory flashed back to the dim hallway, the smell of dirt, the man's enraging, filthy leer. His throat tightened.

'Completely lost his temper,' Pitt went on with a lift of surprise in his voice. 'Hit him!'

Ross swallowed. 'Was he hurt?'

Pitt smiled, pulling the corners of his mouth down in a tiny grimace. 'Pretty good crack on his skull, broken collarbone. He's certainly very angry about it. Put the word about that if the fellow comes back to the Acre he's to be taught a lesson in a way he won't forget! That's how I heard about it—the word around.' Suddenly he looked directly at Ross and his eyes were full of brilliance. 'But you didn't kill him, if that's what you are afraid of.'

'Thank God—I—I—' He stopped, but it was too late. 'I didn't go there for—'

He could not bear anyone, even this policeman, to think he had intended to hire some whore and take her there.

Pitt's face was quite smooth, even friendly. 'No, Mr Ross, I didn't think for a moment that you did,' he said. 'What did you go there for?'

Oh, God! This was even worse. He could not possibly tell him about Christina. His heart pounded at the memory and the room seemed red-edged, whirling far away.

'I cannot say—it is a private matter.' Pitt would have to think whatever he wished. The truth was worse than any imagining.

'Very dangerous, sir.' Pitt's voice was getting gentler and gentler, as if he were speaking to someone in great trouble. 'Three men have been murdered in the Devil's Acre. But I'm sure you knew that.'

'Of course I knew that!' Ross shouted.

Pitt took a deep breath and let it out in a sigh. 'Not a place to go sightseeing, Mr Ross. It's ugly and it's dangerous, and people have paid very highly for their pleasures there lately. What particular curiosity was it that took you to that house?'

271

Ross hesitated. The man was like a ferret, tracking him in all the tunnels of his misery to corner him into some damning truth. Better give him one and send him away with it. That would at least guard the others, the ones he could not bear to tell.

'I had an idea whom it belonged to,' he lied, looking Pitt squarely in his bright eyes. 'I wanted to know if it was true. I hated to think any acquaintance of mine should make his living on the ownership of such places.'

'And was it true?' Pitt inquired.

Ross swallowed. 'Yes, I'm afraid it was.'

'Who would that be, Mr Ross?'

'Bertram Astley.'

'Indeed,' Pitt's face relaxed. 'Was it indeed? So that is where the Astley money comes from. And now of course Sir Beau has it.'

'Yes.' Ross let his breath go. He felt better. Pitt would never know about Christina, that she had gone there to meet Beau Astley in that filthy place. His wife—lying there in— He forced it from his mind, drove it out. Any other pain was better than this. 'Yes, it was,' he repeated. 'Perhaps that will help you in your investigations. I'm sorry, perhaps I should have told you before.'

Pitt stood up. 'Yes, sir, I think perhaps you should. But now that I do know'—his face split in a sudden charming smile—'I'm damned if I can see where it gets me!'

Ross said nothing. There was no emotion left inside him to draw on; he simply watched Pitt walk to the door and out into the hallway to take his coat from the maid.

CHAPTER 8

Pitt stumbled downstairs in the dark and opened the door. Outside on the step, gleaming wet in the lamplight and the rain, a constable stood, water running off his cloak in streams and splashing on the stones. The night was still black, before even the grey smudge of false dawn.

Pitt blinked fuzzily and shuddered with cold as the air hit his body. 'For God's sake come in!' he said irritably. 'What is it now?'

The constable stepped inside gingerly, scattering water over the floor, but Pitt was too cold to care. Gracie was not up yet and all the fires were out. 'Shut that door behind you, man, and come into the kitchen.' He led the way in enormous strides. The linoleum was like ice under his bare feet. At least the kitchen floor was wooden and kept the warmth of something that had once been alive. And the stove would be alight; it always was. With a little riddling and stoking he might even get the kettle to boil. The idea of a cup of steaming tea was the nearest he could get to decent sense. Going back to bed and the refuge of sleep was obviously impossible.

'Well, what is it?' he demanded again, pushing and pulling at the fire furiously. 'And take that thing off'—he gestured at the man's cloak—'before you drown us all.'

The constable obediently divested himself of the cloak and set it down in the scullery. He was a domestic man, and normally would have known what to do without being told. But the news he had brought had swept away his years of training by mother and wife.

'It's another one, sir,' he said quietly,

coming back into the kitchen and handing Pitt the kettle he was reaching for. 'And it's worse than before.'

Pitt knew why he had come, but it would still be ugly to hear. Before the words were spoken, there was always the hope it might be something else.

The pressure was mounting: Athelstan had called for him again—the newspapers were spreading the panic. And he knew that Charlotte, for all her pretended innocence, was using Emily's social position to pursue her own suspicions about Max's women and Bertie Astley's life. If he accused Charlotte of lying, they would have the sort of argument that would wound them both. Besides, he could not prove he was right; he simply knew her well enough to understand her sense of purpose. And, by God, he was going to get the Devil's Acre slasher before she did!

He was still standing in the middle of the kitchen floor with the kettle in his hand. 'Worse?' he said.

'Yes, sir.' The constable's voice dropped. 'I bin round the Acre ever since I joined the force, but I never seen anythin' like this before.'

Pitt poured the water into the pot. The

275

steam rose fragrantly into the air. He took half a loaf of bread out of the big wooden bin. Whatever it was that waited for him, however appalling, would be worse on an empty stomach in the icy morning.

'Who is it?'

The constable handed him the bread knife. 'A man. Things in his pockets says 'e's called Ernest Pomeroy. They found 'im on the steps of a charity 'ouse, Sisters o' Mercy, or something—not Popish—reg'lar church,' he explained hastily. 'Woman as found 'im'll never be the same again. In 'ysterics, she was, poor creature, white as paper and screamin' terrible.' He shook his head in bewilderment and accepted the china mug of tea Pitt handed him. Automatically he put both hands around it and let the heat tingle his numb flesh.

Pitt sliced bread and set it on top of the cooking surface to toast. He reached down two plates, the butter from the cool pantry, and marmalade. He tried to imagine the woman, dedicated to good work, sheltering the homeless and uplifting the fallen. She would be used to death; she could hardly fail to be, in the Devil's Acre. Indecency would be all around her, but she had probably never seen a naked man in her life—perhaps not even imagined one.

'Was he mutilated?' he asked unnecessarily.

'Yes, sir.' The constable's face blanched at the memory. 'Cut to pieces, 'e was, and sort of—well—like 'e'd bin ripped by some kind o' animal—with claws.' He took a deep breath, the muscles in his throat tight. 'Like someone 'ad tried to pull 'is privates off 'im with their 'ands.'

He was right—it was getting worse. Bertie Astley's injuries had been slight, almost a gesture. The thought returned to him that Bertie was not a victim of the same killer, but that Beau Astley had seen the chance to step into his brother's place and lay the blame on a lunatic already beyond the pale of ordinary human decency. It was a thought he tried to reject because he had liked Beau Astley, as one likes from a distance someone one does not know but feels to be pleasant.

The toast was smoking. He turned it over smartly and took a sip of his tea. 'Was he stabbed in the back, too?'

'Yes, sir, just about the same place as the others, one side of the backbone, and right about the middle. Must 'a died quick like, thank God.' He screwed up his face. 'Wot

277

kind o' man does that to another man, Mr Pitt? It ain't 'uman!'

'Someone who believes he has been wronged beyond bearing,' Pitt replied before he even thought.

'I reckon as you're right. An' you're burnin' your toast, sir.'

Pitt flipped the two pieces off and handed one to the constable. He took it with surprise and satisfaction. He had not expected breakfast—even of rather scorched toast, eaten standing up. It was good, the marmalade sharp and sweet.

'Maybe if someone killed my little girl, I'd want to kill 'im bad enough,' he said, with his mouth full. 'But I'd never want to—to tear out 'is—beggin' your pardon, sir—'is privates like that.'

'Might depend on how he killed your girl,' Pitt replied, then scowled and dropped his toast as the full horror of what he had said invaded his imagination. He thought of Charlotte and his daughter, Jemima, asleep upstairs.

The constable stared at him, his light brown eyes round. 'I reckon as 'ow you could be right at that, sir,' he said in no more than a whisper.

Upstairs everything was silent. Charlotte

had not stirred, and the nursery had only a single light burning.

'You'd better eat your breakfast, sir.' The constable was a practical man. This was going to be no day for an empty stomach. 'And put plenty o' clothes on, if you won't think me impertinent.'

'No,' Pitt agreed absently. 'No.' He picked up the toast and ate it. There was no time to shave, but he would finish his tea and take the constable's advice—lots of clothes.

The corpse was appalling. Pitt could not conceive of the rage that could drive a human being to dismember another in this way.

'All right,' he said, standing up slowly. There was nothing more to be seen. It was like those before, but worse. Ernest Pomeroy had been an ordinary-looking man, perhaps less than average height. His clothes were sober, of good fabric, but far from fashionable. His face was bony and rather plain. It was impossible to tell if life had fired him with any charm or humour, if those unbecoming features had been transformed by an inner light.

'Do we know where he comes from?' he asked.

'Yes, sir,' the sergeant on duty answered quickly. 'Got a few letters and the like on 'im. Seabrook Walk. Quite a decent sort o' place, 'bout a couple o' miles from 'ere. I got a sister as obliges for a lady up that way. Not a lot o' money, but very respectable, if you know what I mean.'

Pitt knew exactly what he meant. There was a large class of people who would prefer to eat bread and gravy, and sit in a cold house, rather than be seen to lack for the world's goods, especially for servants. To eat frugally could, by stretching the imagination, be a matter of taste. One might even pretend not to feel the cold, but to be without servants could only mean the depth of poverty. Had Ernest Pomeroy escaped a sad sham of life for a few hectic hours of indulging his starved nature, only to die here in these filthy and equally deceiving streets?

'Yes, I know what you mean,' he replied. 'We'll have to get someone to identify him. Better not the wife—if we can find someone else. Maybe there's a brother, or—' He looked down at the face again. Ernest Pomeroy was probably nearer fifty than forty. 'Or a son.'

'We'll see to it, sir,' the sergeant said. 'Wouldn't want to do that to any woman, even though as she'd only 'ave to see 'is face. Still—all the same. You goin' to see the wife, sir?'

'Yes.' It was inevitable. It must be done, and again it must be Pitt. 'Yes...give me that address, will you?'

Seabrook Walk looked flat and grey in the thin light of morning. Somehow the rain did not make it clean, merely wet.

Pitt found the number he was looking for and walked up to the door. As always, there was no point in hesitating: there was nothing that would make it hurt less, and there might be something to learn. Somewhere there must be something that linked these men: a common acquaintance, an appetite, a place or a time, some reason they had been hated so passionately. Whatever the cost, he must find it. Time would not wait for him. The murderer would not wait.

The narrow flower beds were empty now, just dark strips of earth. The grass in the middle had a lifeless, wintery look, and the laurel bushes under the windows

281

seemed sour, holding darkness and stale water. Immaculate lace curtains hung at all the windows, evenly spread. In an hour they would be obscured by the drawn blinds of mourning.

He raised the polished door knocker and let it fall with a jarring sound. It was several moments before a startled betweenmaid opened it a crack, her pasty face peering out. No one called this early.

'Yes, sir?'

'I have come to speak with Mrs Pomeroy. It is urgent.'

'Oooh, I don't know as she can see you now.' The tweeny was obviously confused. 'She ain't even'—she swallowed and remembered her loyalties to the house—'even 'ad 'er breakfast yet. Could you come back in an hour or two, sir?'

Pitt was sorry for the girl. She was probably not more than thirteen or fourteen, and this would be her first job. If she lost it through annoying her mistress, she would be in difficult straits. She might even end up wandering the streets, less fortunate than the women with the skill or the personality to end up in a bawdy house with someone like Victoria Dalton.

'I'm from the police.' Pitt took the responsibility from her. 'I have bad news for Mrs Pomeroy, and it would be most cruel to let her hear it by rumour, rather than to tell her discreetly ourselves.'

'Oooh!' The girl swung the door wide and let Pitt step inside. She stared at his dripping clothes; even in the face of crisis, her training was paramount. ' 'Ere, you're soakin' wet! Better take off them things and give 'em to me. I'll 'ave cook 'ang 'em up in the scullery. You wait in there, an' I'll go upstairs an' tell Mrs Pomeroy as you're 'ere, an' it's urgent.'

'Thank you.' Pitt took off his coat, hat, and muffler and handed them to her. She scurried out, almost hidden by the bulk of them. He stood obediently until Mrs Pomeroy should appear.

He looked around the room. It was quite a good size; the furniture was of heavy, dark wood without lustre in the thin light. There were embroidered antimacassars on the backs of the chairs, but no extra cushions on the seats. The pictures on the walls were views of Italy painted in hard blues—blue sea, blue sky—with harsh sunlight. He found them ugly and offensive; he had always imagined Italy to be a beautiful

283

place. There was an embroidered religious text over the mantelpiece: 'The price of a good woman is above rubies.' He wondered who had selected it.

On the chiffonier at the side there was a vase of artificial silk flowers, delicate things with gay, gossamer petals. It was a surprising touch of beauty in an unimaginative house.

Adela Pomeroy was at least fifteen years younger than her husband. She stood in the doorway in a lavender robe, trimmed with froths of lace at throat and wrists, and stared at Pitt. Her hair tumbled down her back; she had not bothered to dress it. Her face was fine-boned, her neck too slender. For another few years she would be lovely, before nervous tensions ate the lines deeper and marred the roundness of the flesh.

'Birdie said you are from the police.' She came in and closed the door.

'Yes, Mrs Pomeroy. I am sorry, but I have bad news for you.' He wished she would sit down, but she did not. 'A man was found this morning whom we believe to be your husband. He had letters identifying him, but we will have someone make certain, of course.'

She still stood without movement or

change of expression. Perhaps it was too soon. Shock was like that.

'I am sorry,' he repeated.

'He's dead?'

'Yes.'

Her eyes wandered around the room, looking at familiar things. 'He wasn't ill. Was it an accident?'

'No,' he said quietly. 'I am afraid it was murder.' She would have to know; there was no kindness in pretending.

'Oh.' There seemed to be no emotion in her. Slowly she walked over to the sofa and sat down. Automatically she pulled across her knees the silk of the robe, and Pitt thought momentarily how beautiful she was. Pomeroy must have been a wealthy man, and more generous than his face suggested. Perhaps it was not a meanness he had seen, but merely the emptiness of death. Maybe he had loved this woman very much, and saved hard to give her these luxuries—the flowers and the robe. Pitt felt what could be a quite unjust dislike well up inside him that he could see no agony or grief in her.

'How did it happen?' she asked.

'He was attacked in the street,' he replied. 'He was stabbed. It was probably over very quickly. I dare say there was only a moment of pain.'

Still there was nothing in her face, then a faint surprise. 'In the street? You mean he—he was robbed?'

What had she expected? Robbery was not such an uncommon crime, although it was not usually accompanied by such dreadful violence. Maybe he carried little of value. But then robbers were not to know that, until too late.

'He had no money on him,' he answered her. 'But his watch was still in his pocket, and a very good leather case for cards and letters.'

'He never carried much money.' She was still staring ahead of her, as if Pitt was a disembodied voice. 'A guinea or two.'

'When did you last see him, Mrs Pomeroy?' He would have to tell her the rest; where he was found, the mutilation. Better she hear it from him...

'Yesterday evening.' Her answer cut into his thoughts. 'He was going to deliver a book to one of his pupils. He was a teacher. But you probably know that—mathematics.'

'No, I didn't know. Did he tell you the

name of the pupil, and where he lived?'

'Morrison. I'm afraid I don't know where—not far away. I think he intended to walk. He would have a note of it in his books. He was very meticulous.' Still there was no emotion in her voice except the faint surprise, as if she could not comprehend that such a violent thing should have happened to so ordinary a man. She stood up and went to the window. She was very slight and fragile, like a bird. Even in this apparent state of numbness she had a grace that was individual, a way of holding her head high. Pitt found it hard to imagine her in the arms of the man whose face he had seen in the Devil's Acre. But then so often one cannot fathom the loves or hates of other people. Why should this be comprehensible? He knew nothing of either of them.

'Can you think of any reason he should go to the Devil's Acre, ma'am?' he asked. As usual, it was brutal, but she seemed so emotionless; perhaps this was the best time.

She did not turn, but stayed with her back to him. He was not sure whether it was his imagination that the delicate

287

shoulders stiffened under the lavender silk. 'I have no idea.'

'But you did know that he went there, from time to time?' he pressed.

She hesitated for a moment. 'No.'

There was no point in arguing with her. It was only an impression. He remained silent; perhaps in her speech she would give something away.

'Is that where he was found?' she asked.

'Yes.'

'Was it—the same—the same as the others?'

'Yes. I'm sorry.'

'Ah.'

She stood so long he could not tell if she kept her back to him to hide some overwhelming private feelings, if perhaps he should call a maid to help her, to bring her some restorative, or if she preferred the dignity of being left alone. Or was she simply waiting for him to speak again?

'Can I call your maid to bring something, ma'am?' He broke the silence from his own necessity.

'What?'

He repeated the offer.

At last she turned around; her face seemed perfectly composed. 'No, thank you. Is there anything else you wish to know from me?'

He was worried for her; this dry, calm shock was dangerous. He must have some responsible servant call her doctor. 'Yes, please. I would like the names and addresses of his pupils, and any close acquaintances you believe he may have seen in the last few weeks.'

'His study is on the other side of the hall. Take whatever you want. Now if you will excuse me, I would like to be alone.' Without waiting for his answer, she walked past him with a faint waft of perfume—something sweet and mildly flowery—and went out the door.

He spent the rest of the morning looking through the books and papers in Pomeroy's study, trying to form some picture of the man's life, his nature.

Pomeroy emerged as a meticulous, pedestrian man who had taught mathematics ever since he had graduated with academic qualifications. Most of his students seemed to have been aged about twelve or fourteen, and of quite average ability, except an occasional one of real promise. He tutored families privately, both boys and girls together.

It seemed a conscientious and blameless life, without any outward mark of humour. The flamboyant silk flowers in the withdrawing room could never have been his. In fact, the lavender silk gown with its foam of lace seemed far beyond his imagination—or his financial reach.

Pitt was offered luncheon by a cook who burst into tears every time he spoke to her. Then in the afternoon he copied out all the names and addresses of the current pupils, plus a few of those from the recent past, and those of acquaintances and tradesmen. He took his leave without seeing Adela Pomeroy again.

He went home earlier than usual. He was tired and beginning to feel the chill of the day spread through him. He had been woken to the news of another death, had gone to see the corpse lying grotesquely on the steps of a house of charity, then had had to bear the news of it to the widow whose shock he had been helpless to reach. He had spent the long hours of the day intruding into the details of the man's life, searching it and taking it apart, looking for the flaws that had led him to the Devil's Acre...and murder. He had accumulated a multitude of facts, and none of them told him anything that seemed to matter. He felt helpless, hemmed in on every side by grief and trivia.

If Charlotte made one cheerful or inquisitive remark, his temper would explode.

Pitt spent the next four days picking at ragged edges, trying to unravel enough to find one thread sufficiently strong to evoke something better than the random destruction of a madman.

He spoke to Pomeroy's students, who seemed to think well of their tutor despite the fact that he had spent his entire time instilling into their minds the principles of mathematics. They stood in front of Pitt, each in his own separate, overcrowded parlour. They were sober and scrubbed, and spoke respectfully of their elders, as became well-brought-up children. He thought he even detected beneath the ritual phrases a genuine affection, pleasant memories, perceptions of beauty in mathematical reason.

Occasionally, in spite of himself, ugly thoughts crossed Pitt's mind of intimacies between man and child, of cases he had known in the past. But he could discover no instance where any child, boy or girl, had been tutored alone.

Ernest Pomeroy emerged as an admirable man, even if there was too little humour or imagination to make him likeable. But then it is hard to catch the essence of a man when all you know is his dead face, and the memories of stunned and obedient children who had been grimly forewarned of the consequences of speaking ill of the deceased—and of the general disgrace of having anything to do with the police for any reason. The majesty of the law was better observed from afar. Respectable people did not become involved with the less savoury minions who served to enforce its rule.

Pitt also, of course, asked Mrs Pomeroy if he might look through the dead man's personal effects to see if there were any letters or records that might suggest enmity, threat, or any motive at all to harm him. She hesitated and stared at him out of eyes that still looked frozen in shock. It was an intrusion, and he felt no surprise that she should resent his request. But it seemed that she realized the necessity and that to refuse would be pointless. And of course if she had any guilt or complicity in the murder, she would have had more than enough time to destroy anything she wished before he had first come with the news.

'Yes,' she said at last. 'Yes, if you wish. I do not believe he had much correspondence. I recall very few letters. But if you feel it would be useful you may have them.'

'Thank you, ma'am.' She made him feel peculiarly awkward because her grief was so inaccessible. If she had wept, there was no sign of it in her face; her eyes were smooth, the lids pale and unswollen. And yet she did not move with the stilted, sleepwalking gait of those who are so profoundly shocked that emotion is still petrified inside them—before the shell cracks and the pain bursts free.

Had she loved Pomeroy? More probably it had been one of the many marriages arranged by parents and suitor. Pomeroy was considerably older; he might have been her father's choice rather than her own.

Yet even in this state of limbo between the news of death and the beginning of acceptance of life as it must become, Pitt could see that she was a woman of grace and delicacy. Her clothes were very feminine, her hair soft. Her bones were just a little too fine to appeal to him. But to many men she must have been beautiful. Surely Pomeroy was not the best she could have done for herself?

Had she loved him or was it perhaps a debt of honour? Did her parents know Pomeroy, and owe him something?

He searched through all of Pomeroy's rooms and read every letter and receipt. As Adela Pomeroy had said, his affairs were meticulously kept. From the accounts, the age and quality of the furnishings, the number of house servants, and the stock in the kitchen and pantry, it appeared they lived frugally. There was no sign of extravagance—except the vase of coloured silk flowers in the withdrawing room and Adela's gowns.

Had he bought them as gifts for her, an indulgent expression of his love? He could not imagine it of a man with the face he had seen in the Devil's Acre. But by then he had already been robbed of that quickening that inhabits the flesh, of the capability for passion and pain, moments of tenderness, dreams or illusions.

Even in life we mask our vulnerability. What right had Pitt, or anyone else, to know what this man had felt for his wife? What vain or hopeless ideas still haunted him?

Or was her indifference apparent now because there had long ago ceased to be any real emotion between them? Was his death merely the formal ending of a relationship that was merely a façade? They had been married fifteen years; that much she had told him. There were no children. Had there ever been?

Could that even have been the reason she chose this plain, older man—a kindness to a woman whose moral character had been blemished? Or perhaps who already knew she was barren? Had gratitude turned over the years to hatred?

Had she sought love elsewhere? Was that where the silk flowers and the gowns came from? It was an obvious question, and he would be obliged to search.

He asked her if she had ever heard of Bertram Astley, Max Burton, or Dr Pinchin. The names produced no answering flicker in her face. If she was a liar, she was superb. Neither did he find any mention of the other victims in Pomeroy's papers.

There was nothing to do but thank Mrs Pomeroy and leave with a peculiar feeling of unreality, as if all the time she was speaking she had barely been aware of him. He was an usher in the theatre, and she was watching the main drama somewhere else, out of his sight.

The next obvious thing was to try the Acre again, and the best source was Squeaker Harris. Pitt found him in his grubby attic, hunched over the table by the window—the cleanest thing in the place—so that the winter light could fall onto his paper. Too many careful, suspicious eyes would examine his work. It must meet the highest standards of perfection or he would not remain in his trade.

He glared at Pitt balefully. 'You ain't got no right bustin' inter a man's 'ouse!' he exclaimed as he covered the paper he was working on as inconspicuously as possible. 'I could 'ave yer—fer trespassin'. Vat's agin ve law, Mr Pitt. An' wot's more, it ain't right.'

'It's a social call,' Pitt replied, sitting on an upended box and balancing with some difficulty. 'I'm not interested in your business skills.'

'Ain't yer?' Squeaker was not convinced.

'Why don't you put them away?' Pitt suggested helpfully. 'In case dust falls on them. You don't want anything spoiled.'

Squeaker gave him a squinting glare. Such leniency was confusing. It was very contrary of policemen to be so inconsistent in their behaviour. How was anyone to know where he stood? However, he was glad of the chance to put the half-completed forgeries out of sight. He returned and sat down, considerably easier in his mind.

'Well?' he demanded. 'Wotcher want ven? Yer ain't come 'ere for nuffin'!'

'Of course not,' Pitt said. 'What's the word about these murders now? What are they saying, Squeaker?'

'The Acre slasher? Vere ain't no word. Nobody knows nuffin', and nobody ain't sayin' nuffin'.'

'Nonsense. You telling me there've been four murders and mutilations in the Acre, and nobody's got any ideas as to who did them, or why? Come on, Squeaker—I wasn't born yesterday!'

'Neever was I, Mr Pitt. And I don't want ter know nuffin' abaht it. I'm a lot more scared o' 'ooever done vose geezers like vat van I ever am o' you! You crushers is a nuisance, Gawd knows, bad fer ve 'ealf an' bad fer business, and some of yer is downright nasty at times. But yer ain't mad—least not ravin' mad like ve lunatic wot does vis! I can understand a decent murder along wiv ve next man! I ain't unreasonable. But I don't 'old wiv vis, an' I don't know nobody as does!'

Pitt leaned forward and nearly fell off the box. 'Then help me find him, Squeaker! Help me put him away!'

'Yer mean 'ang 'im.' Squeaker pulled a face. 'I dunno nuffin', an' I don't want ter! It's no use yer arskin' me, Mr Pitt. 'E ain't one o' us!'

'Then who are the strangers? Who's new in the Acre?' Pitt pressed.

Squeaker put on an elaborate air of grievance. 'Ow ve 'ell do I know? 'E's mad! Mebbe 'e only comes aht at nights. Mebbe 'e ain't even 'uman. I dunno anyone as knows anyfink abaht it! None o' ve pimps or blaggers or shofulmen I know 'as got any call ter do vat kind o'fing! An' yer know we screevers don't go in fer nastiness. I'm an artist, I am. Fer me ter get violent wiv me 'ands 'd ruin me touch.' He waved his fingers expressively, like a pianist. 'Dips don't neever,' he added as an afterthought.

Pitt conceded with a smile. Unwillingly

he believed Squeaker. Still he gave it a last try. 'What about Ambrose Mercutt? Max was taking his trade.'

'So 'e was,' Squeaker agreed. 'Better at it, see? An' Ambrose is a nasty little bastard w'en 'e's crossed as many o' 'is girls'd tell yer. But 'e ain't mad! If'n someone'd stuck a shiv inter Max and dropped 'im inter ve water, or even strangled 'is froat, I'd 'ave said Ambrose, quick as look atcher.' His lip curled. 'But you lot'd never 'ave fahnd 'im! Just gorn, va'ts all—Max'd just 'ave gorn, and you rozzers'd never 'ave known ve diff'rence. Nobody but a fool or a lunatic draws attention ter 'isself by cuttin' people abaht an leavin' 'em in gutters fer people ter fall over.' He raised his scruffy eyebrows. 'I arks yer, Mr Pitt—now 'oo'd leave a corpus in front of an 'ouse o' mercy, wiv all vem 'oly women in it—if'n 'e was right in 'is mind, like?'

'Did Ambrose employ children in his brothel, Squeaker?'

Squeaker screwed up his face. 'I don't old wiv vat. It ain't 'ealfy. A proper man wants a proper woman, not some scared little kid.'

'Does he, Squeaker?'

'Gawd! 'Ow do I know? You fink I got vat kind o' money?'

'Does he, Squeaker?' Pitt persisted, his voice harder.

'Yes! Yes 'e does! Greedy little git! Go an' 'ang 'im, Mr Pitt, an' welcome!' He spat on the floor in disgust.

'Thank you. I'm obliged.' Pitt stood up and the box collapsed.

Squeaker looked at the box and his face wrinkled up. 'Yer shouldn't 'ave sat on vat, Mr Pitt! Yer too 'eavy fer it—now look wot yer done! I oughta charge yer fer breakages, I ought!'

Pitt pulled out a sixpence and gave it to him. 'I wouldn't like to owe you, Squeaker.'

Squeaker hesitated, the coin halfway to his teeth. The thought of Pitt owing him was extremely attractive, even tempting. But sixpence now was better than a debt Pitt might let slip from his rather erratic mind.

'Vat's right, Mr Pitt,' he agreed. 'Shouldn't never owe nobody. Never knows as w'en vey might collect at an inconvenient moment.' He raised candid eyes. 'But if'n I 'ears 'oo done the poor geezers—fer sure like—I'll send and tell yer.'

300

'Oh, yes?' Pitt said sceptically. 'You do that, Squeaker.'

Squeaker spat again. ' 'Ope ter die! Oh, Gawd—I didn't oughter said vat! Geez! May Gawd strike me if'n I don't!' he amended—with greater trust in his ability to obtain mercy from the Almighty than from the Acre slasher.

'He can have you after I've finished with you.' Pitt looked him up and down. 'If He can be bothered with what's left!'

'Nah, Mr Pitt, vat ain't nice. Yer abusin' me 'orspitality.' Squeaker was aggrieved, but happily so. It was a feeling he enjoyed. 'Ve trouble wiv you crushers is yer ain't got no happreciation.'

Pitt smiled and went out the door. He picked his way down the stairs carefully, avoiding the rotted ones, and went outside into the cold malodorous air of the alley. Tomorrow he would get a picture of Ernest Pomeroy and take it around the brothels in the Acre.

Charlotte was waiting for him when he arrived home. She was beautiful, her face radiant, hair soft and sweet to smell. She clung to him fiercely as if she were bursting with energy.

'Where have you been?' he asked, holding her hard.

'Only to see Emily.' She dismissed it as a trifle, but he knew perfectly well why she had gone.

She gave him a quick kiss and pulled away. 'You're cold. Sit down and warm yourself. Gracie will have dinner in half an hour. Your coat looks very dirty. Where have you been?'

'To the Devil's Acre,' he said tartly as he eased off his boots and wriggled his toes. He leaned back in his chair and stretched his feet out toward the fire.

Charlotte passed him his slippers. 'Did you learn anything?'

'No,' he lied. After all, it was not definable.

Her face fell into lines of commiseration. 'Oh. I am sorry.' Then she brightened, as if an idea had just occurred to her. 'Perhaps it would be better to approach it from the other point of view.'

In spite of himself, he asked, 'What other point of view?' And then was angry with his gullibility.

But she did not hesitate. 'The point of view of Max's women,' she replied instantly. 'These murders were committed with a great deal of hatred.'

He smiled sourly. It was a ludicrous understatement, and, sitting here in her own safe home, what on earth could she know about it? He had seen the corpses!

'You should look for someone whose life has been ruined,' she went on. 'If Max had seduced some woman, and then her husband had found out, he might well hate enough to kill like that—not only Max but whoever had had anything to do with her disgrace.'

'And how would he find out?' he asked. If she was going to play policeman, let her answer all the difficult, ugly questions that Athelstan would have thrown at him. 'There is no connection whatsoever between Max and Hubert Pinchin. We can't find anyone who knew them both.'

'Maybe Pinchin was the doctor for Max's establishments,' she suggested.

'Good idea. But he wasn't. There's a disbarred old crow who does that—and very lucrative it is, too. He wouldn't share his practice with anyone.'

'Crow? Is that an underworld term for a doctor?' She did not wait for a reply. 'What if the husband came as a customer and found the whore was his own wife?

That way he would know who the procurer was as well!' It was an excellently rational solution, and she knew it. She glowed with triumph.

'And what about the woman?' he said scathingly. 'He just bundled her up and took her back home again? I'm sure he wanted her—after that!'

'I don't suppose so for a moment.' She sniffed and looked at him impatiently. 'But he couldn't divorce her, could he?'

'Why not? God knows, he would have cause!'

'Oh, Thomas, don't be ridiculous! No man is going to admit he found his wife in the Devil's Acre working as a whore! Even if the police weren't looking for someone with a motive for murder, it would ruin him forever! If there is anything worse than death for a man, it is to be laughed at and pitied at the same time.'

He could not argue. 'No,' he said irritably. 'He'll probably kill her, too, but quietly, when he's ready.'

Her face paled. 'Do you think so?'

'Damn it, Charlotte! How should I know? If he's capable of cutting up her pimp and her lovers, what would stop him leaving her in some more respectable gutter when he's ready? So you bear that in mind, and stop meddling in things you don't understand—where you can only do damage by stirring up a lot of suspicions. Remember—if you're right, he's got precious little left to lose!'

'I haven't been—'

'For heaven's sake, do you think I'm stupid? I don't know what you've been doing with Emily, but I most assuredly know why!'

She sat perfectly still, colour high in her cheeks. 'I haven't been anywhere near the Devil's Acre, and to the best of my knowledge I haven't spoken to anyone who has!' she said righteously.

He knew from the brilliance of her eyes that she was speaking the literal truth. Anyway, he did not think she would lie to him, not in so many words.

'Not for want of trying,' he said acidly.

'Well, you don't appear to have got very far either,' she retorted. 'I could give you the names of half a dozen women to try. How about Lavinia Hawkesley? She is married to a boring man at least thirty years older than she is. And Dorothea Blandish and Mrs Dinford and Lucy Abercorn, and what about the new widow Pomeroy? I hear she is very pretty, and she knows one or two people in the fast set.'

'Adela Pomeroy?' He was momentarily startled out of his anger.

'Yes,' she said with satisfaction, seeing his face. 'And there are others. I'll write them down for you.'

'Write them down, then forget the whole thing. Stay at home! This is murder, Charlotte, very ugly and violent murder. And if you go meddling in it you may very well end up dead in a gutter yourself. Do as you are told!'

She said nothing.

'Do you hear me?' He had not meant to, but he was raising his voice. 'If you and Emily go blundering about, God knows what lunatic you'll disturb—presuming you get anywhere near the truth! Far more likely it's a business vengeance in the Acre and nothing to do with society at all.'

'What about Bertie Astley?' she demanded.

'What about him? He owned a block of buildings in the Acre, a whole street. That's where the Astley money comes from, their own private slum.'

'Oh, no!'

'Oh, yes! Perhaps he had a brothel as well, and he was removed by a rival.'

'What are you going to do?'

'Go back and look again, of course! What else?'

'Thomas, please be careful!' She stopped, unsure what more to say.

He knew the dangers, but the alternatives were worse; another murder; public outrage reaching hysteria; Athelstan, afraid for his position, putting more and more pressure on Pitt to arrest someone, anyone, to satisfy Parliament, the church, the patrons of the Acre and other whorehouses all over London. And then terror, fury, and guilt when there was yet another atrocity.

But, perhaps foremost in his own mind, he felt the need to solve this case himself, to solve it before Charlotte, unwinding some thread from Emily's society connections, started to follow it from the other end and ran into something she could not handle. He had forbidden her to meddle not only because her life could be in great danger, but also because he must demonstrate that he did not need her help.

'Of course I shall be careful,' he said stiffly. 'I'm not a fool!'

She gave him a sidelong look and held her tongue.

'And you stay at home and keep out

of it!' he added. 'You've plenty to attend to here without interfering where you can only get into trouble.'

Nevertheless, when he went into the Acre the next day, he took even more care than usual to dress inconspicuously, and to walk with that mixture of sureness of where he was going and the furtive, beaten air of someone whose journey is futile and who knows it.

The day was cold, with gloomy skies and a hard wind blowing up from the river. There was every excuse to pull his hat down and wind his muffler over the bare skin of his face. The sparse gaslights of the Acre glimmered in the murky morning air like lost moons in a sunken, crooked world.

Pitt had a good likeness of Pomeroy, and he intended to find out everything he could about the brothels that catered to customers who liked children. Somewhere in this cesspit he expected to find Pomeroy's reason for being here, and he believed it had to do with a need the man could not or dared not satisfy in Seabrook Walk. Nothing else would have brought such a prim, almost obsessively meticulous

308

creature into this world.

He had begun the day in Parkins' office, gathering all the information the local police could give him about brothels that were known to employ children. He was even offered the names of snouts, and small personal secrets that might allow him to exert a little pressure to assure the truth.

But no one was prepared to say that he knew Pomeroy, or had ever catered to him.

By ten that night, Pitt was cold, bone-aching tired; he intended to try one more house before going home. There was no point in lying about who he was this time; Ambrose Mercutt's doorman knew him. It was his job to remember faces.

'Wotcher want?' he demanded angrily. 'Yer can't come 'ere nah, it's business hours!'

'I'm on business!' Pitt snapped. 'And I'm perfectly happy to come and go quietly, and not disturb your customers, if you'll treat me civilly and answer a few questions.'

The man considered for a moment. He was long and lean and he had half an ear missing. He was dressed in a modishly cut jacket, with a silk kerchief tied around his throat. 'Wot's it worth to yer?' he asked.

'Nothing,' Pitt said immediately. 'But I'll tell you what it's worth to you: continued employment and a nice pretty neck—no ugly rope burns! Can ruin a man's future, a hemp collar.'

The man snorted. 'I ain't murdered no one. Duffed up a few wot didn't know w'en they'd 'ad their money's worth.' He tittered, showing his long teeth. 'But they ain't makin' no complaints. Gentlemen as comes to these parts never do! And there ain't nothin' you can do, rozzer, as'll make 'em. Rather die than lay a complaint against a pimp, they would!' He struck a pose and his voice rose to a falsetto. 'Please Yer Honour, Mr Beak, there's this whore I used, an' I want to complain as she didn't give me value fer me money! I wants as yer should make 'er be more obligin', me lud!' He switched position and put his other hand on his hip, looking down his nose. 'Why, certainly, Lord Mud-in-Yer-Eye. You just tell me 'ow much yer paid this 'ere whore, and w'ere I can find 'er, and I'll see as she gives yer satisfaction!'

'Ever thought of going on the halls?' Pitt asked cheerfully. 'You'd have them in the aisles with that.'

310

The man hesitated; all sorts of glittering possibilities appeared in his mind. He was flattered in spite of himself. He had expected abuse, not appreciation, let alone such a golden idea.

Pitt pulled out the picture of Pomeroy.

'What's that?' the man asked.

'Know him?' Pitt passed it over. There had been no picture of him in the newspapers.

'What of it? What d'you care?'

'That's none of your business. Just believe me, I do care—so much so that I shall go on looking until I find someone who catered for his particular tastes. And if I keep on coming round here, that won't be good for business, now, will it?'

'All right, yer sod! So we know 'im. Wot then?'

'What did he come here for?'

The man looked incredulous. 'Wot did you say? You 'alf-witted or somethin'? Wot the 'ell d'yer think 'e come fer? 'E was bloody bent, the dirty little sod. 'E liked 'em real young—seven or eight, mebbe. But yer'll never prove it, an' I ain't said nothin'. Nah git aht of 'ere afore I spoil your nice pretty neck with a red ring round it—right from one ear to the other!'

Pitt believed him and he did not need proof. He had always known there would be none. 'Thank you.' He gave the man a curt nod. 'I don't think I shall need to trouble you again.'

'Yer better not!' the man called after him. 'Yer ain't liked around 'ere! Vest fer yer 'ealth ter try somewhere else!'

Pitt had every intention of leaving as rapidly as possible. He started to walk briskly, hands in his pockets against the cold, scarf pulled up around his ears. So Pomeroy was a pederast. That was no surprise; it was what he had expected. All he had been looking for was confirmation. Bertie Astley had owned a row of houses here in the Acre—sweatshops, tenements, a gin mill. Max's occupation had never been a secret. All that remained was to establish Pinchin's reason for being here. And then, of course, to find the common link, the place or the person that bound them together—the motive.

It was desperately cold. The wind with its acrid sewer smell made his eyes water. He lifted his head, squared his shoulders, and strode out more rapidly.

Perhaps that was why he did not hear them come up behind him in the shadowy light. He had solved the mystery of Pomeroy in his mind; he had completed his business and had forgotten he was still well inside the Acre. Walking like a happy man, a man with purpose, he was as conspicuous as a white rabbit on a new-turned field.

The first one struck him from behind. There was a stinging blow in the small of his back; his feet were suddenly entangled and the pavement hit him in the face. He rolled over, knees hunched, then straightened with all his strength. His feet met flesh that gave under his weight, falling away with a grunt. But there was another at his head. He lashed out with his fists and tried to regain his balance. A blow landed on his shoulder, bruising but harmless. He threw his weight behind his answering punch and was exhilarated to hear the crack of bone. Then there was a numbing punch in his side. It would have been his back had he not turned and kicked as hard as he could at precisely the moment he was struck.

There was nothing he could do now but run for it. A hundred yards, or two at the most, and he would be on the edge of the Acre and within hailing distance of a hansom, and safety. His side hurt; he must have a terrible bruise there, but a hot bath and a little embrocation would cure that. His feet were flying over the cobbles. He was not in the least ashamed to run; only a fool stayed against impossible odds.

He was short of breath. The pain in his side was sharper. It seemed a mile to the lighted street and traffic. The ghostly rings of the gas lamps were always ahead. They never drew level.

'Now then! W'ere you goin' in such an almighty 'urry then?' An arm came out and caught hold of him.

In a moment of panic, he tried to raise his hand and strike the man, but the arm was leaden. 'What?'

It was a constable—a constable on the beat.

'Oh, thank God!' he exclaimed. The man's face grew enormous and vacant, shining in the mist like the gas lamps.

' 'Ere, guv, you look rough, wot's the matter wive yer? Eh! 'Ere? You got blood all over yer side! I think as I'd better get yer to an 'orspital right quick! Don't want yer passin' out on me. 'Ere! 'Old up a bit longer. Cabbie! Cabbie!'

Through a haze of swinging lights and

314

numbing cold Pitt felt himself bundled into a hansom and jolted through the streets, then helped gingerly down and through a labyrinth of bright rooms. He was stripped of his clothes, examined, swabbed with something that stung abominably, stitched through flesh that was mercifully still anaesthetized by the original blow, bandaged and dressed, then given a fiery drink that scorched his throat and made his head muzzy. At last he was courteously accompanied home. It was midnight.

The following morning, he woke up so sore he could barely move, and it was a moment before he could remember why. Charlotte was standing over him, her hair pulled back untidily, her face pale.

'Thomas?' she said anxiously.

He groaned.

'You were stabbed,' she said. 'They told me it isn't very deep, but you've lost quite a lot of blood. Your jacket and shirt are ruined!'

He smiled in spite of himself. She was very pale indeed. 'That's terrible. Are you sure they're completely ruined?'

She sniffed furiously, but the tears ran down her face and she put her hands

315

up to cover them. 'I will not cry! It's your own stupid fault. You're a perfect idiot! You sit there as pompous as a churchwarden and tell me what I must and must not do, and then you go into the Acre all by yourself asking dangerous questions and get stabbed.' She took one of his big handkerchiefs from the dresser and blew her nose hard. 'I don't suppose for a moment you even saw the slasher after all that—did you!'

He hitched himself up a little, wincing at the pain in his side. Actually, he was not at all sure it was the Acre slasher who had attacked him. It could have been any group of cutpurses prepared for a fight.

'And I expect you're hungry,' she said, stuffing the handkerchief into her apron pocket. 'Well, the doctor said a day in bed and you'll be a lot better.'

'I'll get up—'

'You'll do as you're told!' she shouted. 'You'll not get out of that bed till I tell you you may! And don't you argue with me! Just don't you dare!'

It was three days before he was strong enough to return to the police station, tightly bandaged and fortified with a flask of rather expensive port wine. The wound was healing, and although it was still painful, he was able to move about. Meanwhile the threads of the Devil's Acre murders had drawn closer in his mind, and he felt compelled to return to the case.

'I've put other men on it,' Athelstan assured him, with a worried gesture. 'All I can spare.'

'And what have they come up with?' Pitt asked, for once permitted—even pleaded with—to sit in the big padded chair instead of standing. He enjoyed the sensation and leaned back, spreading his legs. It might never happen again.

'Nothing much,' Athelstan admitted. 'Still don't know what tied those four men together. Don't know why Pinchin went to the Acre, for that matter. Are you sure it's not a lunatic, Pitt?'

'No, I'm not sure, but I don't think so. A doctor could find a dozen occupations in the Acre if he wasn't particularly scrupulous.'

Athelstan winced with distaste. 'I presume so. But which of them did Pinchin practice, and for whom? Do you think he procured these well-bred women for Max that you insist he had?'

'Possibly. Although there weren't many society women among his patients.'

' "Well-bred" is relative, Pitt. Almost anything would appear to be a lady in the Acre.'

Pitt stood up reluctantly. 'Then I'd better go and ask a few more questions—'

'You're not going by yourself!' Athelstan said in alarm. 'I can't afford another murder in the Acre!'

Pitt stared at him. 'Thank you,' he said dryly. 'I shouldn't like to embarrass you.'

'Damn it—'

'I'll take a constable with me—two, if you like?'

Athelstan pulled himself to attention. 'It's an order, Pitt—an order, you understand?'

'Yes, sir, I'll go now...with two constables.'

Ambrose Mercutt was incensed with a mixture of outrage and very real fear that he would be blamed for Pitt's injury, which was now common talk in the Acre.

'It's your own fault!' Mercutt said peevishly. 'Go wandering around places you're not wanted, poking your nose into other people's private business—of course you get stabbed. Lucky you weren't garrotted! Downright stupid. If you pushed everyone around the way you did my people, I'm only surprised you weren't killed.'

Pitt did not argue. He knew his own mistake; it was not in having come into the Acre, but in having forgotten to keep up the appearance, to walk like a man who belonged here. He had allowed himself to become conspicuous. It was careless and, as Ambrose said, stupid.

'And sorry, too, no doubt,' Pitt said. 'Who looks after your women when they get sick?'

'What?'

Pitt repeated the question, but Ambrose was quick to understand. 'Not Pinchin, if that's what you think.'

'Maybe. But we'll speak to all your women, just in case. They may remember something you don't.'

Mercutt's face was white. 'All right! He may have looked after one or two of them from time to time. What of it? He was very useful. Some of the stupid bitches get with child sometimes. He took care of it, and took his pay in kind. So I'd be the last person to kill him, wouldn't I?'

'Not if he was blackmailing you.'

'Blackmailing me?' His voice rose to a

319

screech at the idiocy of the idea. 'Whatever for? Everyone knows what business I'm in. I don't pretend to be something I'm not. I could have blackmailed *him*—I could have ruined his nice respectable practice at Highgate—if I'd wanted to. But the arrangement suited me well enough. When he was killed, I had to find someone else.'

Pitt could not move him from that, no matter what other questions or pressures he put forth. Finally he and the constables left and went to another bawdy house, and another and another.

It was five o'clock when Pitt, tired and sore, came with the two constables to the house of the Dalton sisters. He had kept them until last on purpose; he was looking forward to the warmth, the agreeable atmosphere, and perhaps a cup of hot tea.

Both Mary and Victoria were present this time; he was received with the same domestic calm as before and invited to the sitting room. He accepted the offer of refreshment with rather more speed than grace.

Mary looked at him suspiciously, but Victoria was as civil as before. 'Ernest

Pomeroy did not come here,' she said candidly, pouring the tea and passing it to him. The constables were in the main entrance room, embarrassed and thoroughly enjoying themselves.

'No,' Pitt said, accepting the cup. 'I already know where he went. I was thinking of Dr Pinchin.'

Her eyebrows rose and her grey eyes were like smooth winter seas. 'I don't see all our customers, but I don't recall him. He was certainly not murdered here—or anywhere near here.'

'Did you know him? Professionally, perhaps?'

The ghost of a smile touched her mouth. 'His profession or mine, Mr Pitt?'

He smiled back. 'His, Miss Dalton.'

'No. I have good health, and when I do not, I know well enough what to do for myself.'

'How about your women—your girls?'

'No,' Mary said immediately. 'If anyone is sick, we look after them.'

Pitt turned to look at her. She was younger than Victoria. Her face lacked the power of will, the resolution in the eyes, but it had the same smooth, country look, the short nose and soft freckles. She opened her mouth and then closed it again. The meaning was obvious to Pitt; she did not want to admit to abortion.

'Of course we have doctors sometimes.' Victoria took charge again. 'But we have not used Pinchin. He has never had anything to do with this establishment.'

Pitt actually believed her, but he wanted to stay in the warmth a little longer, and he had not finished his tea. 'Can you give me any reason I should believe that?' he asked. 'The man was murdered. You would not wish to admit acquaintance with him.'

Victoria glanced at her sister, then at Pitt's cup. She reached for the pot and filled it without asking him. 'None at all,' she said with an expression Pitt could not fathom. 'Except that he was a butcher, and I don't want my girls cut about so they either bleed to death or are too mutilated ever to work again. Believe that!'

Pitt found himself apologizing. It was ridiculous. He was taking tea with a brothel-keeper and telling her he was sorry because some doctor had aborted whores so clumsily that they never recovered—and they were not even her whores!... Or was she a brilliant liar?

'I'll ask them myself.' He drank the rest

of his tea and stood up. 'Especially those who've come to you most recently.'

Mary stood up too, hands clenched in her skirt. 'You can't!'

'Don't be silly,' Victoria said briskly. 'Of course he can, if he wants to. We've never had Pinchin in this house, unless he's come as a customer. I'd be obliged to you, Mr Pitt, if you'd not be abusive to our girls. I won't permit it.' She fixed him with a firm eye, and Pitt was reminded of governesses he had met in great houses. She did not wait for his answer, but led him into the upper part of the house and began knocking on one door after another.

Pitt went through the routine of asking questions and showing Pinchin's picture to plump and giggling prostitutes. The rooms were warm and smelled of cheap perfume and body odours, but the colours were gay and the rooms cleaner than he had expected.

After the fourth one, Victoria was called away to attend to some domestic crisis, and he was left with Mary. He was speaking to the last girl, skinny, not more than fifteen or sixteen years old, and plainly frightened. She looked at Pinchin's face on the paper, and instantly Pitt knew she was lying when she said she had never seen him.

'Think hard,' Pitt warned. 'Be very careful. You can be put in prison for lying to the police.'

The girl went pasty white.

'That's enough!' Mary said sharply. 'She's only a housemaid—what would she want with the likes of him? Leave her alone. She just dusts and sweeps. She has nothing to do with that side of things.'

The girl started to move away. Pitt caught hold of her arm, not roughly, but hard enough to prevent her going. She began to cry, great shuddering sobs as if she were overtaken with some desperate, animal grief.

Instantly, in the bottom of his stomach, Pitt knew she must be one of Pinchin's 'butcheries,' one who had lived, but so damaged she would never be a normal woman. At her age, she should have been laughing, dreaming of romance, looking forward to marriage. He wanted to comfort her, and there was nothing he could say or do, nothing anyone could.

'Elsie!' It was Mary's voice, loud and

frightened. 'Elsie!' The little maid was still weeping, clinging now to Mary's arm.

From the end of the passage came the sound of a low singing snarl. Pitt swung around. There, under the gas lamp stood a squat, white, rat-faced bullterrier, with teeth bared and bow legs quivering. Behind him was the most enormous woman he had ever seen, her bare arms hanging loosely, her flat face like a suet pudding, with eyes shrouded in creases of fat.

'Never you mind, Miss Mary,' the woman said, in a soft, high voice like that of a little girl. 'I won't let 'im 'urt yer. Yer just leavin', ain't yer, mister?' She took a step forward, and the dog, bristling, lurched a step forward with her.

Pitt felt horror flood through him. Was he looking at the Devil's Acre slasher? Was it this woman mountain and her dog? His throat was dry; he swallowed on nothing.

'Throw him out, Elsie!' Mary shrieked. 'Throw him out! Throw him hard, go on! Put him in the gutter! Set Dutch on him!'

The great woman took another step forward. Her face was expressionless. She could have had her sleeves rolled up to do laundry or knead bread. Beside her, Dutch's snarl grew higher.

'Stop it!' Victoria's voice shouted from the head of the stairs where she had disappeared a short time before. 'That's not necessary, Elsie. Mr Pitt is not a customer—and he won't hurt anyone.' Her tone became sharper. 'Really, Mary, sometimes you are stupid!' She pulled a handkerchief out of her sleeve and handed it to the maid. 'Now pull yourself together, Millie, and get on with your work! Stop sniffling—there's nothing to cry about. Go on!' She watched as the girl ran away and the enormous woman and the dog turned and trundled obediently after her.

Mary looked sullen, but kept her peace.

'I'm sorry,' Victoria said to Pitt. 'We found Millie in a bad way. I didn't know who was responsible, but perhaps it was Pinchin. Poor little creature nearly bled to death. She got with child and her father threw her out. She worked herself into one of the houses, where someone aborted her. Then, when they threw her out because she was useless to them, we picked her up.'

There was nothing Pitt could say, the situation was beyond trite sympathy.

Victoria led the way back toward the front rooms. 'Mary shouldn't have called Elsie. She's only for customers who get difficult.' Her face was bleak. 'I hope you were not frightened, Mr Pitt.'

Pitt had been terrified; the sweat was still standing out on his body. 'Not at all,' he lied, glad she could not see his face. 'Thank you for your frankness, Miss Dalton. Now I know what Pinchin was doing in the Acre, and where his additional income came from—at least to furnish his cellar. You don't happen to know whom he practiced for, do you?'

'Millie was with Ambrose Mercutt, if that's what you want to know,' she said calmly. 'I cannot tell you anything more than that.'

'I don't think I need anything more.' Pitt came out into the main room, and both constables, scarlet-faced, sprang to their feet, tipping two laughing girls off their laps. Pitt turned to Victoria affecting not to notice. 'Thank you, Miss Dalton. Good night.'

Victoria was equally imperturbable. 'Good night, Mr Pitt.'

CHAPTER 9

General Balantyne could not put the
Devil's Acre murders out of his mind.
He had never heard of Dr Pinchin or
the last victim, Ernest Pomeroy, before
the newspapers made them synonymous
with terror and abomination in the dark.
But the face of Max Burton, with its
lidded eyes and curling lip, raised in him
disturbing memories of other murders,
hideous incidents from the past that he
had never fully understood.

And Bertie Astley belonged to Balantyne's
own class, something less than true
aristocracy, but far more than merely
gentry. Anyone might come by money,
and manners could be mimicked or
learned. Wit, fashion, and even beauty
were nothing; one enjoyed them, but
no one worth a thought was taken in
by them. But the Astleys had breeding;
generations of honourable reputation, of
service to church or state, had made
them part of a small world of privilege

that had once seemed golden—and safe. Occasionally some knave or fool stepped out of it—but no invader had beaten his way in.

How had Bertram Astley's body come to be found in a doorway to a male brothel? Balantyne, of course, was not naïve enough to exclude the possibility that Astley had gone there for the obvious purpose, or that he had been murdered by a chance lunatic. Neither could he dismiss the fear that it was not accident but design that had selected him. He mistrusted the comfortable belief in a random killer that chose two men, Max and Bertie, so dramatically dissimilar, yet both known to him.

He broached the subject to Augusta. She immediately assumed he wished to discuss the Devil's Acre itself, and some plan for reform of prostitution and its ills; her face closed over.

'Really, Brandon, for a man who has spent the best part of his adult years in the army, you are singularly ingenuous!' she said with some contempt. 'If you imagine you are going to alter the baser instincts of human nature by a little well-meaning legislation, then you belong in some nice village pulpit where you can dispense tea and platitudes to unmarried ladies of earnest disposition and do very little harm by it. Here in a sophisticated society, you are ridiculous!'

He was stung. It was not only cruel, but totally unjust. And it was not what he had meant. 'There are many words I have heard applied to the murder of Bertie Astley,' he said cuttingly. 'But you are the first to choose "sophisticated." It is an allusion whose appropriateness escapes me!'

A dull colour marked her cheeks. He had misunderstood her wilfully, and as painfully as she had mistaken him. 'I do not appreciate sarcasm, Brandon,' she answered. 'And you have not the wit to do it successfully. Bertie Astley was an unfortunate victim of whatever lunatic is perpetrating these outrages. What purpose took him to that area we will probably never know, and it is none of our business. Suffer him to be buried in peace, and his family to mourn him decently. It is indelicate in the extreme to remind anyone of the circumstances of his death. I imagine a gentleman would not do so.'

'Then it is time we had fewer gentlemen—

and a greater number of police, or whatever it is that it takes to get something done!' he retorted. 'I, for one, do not desire to see any more mutilated corpses turning up in London.'

She looked at him wearily. 'We have few enough gentlemen already. I would wish there were more, not less!' She turned and walked away, leaving him with the feeling that he had lost the argument in spite of the fact that he was in the right.

The following day, Christina had luncheon with her mother but declined to go calling. Balantyne found himself in the withdrawing room alone with his daughter. The fire was blazing halfway up the chimney, and the room was full of warm, flickering light. It seemed familiar, comfortably timeless, almost as if they could have slipped back into his youth and her childhood, when affection was taken for granted.

He sat back in his chair and stared at Christina as she stood by the round piecrust table. Her face was remarkably pretty: the small features, rounded lips, wide eyes, shining hair. Her figure, in its fashionable dress, still had the freshness of a girl's. She was a strange mixture of child and woman—perhaps that was her charm. Certainly she had had many admirers before she married Alan Ross. And, to judge from the social occasion at which he had seen her, she still had, even if they were now more discreet.

'Christina?'

She turned and looked at him. 'Yes, Papa?'

'You knew Sir Bertram Astley, didn't you.' He did not allow it to be a question, because he would not accept denial.

She faced him when she spoke, but bent her eyes to a china ornament on the table. The subject was trivial, not worth a conversation.

'Slightly,' she replied. 'One is bound to meet most of the people in Society at some time or another.' She did not ask why he had mentioned it.

'What sort of man was he?'

'Pleasant, as far as I could judge,' she answered with a slight smile. 'But quite ordinary.'

She was so confident that he could not disbelieve her. And yet he knew she moved in circles that were neither bland nor artless. She was far less innocent than he had been at her age—perhaps than he was even now?

'What about Beau Astley?'

She hesitated a moment. Was there a touch of colour on her skin, or was it only reflection of the firelight?

'Charming,' she said without expression in her voice. 'Very agreeable, although I admit I do not know him well. It is something of a hasty judgment. If you are expecting me to come up with any profundity, Papa, I am afraid I shall disappoint you. I had no idea Sir Bertram had perverted tastes. I fully thought he was after that silly Woolmer creature, and meant to marry her. And since she has no money at all, and no family to speak of, I can only imagine it was for the most physical of reasons.' She glanced over at him. 'I'm sorry if I shock you. Sometimes I find you incredibly stuffy!'

He was aware that she found him so, but it still hurt to hear it in such words. He did not wish to pursue the matter by defending himself and, at the same time, was conscious that he should. She had no business to speak to him with so little respect.

'Then either he did not go to the Devil's

Acre for the reason supposed—or else he was a man of very diverse tastes,' he said dryly.

She laughed outright. Her hands held the china ornament up in the air; she had beautiful fingers, small and slender. 'You know I quite expected you to be furious! Instead you turn out to have a sense of humour.'

'A sense of the absurd,' he corrected, which was a pleasant feeling. 'If Bertie Astley was as diligent in his pursuit of Miss Woolmer as you suggest, I find it hard to believe he was also satisfying quite different appetites in the Devil's Acre. Or had Miss Woolmer declined him?'

She gave a little snort. 'Far from it. She grasped onto him like a drowning woman. And her mother was even worse. If they can manage it, they'll catch poor Beau now! She's a great lump of a girl, like clotted cream.'

'And "poor Beau" is unwilling?'

Again she hesitated, her fingers tightening on the ornament. 'I really have no idea. As I said before, I do not know them except in the briefest way. It is really none of my concern.' She set the ornament down and smiled, turning from the table to come

334

toward the fire. The light shone on the satin of her dress, gleaming brilliantly for a moment, then falling into rich shadows again.

'Have you ever heard of any of the other victims?' As soon as he said it, he knew it was a ridiculous question, and wished he could withdraw it. 'Apart from Max, of course!' he added by way of making it at least logical within itself, even if it was stupid in the whole.

Perhaps some memory of Max's service in this house stirred in her. She swallowed. He felt guilty for having mentioned it.

'Hardly,' she said casually. 'Wasn't one a doctor and one a schoolteacher, or something? Not exactly my social circle, Papa. Isn't there a saying about necessity making strange bedfellows, or something of the sort?' She laughed a little harshly. 'Maybe they were all possessed of the same vice. Maybe they gambled in the Devil's Acre, and lost. I seem to have heard that Bertie Astley gambled. Not to pay one's debt is a social sin of monstrous proportions, you know. Didn't they teach you that in the officers' mess?'

'They blackballed welshers,' he said soberly, watching her. 'They didn't kill them and—' He hesitated to use a graphic word in front of her, embarrassed for himself, and then ashamed of his embarrassment. Why should he falter around in euphemisms like an old woman? Why should he speak of masculinity in a whisper? 'Castrate them,' he finished.

She did not seem to notice the word. The firelight on her face made her skin warm anyway; he could see no extra blush.

'We are not dealing with officers and gentlemen in the Devil's Acre, Papa,' she pointed out with some sarcasm. 'Blackballing them would hardly serve!'

Of course she was right. Whatever use would that threat be to a man? It would get the gambler not a penny of his debt repaid. The losers would simply go to another place in future—if not in the Acre, then in some slum back room elsewhere. And the man owed would not dare broadcast the fact or he would lose face everywhere, and from then on no one would pay him.

'Actually,' she continued, turning to look at him, 'I would have thought that this method would be most effective. I'm amazed it has needed four men dead to have made the point.'

'It is more than amazing.' He spoke slowly, turning it over in his mind and finding himself inexplicably cold. 'In fact, it is incredible.'

She was not looking at him. The light on her dress accented the slender curve of her body as she turned away. She did not look very different from when she had been seventeen, yet he felt as if she were unreachable. Had she always been so, and only his complacency had allowed him to imagine he knew her because she was his daughter?

'One does not hate someone so passionately over a gambling debt.' He went back to the subject because he had not yet exorcised it.

'Perhaps they are mad?' She shrugged. 'Who knows what it was? Really, it is a most unpleasant affair, Papa. Must we discuss it?'

An apology was on his tongue, and then he changed his mind. 'Do you find you can dismiss it?' he asked instead. 'I cannot.'

'Apparently.' She had an excellent shadow of Augusta's cold scorn. 'Yes, I can. I do not find the goings-on of the denizens of the slums as fascinating as you do. I greatly prefer the society in

337

which I was brought up.'

'I thought you found it tedious.' He was surprised how sharp his own tongue had become. 'I have frequently heard you say so.'

She lifted her chin a little and moved away. 'Do you suggest I should look in the Devil's Acre for a little variety then, Papa?' Her voice was brittle. 'I don't think Alan would care for that! And Mama would be appalled.' She walked over to the bell and pulled it. 'I am afraid that, like most other women, I shall just have to put up with a certain tedium and a great deal of trivia in daily life. But I find your moralizing insufferably pompous. You have not the faintest idea what caused these murders, and I can't think why you want to go on talking about them, unless it is to make yourself feel superior. I don't care to discuss it anymore. As Mama says, it is unbelievably sordid.'

The bell was answered by the footman.

'Please call my carriage, Stride,' she said coolly. 'I am ready to return home.'

Balantyne was filled with a mixture of relief and a sense of loss as he watched her go. Was it the difference between men and women, or one generation and another that set the gulf between their understanding? It seemed these days there were fewer and fewer people he could talk to with ease, and feel that they were discussing something significant, not merely exchanging conventional words that one neither believed in nor cared about.

Why had he wanted to talk about the murders with Christina? Or with anybody? There were a thousand other things to discuss, all pleasant or interesting—even amusing. Why the Devil's Acre?... Because in remembering some of the things Brandy had spoken of, the poverty and the pain, he could understand the hatred that might drive someone to kill a creature like Max—even if the savage mutilation was beyond his understanding. He would have executed the man, simply, with a shot through the brain. But perhaps, after all, if it were his wife or his daughter Max had used in his whorehouse, he might have felt the need not only to kill but to destroy the offender's manhood, the means of his power and the symbol of his abuse. There was a kind of justice in it.

He could not put it from his mind. And there was no one with whom he could discuss it without arousing anger or being accused of fatuity and empty moralizing. Was that how his family, the women he loved, saw him? An insensitive man, pompous, obsessed with a series of sordid killings in an area that he knew nothing about?

Surely Charlotte did not see him like that. She had seemed so interested. Could it have been only kindness? He remembered the letters from Wellington's soldier in Spain, she had affected to find them so exciting. Could that light in her face have been just a politeness? The thought was abhorrent.

He stood up and walked smartly out of the room and across the hallway to the library. He pulled out paper and wrote a letter to Emily Ashworth. She was Charlotte's sister; she would pass on the message tactfully that the soldier's letters were available if Charlotte cared to read them for herself. He sent it off with the footman before he had time to reconsider whether he was being foolish.

The following afternoon, at the earliest hour acceptable for calling, the parlourmaid came in with a message that Miss Ellison was in the morning room, and did the general wish to receive her?

He felt a rush of excitement boil up inside him, sending the blood into his face. That was ridiculous—she had come to see the letters. It was not personal. She would have come just as quickly, whoever had possessed them.

'Yes.' He swallowed and tried to meet the parlourmaid's eyes quite casually. 'By all means. She has come to see some historical documents, so show her into the library, and then bring tea.'

'Yes, sir.' If the parlourmaid found it strange, there was nothing in her face to betray it.

He stood up and pulled his jacket a little straighter. Without thinking, he raised his hands to his cravat. It seemed tight. He loosened it a fraction, and made sure in front of the glass that it was properly tied.

Charlotte was in the library. She turned and smiled as the general came in. He did not even notice the warm reds of her street gown, or that her boots were soaked. All he saw was the light in her face.

'Good afternoon, General,' she said quickly. 'It is most kind of you to allow me to read the letters. I do hope I have not called inconveniently?'

'No—not at all.' He wished she would use his name, but it would be grossly familiar to ask her to. He must behave with dignity or he would embarrass her. He kept his face cool. 'I have no other engagements for the meantime.' He was going to have late tea with Robert Carlton, but that was unimportant; they were old friends and the arrangement was quite informal.

'That is very generous of you.' She was still smiling.

'Please sit down,' he said, indicating the big chair near the fire. 'I have asked the maid to bring tea. I hope that is acceptable?'

'Oh, yes, thank you.' She sat down and put her feet on the fender. For the first time, he noticed how wet her boots were, and that they were quite worn. He looked away, and went for the letters out of the bookcase.

They studied them together for half an hour. The maid brought tea, Charlotte poured it, and they returned to the utterly foreign world of Spain at the beginning of the century. The soldier wrote with such intense honesty that they knew his thoughts, felt his emotions, sensed the closeness of other men and the impact of battle, endured with him endless marches over dry hills, his hunger, and the long hours of waiting followed by sudden fear.

At last Charlotte sat back, her eyes wide, seeing far away. 'You know, with his writing that soldier has given me a portion of his life. I feel very rich. Most people are restricted to one time and place, and I have been privileged to see another so vividly it is as if I had been there but come away without the injury or the cost.'

He looked at her face, alive with pleasure, and felt ridiculously rewarded. The sense of being alone vanished like night when the whole earth whirls suddenly upward toward the sun.

He found himself smiling back at her. Instinctively he put out his hand and touched her for a moment. The warmth of her spread right through him till his whole body felt it. Then reluctantly, he withdrew his hand. It was a moment he dared not linger over. The intensity with which he wished to was warning enough.

What could he say that was honest? He would shatter the moment if he were to descend to platitudes, ordinary and born of someone else's mind. 'I'm glad,' he said simply. 'It mattered to me, too. I felt as if I knew that soldier better than I know most of the people I see and talk to, and whose lives I thought I understood.'

Her eyes moved away from his and she took a deep breath. He observed the smooth curve of her body, her throat, the fine line of her cheek.

'Merely living close to people does not mean you know them,' she said thoughtfully. 'All you know is what they look like.'

Christina came to his mind.

'One tends to believe that other people care about the same things,' she went on. 'It comes as a shock to discover sometimes that they don't. I cannot get the murders in the Devil's Acre out of my thoughts, and yet most of the people I know prefer not to hear anything about them. The circumstances remind us of poverty and injustices that hurt.' She swung around to look at him, her eyes level. She felt a little embarrassed. 'I'm sorry—do you find it unbecoming that I should mention it?'

'I find it offensive and frightening that anyone should be prepared to ignore it,' he said honestly. Would she think him as pompous as Christina did? She could not be more than a few years older than Christina. That was a realization that shot through him with sudden and startling pain. His face flushed and he felt self-conscious. The past hour's comfort fled. He was being ridiculous.

'General Balantyne?' She spoke very gravely, her hand touching his sleeve. 'Are you being kind to me? Are you sure I have not offended you by raising such a subject?'

He cleared his throat. 'Of course I'm sure!' He leaned back hard against the upright of his chair, where he could not feel the warmth of her, or smell the faint aroma of lavender and clean hair, a sweet musk of the skin. Wild sensations stirred inside him, and he strained after intelligent thought to drown them. He heard his voice as if it came from far away. 'I have tried to discuss the matter. Brandy is most concerned, and Alan Ross as well. But it distresses the women.' Already he was becoming pompous!

But she did not seem to notice. 'It is natural Christina should be upset,' she said quietly, looking down at her hands in her lap. 'After all, she knew Sir Bertram Astley, and she knows Miss Woolmer, whom he was engaged to marry. It must be much more painful to her than to you or me. And it is only natural that the police will wonder if Mr Beau Astley could have envied his brother enough to wish him harm, since he stood to inherit both the title and the estates. And of course Miss Woolmer is very fond of him also—I gather he is most charming. As his friend, Christina is bound to feel for him. His situation must be painful because of his bereavement, and most unpleasant in the suspicions that the uncharitable are bound to exercise.'

He considered it, but Christina had expressed no sympathy. In fact, she had given him the impression that she was impatient of the whole affair. But then Charlotte was crediting Christina with the emotions she would have felt herself.

'And, of course, that wretched creature Max Burton used to be footman here,' she continued. 'Although you can hardly care about his fate, it is unpleasant to think that any human being you had known should meet such an end.'

'How did you know it was the same man?' he asked in surprise. He did not recall any mention of Callander Square in the papers, or of Max's previous career. And Burton was not an uncommon name.

The colour rose in her cheeks and she looked away.

He was sorry for embarrassing her, and yet honesty between them, the ability to say what was truly in the mind, was of overpowering importance to him. 'Charlotte?'

'I am afraid I have been listening to gossip,' she said a little defensively. 'Emily and I have been engaged in a great effort to bring the conditions of certain people, especially the young involved in prostitution, to the attention of those who have influence. Apparently one cannot legislate against it, but one can move public opinion until those who practice these abuses find their positions intolerable!' Now she looked up and met his eyes, challenging him to disapprove. Nothing he could say would alter her beliefs in the slightest. He felt a surge of joy well up inside him as he realized it.

'My dear,' he said candidly. 'I should not wish to be able to.'

A flicker of confusion showed in her eyes. 'I beg your pardon?'

'Are you not defying me to try to change your mind, to disapprove of you?'

Her face relaxed into a smile, and he realized with horror how much he wanted to touch her. A unity of minds was not enough; there were things at once too strong and too delicate to be transmitted by such limited means as speech. Things long dormant inside him broke open their barrier with great currents of movement, destroying the balance. He wanted to stretch out this afternoon into an indefinite future with no nightfall, to prevent Augusta from returning and bringing back normality—and loneliness.

Charlotte was looking at him. Had she seen that thought in his face? The light died out of her eyes and she turned away.

'Only on that subject,' she said quietly. 'Because I know I am right. There are plenty of other things in which I might well be obliged to agree with you if you were to find me at fault. I find myself at fault!'

He did not know what she was referring to, and it would be an intrusion to ask. But he did not think she was saying it for effect, a false modesty. There was some sense of guilt that disturbed her.

'Everyone has faults, my dear,' he said gently. 'In those we love, the virtues outweigh them, and are what matter. The qualities less than good we do not choose to observe. We know them, but they do not offend us. If people were without weakness or need, what could we offer them of ourselves that they could value?'

She stood up quickly, and for a moment he thought there were tears in her eyes. Did she know what he was thinking—what he was trying to say—and at the same time not to say? He loved her. It was there in words in his mind at last.

It would be unforgivable to embarrass her. At all costs, he must behave properly. He pulled his shoulders back and sat up straighter. 'It sounds a most excellent work that you and Emily are engaged in.' He prayed that his voice sounded normal, not too suddenly remote, too pompous.

'Yes.' She kept her back to him and stared out the window at the garden. 'Lady Cumming-Gould is also concerned, and Mr Somerset Carlisle, the Member of Parliament. I think we have already accomplished something.' She turned at last and smiled at him. 'I'm so glad you approve. Now that you have said so, I can confess I should have been hurt had you not.'

He felt the heat burn his cheeks again, with a mixture of pleasure and pain. He stood, then picked up the soldier's letters from the desk. He could not bear for her to go, and yet it was equally intolerable now that she should stay. He must not betray himself. The emotion he felt was so profound and so very unreliable inside him that he must excuse her and be alone.

'Please take these, and read them again if you wish.'

She understood the convention well. She accepted them and thanked him. 'I will take the greatest care of them,' she said quietly. 'I feel he is a friend of both of us. I do thank you for a unique afternoon. Good day, General Balantyne.'

He took a deep breath. 'Good day, Charlotte.' He reached for the bell. When the footman came, he watched her go, her back straight, head high. He stood exactly where he had been when she left, trying to keep her presence with him, to wrap himself in a golden cocoon before the warmth died and he was left alone again.

Balantyne did not sleep well that night. He chose to be out when Augusta returned, and when he came back to the house he was already late for dinner.

'I cannot imagine why you wish to walk at this hour,' she remarked with a little shake of her head. 'It is totally dark, and the coldest night of the year.'

'It is quite fine,' he answered. 'I imagine presently there will be a moon.' It was irrelevant. He had walked to put off the time of meeting her and having to step out of his dream and back into the pattern of life. To try to explain that would be cruel and incomprehensible to her. Instead he broached another unpleasant subject.

'Augusta, I think it would be advisable for you to take some counsel with Christina, give her a little advice.'

Augusta raised her eyebrows and sat motionless, her soupspoon halfway to her mouth. 'Indeed? Upon what subject?'

'Her behaviour toward Alan.'

'Do you consider that she is failing in her duty?'

'It is nothing so simple.' He shook his head. 'But duty does not beget love. She is contrary, too unkind with her tongue. I have seen no softness in her. She is quite unlike Jemima, for example.'

'Naturally.' She carried the spoon to her mouth and ate elegantly. 'Jemima was brought up as a governess. One would expect to find her manner a good deal more obedient and grateful. Christina is a lady.'

It was not necessary to remind him that Augusta's father had been an earl, and his own possessed of no distinction but a military one. 'I was thinking of her happiness,' he said steadily. 'One may be a princess and yet not necessarily inspire love. She would serve herself better if she were to charm Alan a little more, and take him for granted a good deal less. He is not a man to be dazzled by appearances, or to have his affections heightened by the awareness that other men find her pleasing.'

Augusta went suddenly quite white, her arm frozen, fingers rigid around the spoon.

'Are you ill?' he said in confusion. 'Augusta!'

She blinked. 'No...no, I am perfectly well. I swallowed my soup a little carelessly, that is all. What did you mean about Christina? She has always been something of a flirt. It is natural for a pretty woman. Alan can hardly take exception to that.'

'You are talking about social customs!' Why did she seem unable to understand? 'I am talking about love, gentleness, sharing things.'

Her eyes widened and there was a shred of bitter humour in them he found confusing. 'You are being romantic, Brandon,' she said. 'I had not expected anything so—so very young of you!'

'You mean naïve? On the contrary, it is you and Christina who are naïve—in imagining that a relationship can survive without honest emotion and the occasional sacrifice to unreason in the name of kindness. You can argue people into a business arrangement, but not into affection.'

Augusta sat still for several minutes, considering what he had said and what she should reply to him. 'I think we should be interfering where it is no longer our concern,' she said at last. 'Christina is a married woman now. Her private life is Alan's responsibility, and you would be trespassing upon his rights if you were to offer her advice, especially about such personal matters.'

He was surprised. That was the last answer he had expected from her. 'You mean you would stand by and watch her destroy her marriage because you consider it interfering to offer her advice? She did not cease to be our daughter just because she became Alan's wife, nor did our affection stop!'

'Of course our affection did not stop,' she said impatiently. 'But if you regard the law, as well as the practices of daily life, you will find that Alan is responsible for her now. For a woman to marry is a far bigger change in all her circumstances than you seem to appreciate. What passes between them is private, and we would be deeply mistaken to interfere.' She smiled faintly. 'Would you have appreciated it, Brandon, had my father offered you advice upon your conduct toward me?'

'I was speaking of advising Christina—not Alan!'

'Would you have accepted it from your own father?'

The thought was an entirely new one to him. It had never occurred to him that anyone else might have concerned himself in the more private aspects of his life. It was appalling—offensive!... But this was a totally different matter. Christina was his daughter, and he was seeking for Augusta, as her mother, to counsel her so that she might amend her behaviour and forestall a great deal of unhappiness for herself.

He opened his mouth to point out all this, then saw from his wife's expression that to her it was precisely the same. He smiled in dry appreciation and looked back at her.

'I would not have minded had your mother counselled you toward affection rather than duty, if she had considered it necessary. Indeed, I have no idea whether she did or not!'

'She did not!' Augusta said a trifle sharply. 'And nor shall I offer advice to Christina unless she asks it of me. To do so would be to assume that I know what passes between them, and would require an explanation from her as to things which are extremely personal. I shall not place her in that position, nor do I wish her to believe me inquisitive.'

He could think of nothing more to say. They were arguing in words; they were not really even speaking of the same emotions. He let the silence close the subject, and he did not raise it again. He could not speak to Christina himself; he did not know how to begin, how to avoid her either laughing at him or becoming offended. But he could speak to Alan Ross.

Feeling he could not afford to wait for an opportunity to present itself, Balantyne went the following day to visit Alan Ross, at a time when he believed it likely Christina would be out. Even if, by misfortune, she was at home, it would not be awkward to excuse himself from her presence and talk alone with Ross.

It was not an interview he looked forward to, for he had abandoned any idea of trying to be oblique. Since his own emotions had been stripped of their usual protections of ritual and words, he found it surprisingly easier now to contemplate speaking honestly.

Christina was not at home. Alan Ross welcomed him and showed him into his study where he had been writing letters. It was a pleasant room, entirely masculine, but obviously a place where someone spent a great deal of time and kept personal possessions that were both treasured and frequently used.

They exchanged trivialities for a few

minutes. Normally it would have been a comfortable introduction into any of a dozen subjects of mutual interest, but today Balantyne was too conscious of the reasons for his visit to descend to mere companionship. As soon as the footman had left the tray with sherry and glasses, he turned to Ross.

'Did you know Bertie Astley well?' he asked.

Alan Ross seemed to pale. 'Not very,' he said quietly.

Balantyne waited, unsure how to continue. Was there pain underneath that polite reply, the memory of Christina laughing, flirting, being entertained? Somehow he imagined both the Astleys as fashionable and witty, amusing in a way that Alan Ross had never been. He was a graver man, deeper and infinitely harder to win.

'I never met him,' Balantyne went on. 'Do you think he was where they found him of his own accord?'

Ross smiled slightly and his blue eyes met Balantyne's. 'I should be surprised. He seemed eminently normal on the occasions I saw him.'

'You mean he flirted a great deal?'

Ross's smile widened tolerantly. 'No

more than usual for a young man who feels the noose of matrimony closing round him, and wishes to taste of freedom to the full while he still may. Miss Woolmer's mother has a fearsome grip.'

Balantyne remembered his own last few weeks of freedom, before he had asked Augusta's father for her hand. He had known he was going to, of course, but it was still sweet to play with the idea that he might not, to savour in imagination all sorts of other possibilities he would never indulge.

He looked across and caught Ross's eyes. They understood each other perfectly. 'I suppose Christina is very distressed by his death.' It was more an observation than a question. It would account for the strain he saw in her. She hated mourning and would absorb the sorrow in her own way.

'Not especially, though she was rather fond of him,' Ross replied. Ross had turned away and his face was tight. 'She was fond of a number of people,' he said quietly.

Balantyne felt the sweat prickle on his skin. Fond of? Was that a euphemism for something much coarser, more promiscuous? Or was it only his own rush of feeling for

Charlotte, the strong physical desire that made his face burn at the memory, that put in his mind far uglier thoughts of Christina? Had she been drenched with that hunger, but without the love?

He looked at Ross's face, still turned toward the fire. As he had observed before, it was a private face, strong-boned but with a very vulnerable mouth. To intrude into his emotions would be unforgivable.

In that moment Balantyne believed he understood what Ross would never say: Christina was a loose woman. How it had come about he would never know. Perhaps Ross had expected too much of her, a maturity, a delicacy of which she was not capable. Perhaps he had compared her with Helena Doran. A mistake—you should never compare one woman with another. And yet, dear God, how easy to do when you have loved! Was there not at the back of his own mind, painful and bright, a memory of Charlotte's eyes looking at him that would forever be a comparison with every other relationship—and a damning of it?

He must think of Christina. Christina as a young bride would have been confused, hurt, not knowing in what way she had failed to please Ross. A man should teach a woman gently, be prepared to wait while she learned such an utterly new life...the physical...His thoughts stopped. Or was it new to Christina? Memories floated back from the time of the murders on Callander Square, things Augusta had refused to discuss. She had dealt with so much, been so competent—and never told him.

Was Christina seeking from other men the reassurance that she was desired because the husband she loved had rejected her, shut her out? Or was she simply a vain and immoral woman for whom one man was not enough?

But whatever the desire, surely faithfulness...

What sort of faith did he keep with Augusta? It was the knowledge of hurting Charlotte that had kept him from excess yesterday, from touching her, from holding her—and— And what? Anything—everything! And it was selfishness, fear of the rejection he would see in Charlotte's eyes, her horror when she understood what he really felt. It was not any thought of Augusta.

And, more than that, Charlotte would have been irreparably hurt to know what storms she had created in him. He would lose her, she would certainly never come to Callander Square again, never be alone with him to share even the sweetness of friendship. Would she think him ridiculous? Or, worse, pitiful? He thrust the thought away; there was nothing absurd in loving.

But what about Christina? Had she inherited from him this betraying hunger? He had never talked to her of fidelity or modesty; he had left all that sort of thing to Augusta. It was a mother's duty to instruct her daughter in the conduct of marriage. For him to have done so would have been indelicate, and would have caused only embarrassment.

But he could have spoken of chastity— simple morality. And he had never done so. Perhaps he owed Christina a great deal? And heaven knew what he owed Alan Ross!... He looked up and saw Ross's eyes, waiting for him. Could he have any idea what had been passing through his thoughts?

'She knew Adela Pomeroy,' Ross said with a slight frown, as if it puzzled him.

The name meant nothing to Balantyne. 'Adela Pomeroy?' he repeated.

'The wife of the last man who was

murdered in the Acre—the schoolteacher,' Ross explained.

'Oh.' He thought for a moment. 'How on earth did Christina come to know a schoolteacher's wife?'

'She's a pretty woman,' Ross answered painfully. 'And bored. I think she sought diversion in'—he moved his hand slightly—'in wider company.'

Whatever did he mean by that? Thousands of women were probably bored now and then. You could not simply extend your social circle upward unless you were remarkably pretty, and willing to... Then was Adela Pomeroy another loose woman? But if so, why was it Ernest Pomeroy who was killed? It should have been Adela. And Bertie Astley—had he been Adela's lover? And what connection had the doctor with any of them?

Were they all victims of the same lunatic? Or perhaps was one a crime fitted in and made to look like the others, an opportunity taken brilliant advantage of: to inherit a title and an estate; or to be rid of a tedious husband; or—and the sweat broke out on his body at the thought—to avenge a cuckolder of one's bed, one's home.

'What was the doctor's wife like?' he

asked huskily, swallowing.

Ross looked away. 'I've no idea. Why?'

Balantyne's face was stiff. 'No reason. My mind was wandering,' he said lamely. He forced the thought away; it was unworthy of such a man.

Ross offered him the sherry, but he declined it. Its warmth did not reach deep enough inside him. He noticed that Ross himself took none either. How long had he known Christina's nature? He cannot have understood it when he married her. Had the knowledge come slowly, a gathering pain? Or in a single act of discovery, like a sharp wound?

He looked at Ross's face. It would be unpardonable to discuss the subject with him. It was his own private grief, and no matter what Balantyne might guess, he must be silent. He could not bear Ross to know—even for an instant—the thoughts that had come to him.

He wanted to run away, to exist in some fantasy land where he could be with Charlotte, talk with her, see her face, touch her, learn to share a multitude of things.

No doubt Alan Ross would like to be in just such a place, with someone clean and generous. But he understood duty, and so far he had found the courage to fulfill it.

Balantyne sat quite still. His mind fumbled for something to say, anything that would let Ross know that he was not alone; that, far from pity, he felt the most intense admiration for him, and a regard that was perhaps as close to love as one man comes for another. But no words were right; they had all been used too lightly. None of them conveyed the reality of the pain.

The two men sat for a long time, the untouched sherry decanter between them, the logs settling in the hearth. Finally, Balantyne stood up. Christina would doubtless soon be arriving home, and he did not wish to see her.

His goodbyes were trivial, the same things he always said, and Ross gave the same replies. But once, as they shook hands, he had the feeling for a moment that perhaps the unsaid things had been understood after all—at least the good things. And there would be other times, other chances to show a gentleness, to allow Ross to perceive that he cared, not blindly, but because he suffered some of the same loneliness, the same ties to duty that would destroy him if he let them go.

'Good afternoon, sir,' Ross said with a faint smile. 'Thank you for calling.'

'Good afternoon, Alan. Pleasure to see you.'

Neither of them mentioned the women. There was no message, no regards.

Balantyne turned and walked away into the sharp winter afternoon. He had not brought the carriage. He preferred the isolation and the exercise, the wind hard on his face, and it would take longer to get home.

CHAPTER 10

Charlotte did not tell Pitt that she had been to see General Balantyne again. In fact, she had not specifically told him of any of her visits, although she knew he was aware of them. Since he had been brought back from the hospital, white-faced, his clothes soaked with blood, she had realized he wanted to catch the Devil's Acre murderer so desperately that he would take clumsy risks. She still went cold at the thought of how nearly the risks had cost him his life. It was something she normally refused to think about—the chances of his being injured, or even killed. To dwell on it was too frightening, and there was nothing she could do to alter it.

She knew he disapproved very strongly of her becoming involved in the case in any way, even so peripherally as visiting the Balantynes. And, to tell the truth, she felt some guilt because she had enjoyed the glamour of wearing Emily's dresses, of swirling around in great spaces full of lights and music and brilliant colours. It was wonderful to show off—just a little!

She very honestly liked General Balantyne. That was the worst and most thoughtless thing she had done. She had never considered that he might really feel anything deeper for her than a return of her friendship. Naturally, she had wanted him to admire her, to think her beautiful and exciting; she simply had not believed that he would.

But this time she had seen in his face that soft, intensely personal gaze, unwavering and peculiarly naked. She knew it was no longer a social game to be stepped into or out of as the occasion suited.

Of course she could not tell Pitt; it was

out of the question. When he came in that night tired and cold, his side so sore he moved stiffly, she brought his supper through to the parlour for him on a tray and waited in silence while he ate.

At last her curiosity and anxiety overcame good sense and, as usual, her tongue won. 'Do you know anything yet to connect all the victims?' she asked, trying to sound casual.

He gave her a sceptical look and pushed the tray away. 'Thank you, that was very good.'

She waited.

'No!' he said emphatically. 'They all had their own business in the Acre, and so far I don't know anyone who knew them all.'

'All had business?' she asked, trying to keep her voice level. He had not told her that before. 'Max kept a brothel. But what about the others?'

'Pinchin performed abortions—'

'For Max?' she interrupted eagerly.

'Not so far as I know, but it's possible.'

'Then maybe some society woman—' She stopped. Apart from the fact that the idea was not a very good one, she had betrayed herself with her interest—and cut off any more information he might have given her. 'I'm sorry.'

'Accepted.' His mouth curved in a slow smile. He closed his eyes and slid farther down in his chair.

Charlotte clung to her patience with almost infinite effort. She smoothed her face into a calm expression and counted up to a hundred before she spoke again. 'What about Pomeroy? Don't tell me he was teaching prostitutes how to keep their accounts?'

His smile widened in spite of himself, then suddenly vanished altogether. 'No, he was a pederast...poor rotten inadequate bastard!'

Another hundred seconds went by. 'Oh,' she said at last.

'And Bertie Astley owned a whole row of tenement houses, sweatshops, and a gin mill,' he added. 'Now you know it all, and there is nothing whatsoever you can do.'

She tried to imagine Pomeroy. What kind of man hungered for the immature bodies of children too young to want anything but safety, approval, and comfort? They would ask nothing of him, and display neither hunger nor criticism. Certainly, God knows, they would never laugh at him if he was clumsy or inadequate.

And what of them, dreading every night when some new man would fondle their bodies and become strangely more and more excited, culminating in a final desperate and violently intimate act they would neither understand nor participate in. She shivered in spite of the fire, hunching up as if she were threatened, feeling sick.

'Leave it,' Pitt said quietly from the chair opposite. His eyes were open now and he was looking at her. 'Pomeroy's dead. And you'll not stop pederasty—'

'I know.'

'Then leave it.'

But Charlotte could not leave it. As soon as Pitt had gone the following morning, she instructed Gracie for the day, then put on her warmest cloak and walked to the public omnibus stop where she took the next bus going in the direction of Paragon Walk.

'Well?' Emily asked as soon as she arrived. 'What have you learned?'

She told Emily about Pitt being stabbed. She had not seen her since it happened.

'That's terrible! Oh, my dear, I'm so

sorry! Is he all right? Do you need anything?'

'No, thank you. Oh—' It was an offer too good to decline. 'Yes, if you have a bottle of good port.'

'Port?'

'Yes. It is an excellent restorative, especially in this weather.'

'Wouldn't you prefer brandy?' Emily was feeling expansive, and she liked Pitt.

'No, thank you. Port will do very well. But you can make it two bottles, if you like.'

'Has he discovered anything? Was it the Devil's Acre slasher? Did he recognize him?'

'He thinks it was just ordinary thieves. But he does know quite a lot now.' She recounted the reasons Pinchin and Pomeroy had had for being in the Acre.

Emily sat silent for several minutes. 'Perhaps that explains why Adela Pomeroy looked for lovers in the fast set,' she said at last. 'Poor woman. Although whatever her husband was, it hardly warrants indulging in a creature like Max!'

'Are you quite certain Adela Pomeroy looked for lovers in the fast set?' Charlotte asked, then instantly regretted it. She was afraid of the answer. 'And even if she did, it doesn't mean she had anything to do with Max!'

'No, I know that. But I've taken a lot of trouble lately to be sure just who is in that circle.'

'Emily! You haven't—?'

'No, I haven't!' Emily said icily. 'Which brings me to another subject. Investigating is one thing, Charlotte, but your behaviour with General Balantyne has been completely irresponsible. You criticize Christina Ross for flirting, quite rightly, but the only difference between you and her is that you have confined your attention to one man! And that does not make it better. Indeed, for the damage you may do, it makes it a great deal worse.'

Charlotte felt the heat of shame burn inside her so painfully that she could not look at Emily's face. She already knew how deeply she was at fault, but to have Emily tell her so made it the sharper. 'It was unintentional,' she said defensively.

'Rubbish!' Emily snapped back. 'You wanted some adventure, and you took it. You did not foresee the result because you did not bother to look!'

'Well, if you are so excessively clever, why

didn't you tell me?' Charlotte demanded, swallowing on the lump in her throat.

'Because I didn't see it either,' Emily admitted. 'How was I to know you'd behave like a complete fool? You never used to be able to flirt to save yourself!'

'I was not flirting!'

'Yes, you were!' Emily sighed and shut her eyes. 'Maybe you are just too stupid to realize your own success, I grant you that. But I'm never going to take you out anywhere again. You're a disaster.'

'Yes, you will, because you couldn't bear to be left out of it if there were another society murder and Thomas got the case.'

Emily looked around at her.

'I know I behaved badly,' Charlotte went on. 'It doesn't help to have you tell me. I'd undo it if I could.'

'You can't! We might as well put it to some use. What else do you know? I've been wondering if all the murders were committed by the same person. Or, even worse, if only one of them really mattered.'

'What do you mean—mattered? How can a murder not matter?'

'If only one mattered to the murderer,'

Emily said deliberately. 'What if Beau Astley wanted to kill his brother for the money? I believe there is quite a lot of it. If he killed Bertie ordinarily, he would be the first suspect himself. But if Bertie were only one of several deaths, all the others having no connection with Beau at all—'

'That's ghastly!'

'Yes, I know. And I like Beau Astley better each time I see him. But murderers, even lunatics, are not necessarily personally objectionable. And unfortunately plenty of totally worthy and sane people are.'

Charlotte had found this painfully true. 'Bertie Astley owned a whole row of houses in the Acre. That's where the Astley money comes from.'

'Oh.' Emily let out her breath in a sigh. 'I suppose I should have thought of that.'

'I don't see where it helps very much.'

'Who does Thomas think it was?'

'He won't tell me.'

Emily considered in silence for a while. 'I wonder—' Charlotte began.

'What?'

'I'm not sure.' She was thinking of Christina. If Christina had also been one of Max's women—young, hungry, dissatisfied because Alan Ross did not give her the

373

fierce, total love she wanted, the essence of him was always just out of reach—had she looked to prove herself with other men, and so been drawn into one affair after another, in an endless pursuit?

And if Ross had found out—And why should he not? It would surely be simple enough, once he suspected.

'Don't be stupid,' Emily said impatiently. 'Of course you're sure. You may not be right, but you know what you mean!'

'No, I don't.'

'Oh, Charlotte!' Emily's face softened. 'You can't hide from it—not once you've realized. Of course it could be Balantyne.'

'The general!' Charlotte was appalled. 'Oh, no! No, it couldn't!'

'Why not?' Emily said gently. 'If Christina is one of Max's women, he wouldn't be able to bear the disgrace. He's used to discipline and sacrifice. Soldiers who disgrace themselves find a gun and take the honourable way out. Somehow it evens the balance for them—they can be looked on with an obscure kind of respect. He would do that for Christina, wouldn't he?'

'But Christina wasn't shot! Why would he do that to all those other people? It doesn't make any sense!' It was a protest

374

in the wind, and she knew it.

'Of course it does.' Emily put out her hand and touched Charlotte. 'He fought in Africa, didn't he? He's seen all kinds of savage rituals and atrocities. Perhaps it isn't so terrible to him. Maybe Max came back to her, saw her at some party or out somewhere, and approached her—and she became one of his women. That would be reason to kill Max, and dismember him that way.'

'Why Bertie Astley?' It was a silly question. The answer was obvious—he had been her lover. Emily did not even bother to reply.

'All right—then why Pinchin?' Charlotte went on.

'He might have done an abortion on her, and perhaps she cannot have any children now.'

'And Pomeroy? What about him? He only liked children!'

'I don't know. Perhaps he knew about it. Maybe he saw something.'

'I don't believe it. I don't believe General Balantyne would—that he could!'

'Of course you don't. You don't want to. But, my dear, sometimes people one cares for very much can do horrible things. Heaven knows, we even do them ourselves—ugly, stupid, and painful things. Perhaps this just grew from a small mistake till it became...'

Charlotte took a long, deep breath and shook her head. She could feel the tears aching in her throat.

'I don't believe it. It could have been Alan Ross. He had more reason, and he would be more likely to find out. Or it could just as easily be any other woman's husband. We must find out more! When we do, it will prove it wasn't the general or Alan Ross. Who else is in that fast set?'

'Lots of people. I've already told you a dozen or more.'

'Then we must find out who their husbands are, their fathers, brothers, their lovers, and then establish where they were on the nights of any of the murders.'

'Wouldn't it be easier to have Thomas do that?' Emily asked reasonably.

'I can't tell him we are involved. He's angry enough already with the little he knows. You don't have to find out where they were on each of the nights—any one of them will do!'

'Oh, thank you very much! That makes it so much easier—a mere bagatelle! And what are you going to be doing in the meantime?'

'I'm going to see General Balantyne. I'll prove it wasn't him. Or Alan Ross.'

'Charlotte—be careful!'

Charlotte gave her a withering look. 'And what do you imagine they are going to do to me? The very worst they are likely to do is lie a little. They can hardly drum me out of society, since I am not in it. You get started on your own investigations. If you are nice to George, you can persuade him to do at least half of it for you. Good day.'

She arrived at the Balantyne house at the appropriate hour for calling, partly for convenience of being allowed in but mostly because that was when she was most likely to find the general alone. Lady Augusta would be out making her own calls.

The footman opened the door and regarded her with expectation.

'Good afternoon,' she said firmly. For heaven's sake, she must remember they knew her as Miss Ellison! She had nearly announced herself as Mrs Pitt. That was a lie that would have to be explained, but it was too painful to contend with now.

'Good afternoon, Miss Ellison,' the footman said civilly. If he noticed her plain clothes or her wet boots, scuffed at the toes, he affected not to. 'Her Ladyship is not at home, but the general is in, and Miss Christina.' He held the door wide in mute invitation.

Charlotte accepted with alacrity, hoping he attributed it to the withering wind and the hard-driving snow rather than an unbecoming eagerness to visit.

'Thank you,' she said with what she trusted was a compensating dignity. 'I should be grateful to speak with the general, if I may.' She had already thought of her excuse. 'It is with regard to the letters from the Peninsular War that he lent me.'

'Certainly, ma'am, if you care to come this way.' He closed the door against the ice-whirling dusk, and led her to the withdrawing room. It was empty, but a fire was burning hard. Presumably the general was in the library, and perhaps Christina was with him. That was a contingency Charlotte had not considered. She would much rather not speak in Christina's presence. Christina would be far too quick to understand,

and she was possessive of her father. She would end the whole visit as quickly as was decent, it would descend to a painful battle of wits. Charlotte would have to try to bore her away with whatever details of soldiering she could bring to mind!

The footman left her. Several minutes later, he returned and conducted her to the library. Thank heaven Christina had already gone, perhaps finding even the thought of Charlotte and her letters too tedious to bother with.

General Balantyne was standing with his back to the fire. He was tense, his eyes on the doorway, waiting for her.

The footman disappeared discreetly, leaving them alone.

'Charlotte—' He was unsure whether to step toward her or not. Suddenly he was awkward, his feelings so close to the surface that they were embarrassing, even frightening.

She had prepared some scrambled comment about the letters. Now they were not necessary; she had no excuse to prevaricate. Her mouth was dry, her throat tight.

'The footman said something about the letters.' He was trying to help her. 'Have you discovered something?'

She avoided his eyes and looked at the fire.

Then he realized that she was cold and wet, and that he was taking all the heat. He moved away quickly, his face softening. 'Come, warm yourself.'

She smiled. At any other time, such an act would have mattered. All her life she had been accustomed to having a man automatically assume the place nearest the fire.

'Thank you.' She walked over and felt the heat tingle pleasantly on her skin. In a moment it would penetrate through her wet skirt and boots to her numbed feet.

There was no point in putting it off any longer. 'I didn't come about the letters.' She stayed facing the flames, watching them, avoiding his eyes. He was close behind her, and at all costs she did not want to look at him. 'I came about the murders in the Devil's Acre.'

There was a moment's silence. For an instant her anxiety had made her forget Pitt. Balantyne had assumed, because Emily had introduced her as Miss Ellison, that her marriage had failed—and she had never disillusioned him. Now she thought of it with a flood of shame. She turned.

He was still looking at her, the bright, desperate softness in his face unmistakable and wide open to every wound. And yet not to tell him now would be inexcusable. Every time she came here, she made it worse. There was nothing she could do to soften the injury. Everything—attempts at gentleness, shame, pity—would either humiliate or embarrass him.

She began quickly, before she had time to draw back. 'I have no excuse to offer, except that I care very much about finding who killed those men in the Devil's Acre, and the whole system of prostitution and—'

'So do I!' he said fervently, then realized the agony in her face. 'Charlotte? What is it?' He stood still, but she felt as if he had come closer, so intense was his concentration, his awareness of her.

'I have been lying to you.' She used the harshest, most abrasive word. It was cowardly to look away. She also needed to hurt herself. She met his eyes. 'Emily introduced me as Miss Ellison because she wished you to think of me as a private person. And I allowed her to, since Max used to work in this house and we thought we might learn something here.' Still she left out their suspicions of Christina.

Slowly the dawn of a new pain came over him, then a scalding embarrassment. He had pushed Pitt, the whole episode of her marriage, out of his mind. He had wished something—or dreamed something? Now it all shattered around him.

'I am still married to Thomas Pitt,' she whispered. 'And I am happy.'

His face burst hot. He turned away from her for a moment, wanting to hide.

She had used him. Now she felt a bitter shame, and pain, because she cared for him. It mattered intensely to her what he thought of her. If he despised her for it, she would feel the mark as long as she could imagine.

'I'm very ashamed,' she said quietly. Should she pretend she did not know he loved her? Would that save his pride by allowing him to withdraw it as if it had not existed? Or would it only further insult him by devaluing what was the greatest gift he had to offer?

She tried to read his face, but all she could see was the softness in his eyes, hot confusion, blurred. The light of the lamp on the wall reflected on the bones of his cheek. She wanted to touch him, to put her arms around him—but that was ridiculous! He would be offended, perhaps even repelled. He would not understand that although she loved Pitt, she also felt for him something individual and profound. He might even take it for pity, and that would be the most dreadful of all.

'I lied by omission,' she went on, to break the silence. 'I said nothing untrue!' It sounded like an attempt at excuse.

'Please don't explain.' He found words at last, his voice a little husky. He breathed deeply in and out. 'I care about the murders also—and the Devil's Acre. I imagined you had not come about the letters. What did you come for?'

'But I do care about the letters!' Now she was sounding like a child, and the tears were spilling over. She sniffed and reached for her handkerchief. She blew her nose and looked away from him. 'There is some very disturbing information. I—I thought you would wish to know immediately.'

'I—?' Already he understood that there was something else that would hurt him, something further. An instinctive sense of it made him move a little away from her, allowing her to sit down without seeming to rebuff him. It was a delicacy of emotion he had not known before. 'What have you discovered?' he asked quickly.

'Max was keeping two houses.' She hesitated to use the word 'whore.' It was too ugly, too close just now.

He did not seem to grasp the meaning of it. 'Indeed?' The confusion showed in his voice. They were being formal, as if the past moment's intimacy had not happened. It was easier for both of them.

She rushed on before there was time to think of emotions. 'One was ordinary, like in the Devil's Acre. The other was for very high-class customers.' She smiled bitterly, although her face was toward the fire. 'Carriage trade. He even provided women of good birth, very good indeed, on occasion.'

He was silent. She tried to imagine what was in his mind: incredulity, horror— knowledge? Pain.

She breathed out slowly. 'Adela Pomeroy was one of them.'

Still he said nothing.

'Pomeroy was a pederast. I expect—' She stopped. She was trying to excuse the woman. Why? To excuse Christina also, for him? He did not deserve patronage. Again, almost overwhelmingly, she wanted to hold him tightly in her arms, to touch softly the unreachable wound—as if anything she could do would ease it! It was idiotic. She would only intrude on his embarrassment and hurt, preposterously overrating the affection he had felt for her, which was perhaps already destroyed by her duplicity—and by this much closer threat.

'I'm sorry,' she said, still facing the fire.

'What about the others?' he asked. She could not read his voice.

'Dr Pinchin performed abortions on prostitutes, not always successfully. He took his payment in kind. Mrs Pinchin was very grim and very respectable.'

'And Bertie Astley?' he persisted. He was being very objective, covering his feelings for her...or Christina, or anyone, by seeking to understand the facts.

'He owned a row of houses in the Acre—tenements, sweatshops, a gin mill. Of course, Beau Astley might have killed him for the money. They bring in a lot.' She looked at him.

'Do you believe that?' He appeared perfectly calm, except that his facial muscles were tight and his left hand was clenched by his side. For an instant, she caught the brightness in his eyes before he looked away.

'No,' she said with an effort.

The door burst open and Christina came in, her face white, her eyes brilliant. She was wearing an outdoor cloak and carried a large, handsome reticule.

'Why, Miss Ellison, how delightful to see you again!' she said a little loudly. 'I declare, you are the most studious person I have ever known. You will be able to deliver lectures upon the life of a soldier in the Peninsular War to learned societies. That is what you are discussing again, is it not?'

The prefabricated lie came to Charlotte's lips instantly. 'My knowledge is very slight, Mrs Ross. But I have a relation who is most interested. I wished to show him the general's letters, but before doing so, I came to request his permission.'

'How diligent of you to come in person.' Christina moved over to the desk and, her eyes still on Charlotte, opened one of the drawers. 'A lesser woman would have resorted to the penny post! Especially on such a dreadful day. The streets are white with snow already, and it is growing heavier by the moment. You will become quite frozen going home!' Her face twisted a little. She took something from the drawer and put it into her reticule, closing the catch with a snap.

The general was too angry at the slight to Charlotte to bother to inquire what she had taken. 'I shall send Miss Ellison home in the carriage, naturally,' he snapped. 'No doubt you brought your own and will not need one of mine?'

'Of course, Papa! Did you imagine I came in a public omnibus?' She walked to the door and opened it. 'Good day, Miss Ellison. I hope your—relation—enjoys the Peninsular War as much as you appear to do.' And she went out, closing the door behind her. A moment later they heard hooves on the pavement outside and the slam of a carriage door.

'It seems she has borrowed something of yours,' Charlotte remarked, more to break the silence than because it mattered at all.

Balantyne went to the desk and opened the drawer she had taken the object from. For a moment his face was puzzled. There were lines of pain in it, a new and delicate vulnerability to his mouth.

Christina had been one of Max's women. Charlotte knew now that Balantyne either knew it or guessed it. What about Alan Ross?

Balantyne stood perfectly straight, his eyes wide, his skin drained of blood. 'She's taken my gun.'

For an instant Charlotte was paralyzed. Then she leaped to her feet. 'We must go after her,' she commanded. 'Find a hansom. She has only just left. There will be marks in the snow—we can follow her. Whatever she means to do, we may be in time to stop her—or—or if it is good, then to help her!'

He strode to the door and shouted for the footman. He snatched from the man's hands Charlotte's coat, ignoring his own. He grasped her arm and pushed her to the door. The next moment they were outside in the whirling snow, blinded by the dusk and the dim lamps, stung by the slithering snowflakes turning to ice.

Balantyne ran across the road onto the snow-covered grass under the trees. Christina's carriage was still in sight on the far side of the square, slowing to turn the corner. There was a hansom moving from pool to pool of light along the west side.

'Cabbie!' Balantyne shouted, waving his arms. 'Cabbie!'

Charlotte scrambled through shrubs and grass, soaked to her ankles, trying to keep up with him. Her face was wet and numb with cold, and though her gloves were locked in her reticule, her fingers were too frozen even to fish for them. All her efforts were concentrated on keeping up with him.

Sir Robert Carlton was already in the cab.

Balantyne pulled the door open. 'Emergency!' he shouted above the wind. 'Sorry, Robert! I need this!' And, relying on long friendship and a generous nature, he held out his hand and almost hauled Carlton out, then grabbed Charlotte by the waist and lifted her in. He then ordered the cabbie to follow down the far street where Christina's carriage had disappeared. He thrust a handful of coins at the startled man, and was almost thrown to the floor as the driver was transformed into a Jehu at the flash of gold.

Charlotte sat herself up in the seat where she had landed and clung to the handhold. There was no time or purpose in trying to rearrange her skirts to any sense of decorum. The cab was hurtling around the corner from the square, and Balantyne had his head out the window, trying to see if Christina was still ahead of them, or if in the maelstrom of the storm they had lost her.

The horses' hooves were curiously silent on the soft padding of snow. The carriage lurched from side to side as the wheels slid, caught again, and then swerved. At any other time Charlotte would have been terrified, but all she could think of now was Christina somewhere ahead of them, holding the general's gun. Fear sickened her, excluding all thought of her own safety as her body was flung from side to side while the cab careened through the white wilderness. Was it Alan Ross she was going to kill? Was it he, after all, who had murdered first Max, and then the others—and at last Christina knew it? Was she going to shoot him? Or offer him suicide?

Balantyne brought his head in from the window. His skin was whipped raw from the wind, snow crusted his hair.

'They're still ahead of us. God knows where she's going!' His face was so cold that his mouth was stiff and his words blurred.

She was thrown against him as the cab wheeled around another corner. He caught her, held her for a moment, then eased her upright again.

'I don't know where we are,' he went on. 'I can't see anything but snow and gas lamps now and again. I don't recognize anything.'

'She's not going home?' Charlotte asked. Then instantly wished she had not said it.

'No, we seem to have turned toward the river.' Had he also been thinking of Alan Ross?

They were lurching through a muted world with muffled hoofbeats and no hiss of wheels. There sounded only the crack of the whip and the cabbie's shout. Vision was limited to the whirl of white flakes in the islands of the lamps, followed by raging, freezing darkness again till the next brief moon on its iron stand. They were slowed to a trot now, turning more often. Apparently they had not lost her, because the cabbie never asked for further instructions.

Where was she going? To warn Adela

Pomeroy? Of what? Had she hired some lunatic to kill her husband?

Answers crowded into Charlotte's head, and none of them could be right. She put off again and again the one she knew in her heart was the truth. Christina was going back to the Devil's Acre! To one of the whorehouses...and murder.

Beside her, Balantyne said nothing. Whatever nightmare was in his mind he struggled with it alone.

One more corner, another snow-blanketed street, a crossroad, and then at last they stopped. The cabbie's head appeared.

'Your party's gone in there!' He waved his arm and Balantyne forced open the door and jumped out, leaving Charlotte to fend for herself after him. 'Over there.' The cabbie waved again. 'Dalton sisters' whorehouse. Don't know what she's doin', if'n yer ask me. If 'er 'usband's gorn in there, she'd best pretend she don't know—not goin' a-chasing after 'im like a madwoman! 'T'ain't decent. 'T'ain't sense neither! Still—never could tell most women nothin' fer their own good! 'Ere! Best leave the lady in the cab! Gawd! Yer can't take 'er in there, guv!'

But Balantyne was not listening. He

strode across the glimmering road and up the steps of the house where Christina's footsteps still showed in the virgin snow.

' 'Ere!' The cabbie tried once more. 'Miss!'

But Charlotte was after him, running with her skirts trailing wet and heavy, catching Balantyne on the step. There was no one to bar their entrance. The door was on the latch and they threw it open together.

The scene inside was the same large hall, with its red plush furnishings, gay gaslights, and warm pinks, that Pitt had seen. It was too early in the evening; there were no customers here yet, no lush, soft-eyed maids. Only Victoria Dalton in her brown tea gown and her sister Mary in a dress of blue with a wide lace trim. And in front of them stood Christina with the gun in her hands.

'You're madwomen!' Christina's voice choked, her hands shook. But the barrel of the gun still pointed at Victoria's bosom. 'It wasn't enough to kill Max, you had to mutilate him—then you killed all the others! Why? Why? Why did you kill the others? I never wanted that—I never told you to!'

Victoria's face was curiously expressionless, ironed out like a child's. Only her eyes showed emotion, blazing with hate. 'If you'd been sold into prostitution when you were nine years old, you wouldn't need to ask me that! You whore around for fun—you let animals like Max use your body. But if men had relieved themselves in you since you were a child on your mother's lap—if you'd laid in your bed and heard through the cardboard walls your seven-year-old sister scream when they thrust into her with their great naked, obscene bodies—swollen, panting and sweating, their hands all over you—you'd take joy in stabbing them, too, and tearing off their—'

Christina's hands tightened and the gun barrel came higher. Charlotte lunged forward, kicking. She was too far away to reach the gun, but she knocked Christina off her feet and the gun fell, unexploded, onto the floor.

There was a scream of rage, and Charlotte felt strong, clawlike hands tearing at her. The floor hit her hard on the thigh, skirts smothered her. She reached for anything to strike or to pull. Her hands found hair, twisted into it, and jerked.

There was a scream of pain. Another body landed heavily on top of her, more skirts, boots in her thigh, kicking hard.

There was more shrieking and Christina's voice swearing. Charlotte was pinned to the ground, half suffocated by mountains of fabric and the weight of bodies. Her hair was undone, streaming down her back, over her face. A hand grasped at it and pulled. Pain ripped through her head. She punched back, her fists closed. Where was the gun!

'Stop it!' Balantyne's voice thundered above the din. No one took any notice.

Christina, on hands and knees on the floor, was screaming at Victoria Dalton, her face contorted with rage. Mary Dalton swung her hand back and slapped Christina as hard as she could, the ring of it singing in the air. Christina scrambled to her feet and aimed a kick. It caught Mary on the shoulder, and she fell over onto her back, moaning.

Victoria lunged for the gun, but Charlotte threw herself on top of her, jerking her head back hard by the hair. Charlotte's skirt was torn to the waist, showing her underwear and a long stretch of white thigh. Shouting, though she was unaware of it, she looked frantically for the gun.

Suddenly it went off with a deafening roar. They all froze, as if each one of them had been hit.

'Stop it!' Balantyne commanded furiously. 'Stand up! I'll shoot the first one to disobey me!'

Very slowly they climbed to their feet—scratched, clothes ripped, hair wild. Charlotte tried to tie her skirt together to hide the expanse of her thigh.

'Oh, my God!' Balantyne was holding the gun, his face so pale the bones of his cheeks looked sharp, his jaw white.

Christina took a step forward. 'Stand still!' His voice was like a knife cut.

Charlotte felt the tears well behind her eyes. She guessed the answers now, and there was nothing she could do: nothing for Balantyne, nothing for Victoria or Mary—nothing for Alan Ross.

'These women killed Max Burton?' He was talking to Christina as if the others were not there.

'Yes! They're insane! They—' She stopped, gulping, horrified at his face.

He turned to Victoria Dalton. 'Why now? Why did you wait so long?'

Victoria's face was hard, glittering. 'She

paid me to,' she said levelly, crucifyingly honest. 'First she fornicated with Max herself, and then she whored with other men for him... Then, when he started to get greedy and blackmail her, she got frightened. She needed to be rid of him.' Her face twisted with pity—pity for Ross—and contempt for Christina. 'She was afraid her husband would find out, poor sod! She only kept one lover: Beau Astley.'

Charlotte stared at Balantyne. His face was white with pain. But there was no struggle in him, no attempt to reject the truth. 'And why Dr Pinchin?' he asked, still holding the gun up.

'He deserved to die,' Victoria replied coldly. 'He was a butcher!'

'And what did Bertie Astley do that you executed him?'

Victoria's lip curled in scorn. 'He owned all that street. He let it out a room at a time for rich men and their whores that wanted privacy. He was collecting rent. His family kept up their fine drawing rooms and their safe white ladies on the profits of our filth!'

'And his brother should have been grateful! He should have paid us—' Mary began, but Victoria swung around and slapped her hard across the face, leaving a red welt.

In that instant, Charlotte moved forward, reaching for the gun; her hands clasped over Balantyne's and swung it around to aim at Victoria.

Victoria swept her arm over a side table. There was a brief gleam of light on blades, and scissors came down in Christina's chest, blood billowing out. The gun fired into the ceiling.

Balantyne caught his daughter as she slowly sank to her knees and crumpled down into a little huddle. He held her in his arms.

Charlotte picked up a footstool and hit Victoria with it as hard as she could, knocking her over and leaving her stunned and motionless on the red carpet. Then she stood in the middle of the room, the stool still in her hands. Mary, seized with fear now that she was alone, turned and bent over Victoria, crying like a lost child.

Where was Pitt? It was all too much; the pain was too persistent and too hard. She was exhausted of anger, of anything but pity, and her body ached with bruises. Tears were running down her face, but she was too empty to sob.

Balantyne let Christina go gently onto the floor. Her eyes were closed; the lace front of her gown was scarlet with blood.

Charlotte reached out and touched her hand to Balantyne's head, feeling the texture of his hair under her fingers. She stroked it for a moment, once, then again more softly. She turned away and saw a police constable standing in the doorway, and behind him the familiar, beautiful scarecrow figure of Pitt. Of course—the shots! Pitt must have left policemen outside; he had worked it out without her—this had been unnecessary.

He came in slowly, pushing past the constable who was fishing in his pockets for handcuffs for Mary and Victoria. He did not speak to Balantyne. There was nothing to say that would mean anything to his horror or his grief now—and Christina was beyond them all.

Gently he put his arms around Charlotte and held her. He touched her hands, her arms, pushed back her hair.

'You look ridiculous!' he said in sudden fury when he knew she was not injured, when he felt her bones were whole, her body strong. 'Good God—you look terrible! Go home! And don't you ever dare do this again! Not ever! You damn well do as you're told! Do you hear me?'

She nodded, too overwhelmed with horror and pity, and a sense of her own safety in his love, to look for any words.